The
PICKLE BOAT
HOUSE

LOUISE GORDAY

Beverly

There are some bonds
that death cannot sever.

Louise

Freshman year — 40 yrs ago !

ISBN: 978-148189911

Cover design by Radoslaw Krawczyk
photos on cover: fotolia.com. © Winzworks/Dreamstime.com

Book interior layout and design by James Arneson of Jaad Book Design - www.jaadbookdesign.com

Printed in the United States of America

FOR MY FAMILY
YOU MAKE ALL THINGS WONDERFUL

Special thanks to Michael J. Carr (editor) and Michael Aschenbach (developmental editor). You are both amazing!

I am indebted to the following friends who shared their time and gave me their unwavering support: Angela, Carol, Chris, Ellen, Liz, and Priya.

CONTENTS

The
PICKLE BOAT
HOUSE

ONE

FUGUE AND EXPOSITION

As the orange passenger jet roared overhead, sinking toward the runway beyond, James loosened his grip on the wheel a little. But even the blare of Beethoven's op. 123 Credo couldn't put him in the zone. Pity—it was one of his favorites. Arrival time was 12:35 . . . right? It was important; he had a three o'clock meeting. James turned the radio off and pulled into short-term parking. Lucky day! An empty space, right up front. He whipped his car into the spot and headed for Terminal A.

The airport was a sea of faces trailing wheeled appendages. "Sam, Sam, Sam," James mumbled, spinning his key ring on his finger as he surveyed the moving mass. "Come out, come out, wherever you . . ."

"Paging James Hardy. Paging James Hardy."

James whirled around at the sound of the familiar voice and spied Sam in the distance, hands cupped to his mouth. Khakis and a polo shirt—the guy was finally maturing.

"Sam! Great to see ya, bud." James pulled his friend into a bear-hug. "Glad you called. How long's your layover?"

"Let's see, 12:50 . . . got about an hour to kill. I remember you every time I pass through Baltimore, but this is the first time I ever thought about calling. I'm surprised you squeezed me in, being a big-shot lawyer and all. Dressing for success, too," he said, eyeing James's navy suit and mirror-polished Florsheim wingtips. "Looking sharp for a twenty-four-year-old."

"Oh, please! Yours will be the first ass I sue when I get a real job."

"Let's go get you a latte and me a strong cuppa joe, and I'll tell you about the latest corporate shit-fest. You'll soil your legal briefs when you hear what the assholes in my company are trying to do." Sam grabbed James by the elbow and steered him toward the coffee kiosk. "Large dark roast, please." He turned his attention back to James. "Talked to Mark and Jay a few weeks ago. They want us all to meet up in Myrtle Beach in August."

"Not sure about August—may have a job. Interview today," James said, pulling on his lapels. "The place has great credibility. I want this one bad. Small coffee," he said to the barista. He followed Sam to a table at the entrance where they could people watch while keeping an eye on the digital clock on the arrival/departure board.

"So, dressed to *impress*," said Sam. "When's your birthday, August? Expect a Baysox T-shirt. You're gonna need me to keep you grounded."

"Acceptable," James said, dumping sugar into his cup. "Sox are holding their own this year. Don't even think about a United jersey—guys are stinking up the division. They traded everybody away. How are your parents?"

"Good. Yours?"

"Peas in a pod," James replied. "Dad and I are going skydiving on my birthday. Mom's seeing how long she can keep me tied to her apron strings. If she only knew how long ago I cut those!"

Sam laughed. "So this job—you want it, eh?"

"Yep, this is the one—small firm, populist minded. The big corporate offices don't care. If I get this one, I can stay local. I might even be able to live in my great grandparents' house in Nevis, rent free."

"The pickle boat house? Sweet! I loved summer vacations there. Nevis is like one of those fifties sitcom towns, you know? I swear the Beav lived around the corner. Dude, we used to get into such trouble."

"Hah! I remember. It was awesome. We were such idiots—climbing out the window at night. I don't think they knew where we were half the time. Mom still goes down there quite a bit. She's collected a lot of turn-of-the century memorabilia from when Nevis was a hopping resort. She has grand plans to open a museum one day."

"Dontcha miss those carefree days? Hey, check this guy." Sam pointed across the concourse to a well-dressed man with an attaché case. In a hurry, he wove his way in and out of the human traffic on the people mover, with little regard for feet, shoulders, or even small children. "What a dick. If I was in front of him, I'd do my passive-aggressive best to box him in and not let him by."

James laughed. "Always looking for trouble." People movers—they worked best when slowpokes stayed right and the type A's could progress at will in the left lane, like the autobahn. But it took just one jerk like him to give all left-laners a bad name." James watched with fascination as the man bullied a series of people in front of him to move right. He gave the guy the full once-over. "Cold eyes. Wouldn't touch that dude with a ten-foot pole."

As they each reached the bottom of their cups, Sam said, quite out of the blue, "In all seriousness, James, promise me one thing: when you get your job with some hot-shot firm, you won't turn into that guy." Don't ever lose a sense of where you've come from or develop that sense of entitlement. Use your gifts for the good of people. In fact," he said, pulling a pen out of his carry-on and scribbling on his napkin, "put this in your wallet, and when you suspect you might be getting a fat head, read it." He ripped the corner off the napkin and slid it into James's shirt pocket."

"Okay, *Mom,* I promise. Y'know, the dude is probably just late and stressed. Wait until he spends an eternity waiting for his luggage. And speaking of late, Sam, I gotta roll. It's one forty. No rest for the wicked."

Sam grinned. "Gotcha. Only slow down a little, okay? Smell the roses."

"Ah, I'll rest when I'm dead."

"Not planning on dying young, are we?"

James shrugged. "Definitely not in my plans, but time waits for no man."

Sam leaned forward. "Then don't be a man for a while, bro," he whispered, and raised his eyebrows as he extended his hand and gave James the super-secret handshake they had made up when they were kids.

"Grow up, dumb-ass," James said, laughing. "I'll call you."

"Thanks for the company, and good luck today. I'll let you know about August. Text me." Sam watched James move out into the throng of travelers. For the briefest moment, he wanted to ditch his flight and spend the rest of the day with his best friend. Why was this good-bye so hard? He stood rooted, trying to freeze in time the retreating image before it disappeared into the crowd. Jeez, what *was* with this nostalgia thing?

James hit the freeway with the Jeep's pedal down, the road clear, and a lot of information floating around in his brain. Interview suit, check. Directions, check. Plenty of time still? He checked his watch: 1:55. A little close—maybe the visit wasn't such a great idea. He pulled Sam's limp folded napkin out of his pocket and flipped it open. Scrawled in small capital letters were three words: "pickle boat house." He smiled and tucked it back into his pocket, then cranked up the radio to keep his mind occupied. It was almost two; he could catch the news.

James's eyes returned to the road just in time to see the rear end of a stalled car rapidly approaching. "Where'd you come from? Christ!" He jerked the wheel, and the car lurched right, hugging the edge of the asphalt. Hitting loose gravel there, the jeep zigzagged back and forth across the lanes as James fought to maintain control. Careening off the road on two wheels, the car hit an embankment and went airborne, doing a half roll before it came to rest upside down in a creek. It seemed to float on the surface for a brief moment before sinking into the sparkling, flowing water. Then all became strangely quiet.

In those last moments, James had no sudden rush of life's experiences. He just felt himself floating weightlessly, willingly, toward the brightest, warmest light he had ever seen. Confusion ... somewhere a bus accident, humming lights, frantic medical personnel ... and through it all, a strange sense of detachment overwhelmed him.

Meanwhile, at the airport, Sam had grabbed a seat at his departure gate, the constant human flow had morphed in new shapes, and the man with the cold eyes had claimed his luggage.

As he stepped off the curb toward the rental cars, supremely indifferent to those around him, he never saw the city bus, rounding the corner with its own kind of indifference. As the digital clock on the arrival/departure board changed to 2:00 p.m., the bus hit him and the woman three steps ahead. Floating weightlessly toward the lovely white radiance, in that eye blink, the summed experience of the man's life passed before him. Ryan Llewellyn Thomas had been assessed the price for the life he lived.

At two o'clock that day, the light at the end of the passageway shone for many people. It was certainly nothing unusual for more than one soul to traverse its length at exactly the same moment. But it was rare to have two men so very different in temperament and virtue traveling together. And it was almost unheard of for one soul to be cast back to Earth, into the body of his traveling companion, for a second chance in the world.

TWO

BECAUSE

The town overlooked the bay, the boom now a distant memory. Once city folk, eager for their summers at the bay's edge, flocked by train to dip their toes in the surf and cool off in its breezes. Now seagulls and cormorants roosted in the pylons. It was quiet except for the lapping of the waves against the seawall and the hyenalike laugh of the gulls—a laugh that echoed off the weather-worn hulls of the few boats still moored along the bulkhead. Gone were the little white ticket booth, the great carousel, and First and Second Streets, claimed long ago by fifty-year storms that had consumed more than just the beaches. Only the bungalows remained, like mismatched seashells of faded pink, gray, and brown. The town of Nevis was a place still awaiting its renaissance.

The moving van crested the hill, and the sparkling waters of the Chesapeake Bay stretched out below. The scene beckoned like an empty canvas yearning for the artist's brush.

The excitement Vanessa had always felt as a small child coming here to visit her grandparents now gave way to a sense of anxiety and vulnerability. She couldn't remember the last time she had moved. It was probably better that way; remembering would dredge up other memories that were just too painful. Vanessa was going to get through this only if she shut out everything. Her life was blank like that artist's canvas, ready to start a new story: her own personal renaissance—a second life.

"Joe, you might want to slow down through here," Vanessa said to the truck driver. "This is the stretch where they nail you for speeding."

"The last thing I need is a ticket, Ms. Hardy," said Joe, slowing down. "Thanks. I'd get fired for sure. Zero-tolerance policy, you know?"

"Call me Van. Seriously, this is the perfect spot for a cop to hide. My granddad swore the highway people designed it that way—had it 'on good information.' I can remember sitting in the front seat between Dad and Granddad, bouncing along with the ruts in the road. The hum of the engine would lull me to sleep, and then, *bang*, I'd jolt awake to the sound of Granddad cussing out a cop for trapping speeders from the perfect spot." Van smiled. The old man had hated an uneven playing field. She loved that about him.

Van mentally acknowledged each street as the truck lumbered through town to the bungalows sitting along the boardwalk. Good utilitarian names like Mill Swamp Avenue and Polling Place Road bespoke the long history of the place.

"That George Washington, he got around, didn't he?" The driver chuckled as they passed one of several historic markers. "This is a nice area. I've been trying to buy a house down here, but they're sold and off the market almost before I can get a bid in."

"Really?" said Van. "I think you need a new real estate agent. It shouldn't be that hard to get something down here."

"Maybe, but it's happened to me enough times, I'd all but given up. Finally, I got wind of a house on Third Street that was going on the market. I called the owners directly, and we're going to settle next week. It was a fair deal all the way around. I couldn't be happier."

"Well, neighbor, I'm on Third Street. Whose house—"

Joe frowned. "You smell something burning?" He checked his rearview mirror. "Not us."

Van sniffed deeply several times and shook her head. "Sorry. I don't smell anything, but then, I'm just getting over a cold. Can you still smell it? Maybe we should pull over."

"Yeah, it's getting stronger, but I don't think it's us. Maybe someone's burning trash."

As they turned down Third Street, Joe suddenly slammed on his brakes. "Son of a bitch! That's *my* house!" he wailed. Ahead of them smoldered the burned-out hull of a house, with a fire truck and a pumper parked in front, blocking most of the roadway.

"Oh, my God, only one house? What about mine?" Van craned her neck to see past the emergency equipment. "If they let us through . . ."

A fireman stepped out toward the truck and hailed them to stop. Before he could say anything Van jumped out of the truck, with Joe pelting out the other side.

"What's going on?" she asked.

"She went up so fast, we couldn't do much except watch her burn. Pickle boat house is fine, though, Miz Hardy. That's the first thing John asked about when we heard the address. We're just watching for flare-ups now."

Joe stood frozen, watching his dreams turn to soot and cold ashes.

"Faulty wiring?" Van asked the firefighter. "The house has been empty."

"No ma'am. The speed it went up—never seen anything like it. Somebody packed gasoline-soaked rags around the back section of the house. Arson," he said, shaking his head. "Need you folks to move along now. Gotta keep the road clear."

"Sure. Come on, Joe," said Van, pulling the shell-shocked driver back toward the truck. "It's a good thing you hadn't settled yet. This isn't your problem now."

"Such a beautiful house," Joe lamented, his eyes brimming with tears. "It's like somebody just doesn't want me to have a house. Who could hate me that bad?"

"No, it wasn't anything you did. Just bad luck—some kook that likes to watch things burn . . . You know, you could buy the lot and build a new house."

"No," he said, shaking his head sadly as a single tear broke free and rounded his cheek. "Let the kook have it. It's bad luck now."

Van nodded. "Arson. This could be *everyone's* problem."

Joe drove a stone's throw farther down the street and pulled into a tiny driveway. Between two larger, more modern houses sat a small, well-kept bungalow, its empty rooms beckoning for a beating heart as it looked out across the bay. It hadn't changed much since her great grandmother stood on the widow's walk, waiting for the fishing fleet to return to shore. Humble in looks, it was a solid house that had endured every hurricane and nor'easter that nature threw its way over the years. A roofed porch, supported by green carved pillars and white bannisters, crossed the front of the long, narrow white house. A kitchen and parlor below and two bedrooms at the top of the stairs made a comfortable space for someone who wanted to be alone.

Van looked forward to hiding away in her own quiet little space. It certainly wouldn't take her and Joe long to move her in. She had taken very few things from the house when she walked out on Richard. She wanted a clean break. A separation would do them both good, but in reality she was thinking just for herself. She didn't care anymore what he wanted. She had to save herself, and if she felt the same way after she put herself back together, divorce was inevitable.

She and Richard had met at college. He liked her long brown hair, and she loved his sense of humor. But, it was a much deeper connection than that. It was love at first sight—the kind that came out of nowhere and had total control once it seized you in its velvet grip. They had a beautiful first life together, and Van was the happiest person in the world.

But life's beauty was fleeting, and when her and Richard's 24-year-old son was killed in a car accident it evaporated utterly. From the very first, Van realized that she and Richard would grieve differently. He suffered in seclusion and compensated without her, whereas she reached out everywhere. She bought books about loss, grief, and near-death experiences, and the Catholic-faith TV channel became her constant companion. She prayed to God just to get down the hall to the bathroom and back, spent lunchtimes in prayer at the local church—anything to get her from one minute to the next. That first Christmas without him—no tree, no presents; just standing in the surf reciting the rosary. It was unimaginably hard on both of them.

She couldn't fathom why a romantic love so right, so seemingly destined, could turn out so wrong. Van would have given her life for Richard, but she found out that the sentiment didn't run both ways. He cheated on her. Van could have forgiven him had he confessed and admitted to a mistake, a lapse in judgment, but that never happened. Instead, it became a question of admitting when caught, and with never a reason why or an apology that meant anything. She didn't even know how long they lasted or how many there were.

Neither could be blamed for what happened. Their relationship was consumed in the fires of their grief. The simple fact that they both had survived to walk away from each other said something.

Why did beautiful marriages crumble, 24-year-old sons die, terrible things happen? Van had concluded that like so much of life, the answer to "why" was simply "because"—no more, no less. It just was, and if she could accept that, then maybe she could go on. If not, she would spend the rest of her life in hell, trying to rationalize something that could never make sense. In the end, she was learning to control the pain—or, more accurately, learning not to let *it* control *her*. The less it controlled her, the less she would keep living and reliving, steeping herself in, the loss. It was always there, though, like a hibernating viper waiting to rear its poisonous head.

Time could heal, but it could also, and quite unexpectedly, rip open a still-raw wound. A world that didn't pause to reflect on a life, or bow its head in even momentary remembrance, was a painful place to inhabit. Van needed that pause to remember, and closure to heal. Perhaps she could find it in the pickle boat house.

THREE

NOT A LEG TO STAND ON

On the corner of Bayside and Seventh Streets stood a short row of little stores hiding from the sun beneath striped green awnings. Betty's Bakery, on the end, had been around for years. Fancy cupcakes with curlicue icing and sprinkles still drew the locals. Many a serious discussion in town was had, and many a business deal sealed, over a cup of Betty's best, or sweet tea and a blueberry muffin. And, of course, no May wedding was complete without a cake with Betty's strawberry cream filling and fancy petit four favors.

Van maneuvered around a group of cyclists as they propped their bikes up against Betty's and took their helmets off. Their sleek aerodynamic shirts and padded chamois shorts screamed "Passionate cyclist!" Not of Nevis, this bunch was merely passing through. A Pavlovian bell on the back of the door elicited a smile from Van as she entered. Some good things never changed.

"Morning, Betty. Baking blueberry muffins and wheat bread this morning? Smells so-o-o good! I could put on five pounds just breathing."

A plump little woman with graying hair gathered back into a bun, Betty pulled herself up from behind the pastry case. Curly tendrils and a tender smile softened her many wrinkles. Like all the bakers before her, she was known simply as "Betty." Everyone in town was on a first-name basis, connected either through growing up together or through the friend of a second cousin on their mother's side. And every one of them loved Betty.

"Morning, Van. If it's Sunday, it must be muffin day, huh? The usual's in the bag there, on the house." I didn't burn as many today." She flashed the teasing eyes of a feisty woman.

"I see another peloton, off on one of their secret missions. Ever wonder where they're from, where they're going?"

"No, that's all kind of lost on me. Maybe I'm just getting too old. Cars are quicker and a whole lot safer."

"Yeah—unless you're on a bike. I'd rather get my thrills in a spinning class at the Y. They are good for business, though," Van said, absentmindedly watching them through the storefront window. She turned back to Betty and, with a smile, picked up her bag and headed out toward the boardwalk, dodging the knot of cyclists coming through the door. The rich smell of blueberries began to melt away her self-control, and she finally popped a warm piece into her mouth. Nobody made muffins like Betty.

It was one of those beautiful, indelibly clear blue late-summer days. Calm water undulated in gentle, sparkling waves of shimmer. Van walked down the boardwalk toward her favorite bench. She spent a lot of time there, for it gave her a chance to clear the emotional clutter and contemplate details on the various projects she was involved in. Lately, there was more clutter than details. She had to clean house emotionally or face endless hours recreating the wheel. Van had always considered herself to be strong, nonconformist, and thoroughly independent. Everything she needed, she could draw from within. Those qualities had always supported and sustained her—until now. Now she was having a hard time being strong, and when she faltered there would be no one there to catch her. Introversion had effectively isolated her from friends and social ties.

She shooed away the gull perched on the backrest, and sat down, giving the muffin her full attention. Eating on the board-walk was something she usually avoided, and not just because it was prohibited—the fishy-smelling wrack and flotsam along the rocky shore could turn any but the most cast-iron stomach against the very thought of food. Warm blueberries had a certain masking quality, though. She tossed the leftovers out into the water and watched as the ever-observant geese scrambled and fought over the goodness.

Nothing helped better with that inner clutter than the heal-ing effects of the sun. *Mmm,* she could stay like this forever, she decided as she stretched out her legs. Little black dots moved lazily across the inside of her fiery eyelids until preempted by daydreams of a previous life. She was back on the bay with her grandfather, John, the boat dipping in rhythm with the swells, as a giggly girl poked a long-poled net at a jellyfish.

But other important people, such as her son, often inhab-ited her daydreams. Boyish laughter reverberated through the stillness in her, and she turned her mind's eye onto a little boy as he unwrapped his arms from around his grandfather's neck and slid down his strong old back to the safety of the top porch step. The little boy turned and gave her a big, goofy smile, his gray eyes sparkling. Van smiled back but suddenly felt herself pulled back to the now sounds of the boardwalk. It was becom-ing more crowded, less lonely perhaps, as the morning got going and the locals began to stir.

Van couldn't concentrate anymore amid the growing distractions, so she gathered up her things and headed for home. A local fisherman stood leaning his shoulder against the boardwalk railing as his practiced hands baited a hook. He nodded as she passed. "Morning, Miss Van. Catching your rays early, I see. No Lulu today?"

"Spence, happy Sunday. Nah, left Lulu at home." Van tried to keep her eyes off the wriggling lugworm trying to escape the grimy fingers holding the hook. The little worm didn't have a chance against the experienced fingers of the fisherman. "Couldn't take the happy dance this morning. I'll make it up to her later."

Van walked over to the old man and peered into his catch bucket. "Are they biting this morning?"

"Nope, not a good day, Miss Van. 'Bout ready to call it a day. Not like the good old days when they were biting as soon as your bait hit the water. Can't expect nothing to last forever, I guess." Spence stooped down and addressed the Bay retriever that lay snoozing at his feet. "Well, Chessie, it just isn't much of a morning without little Lulu, is it?" The dog momentarily opened his eyes and thumped the boards with his tail before resuming his snooze.

Van smiled to herself as the old man baby-talked his constant companion. She scratched Chessie behind the ears and slowly pushed herself away from the railing. "I'll tell her you missed her," she said over her shoulder as she walked away.

Most of the locals walked the boardwalk at some point during the week. She could set her watch by the older, retired residents who came every day—in the early morning or after sunset in the hot months, just after noon in the cold ones. Often they came hand in hand or arm in arm with their mate. On her good days, they brought a smile to Van's lips; on bad days, a tinge of envy and regret into her broken heart.

The Morgans were one such couple. Grace had been a Sunday school teacher and Harry a truck driver. They had grown silver haired together and completed each other's sentences, if they found it necessary to talk at all. This morning, they approached Van with a slow and steady gait, hand in hand.

"Good morning, Mr. and Mrs. Morgan. Nice to see you out today," Van said as they came face-to-face on the boardwalk.

"Morning, sugar," replied Mrs. Morgan. "Good to see some young people out enjoying God's beautiful day."

"Yes ma'am." Everyone looked like a youngster to Mrs. Morgan. "It certainly is too beautiful to waste being inside."

"I'm glad we caught you, dear. Harry and I are going to be moving soon. We got a very generous offer for our house. We just couldn't refuse it. In the next month or so, we'll be heading down Angela and Duke's way in Virginia. We wanted to make sure we thanked you for all your kindness. I thought you might like to drop by before we leave, and take a peek at some of the older things we're not taking with us. There are still some things of Mother's you might want—for your Nevis collection, of course."

"Oh, I'm so sorry to see you go," Van said. "I apologize. I didn't even realize you had your house up for sale."

"Oh, we didn't. Out of the blue, an out-of-towner offered good money, all cash. Like I said, it was too good to pass up. It's time. Being on our own is almost too much to handle. We're both looking forward to being near the grandkids."

"It sounds lovely, Mrs. Morgan. Anytime you can get good money for land in Nevis, you have to give it some thought.

I'll make sure to stop by before you go. Would it be okay if I brought my genealogy charts of your family, just to make sure I've got it all down?"

"It would be a pleasure. Bring it all over, and we'll look at it one last time. Come on, Harry," she said to her husband. "We'll be all off schedule before long." Harry never said a word, but tipped his ball cap to Van, and they continued past her on their daily ritual.

❧

When Van got home and rounded the corner of her house she was surprised to see a woman hanging by her fingertips from the side window of the house next door. Her legs were flailing wildly as she tried to recover her footing on a box just out of reach. Van could hear her beginning to squeak.

"Can I help you there?" Van shouted as she scurried to grab the woman's waist. She helped her get earthbound again, easing her back onto the box.

"Damn it! You are not going to *believe* what I just did," the woman fumed, tossing her bobbed red hair. "I just locked myself out of my house—so damn-fool stupid today. But just today, of course," she said with a laugh. "Would you mind if I used your phone to call my daughter? She can bring me the spare key."

"No problem. We can have a cup of tea while you wait."

"That would be nice, thanks. "I'm Jean, by the way—just moved in."

"Vanessa Hardy. I saw all the comings and goings. I was wondering who the new owners were."

"Owner. Just me. Kicked the bum to the curb and partway down the street a few years back."

"Oh, sorry."

Jean shrugged. "Well, you shouldn't be. I'm sure not."

They worked their way around a flower bed overflowing with roses and daisies. Just above the vibrant floral display, a single mourning dove circled endlessly around the top of a little birdbath while a cat, crouching amid the daisies, monitored its progress. The cat looked up as the two women climbed the stairs, and gave a single plaintive mew.

"Hi, there, Mouse," Van said, pausing to stroke his head.

"Mouse? Where!" Jean screeched, scooting behind Van.

"No," Van said. "He doesn't *have* a mouse; his *name* is Mouse! He's the resident stray. You'll be friends before long. He hits up everybody for basics—thinks it's his inalienable right to sit on everyone's porch. He loves driving all the indoor dogs crazy. That's my haughty, naughty boy!" Mouse began to rub back and forth against her legs as she tried to get to the door.

"Who's the silent sentinel?" Jean asked, nodding toward the staring man sitting on the porch next door.

Van didn't even have to turn around to know exactly whom she meant. "Ernest Pickett, self-anointed neighborhood watch. If you want to know what's going on in your life, just ask him— he'll know more about your business than you do."

Mr. Pickett rose out of his chair. He hugged to his chest a dainty white teacup poodle with a pink collar. "Tell your gardener to stay off my grass," he said, glowering at the women. "I'm gonna call the cops. I don't pay my taxes for you to stomp around on my lawn." His eyes burned with malice.

"Yes, Mr. Pickett, I'll take care of it," Van politely shouted back at him as she winked at Jean.

"You have a gardener?"

"Nah, he means the older gentleman who does odd jobs around here. No one but Mr. Pickett would call him a gardener. You'll meet Charlie. He's wonderful."

Van was barely inside the door before she was accosted by a tiny Yorkshire terrier. It began to dart, scamper, and twirl like a dervish in the entryway as she came inside.

"Hi, sweetie, I'm glad you missed me. Move out of the way, now. Mommy has company." Van scooped her up with one hand and kept moving toward the kitchen.

"Oh, what an adorable puppy!"

"Adorable pain! Lulu doesn't have much puppy left in her anymore. She's been my best bud for a while. My huggie . . ."

Van continued toward the kitchen and plopped Lulu into the dog bed by the back door. "The phone's right there by the window," she said, motioning across the kitchen.

Jean walked over and chuckled at the white rotary phone hanging on the wall. It was refreshing to see that someone besides her didn't live and die by the latest technology.

"Marla, Mom . . . No, everything's okay. Listen, would you please come over at lunchtime and let me back in my house? I accidently locked myself out . . . Under the flower pot . . . No, you must not have put it back . . . No, no other way. Please. You can stay for lunch if you like . . . Well, okay, thanks. Bye." Jean hung up the phone with a little sigh.

"Is she busy?"

"No, doesn't care. Unless she gets something out of it—then she cares. It's okay, though. We're working on it," she said, putting a weak smile back on her face. "You have kids?"

"One. Deceased."

"Oh, I'm so sorry."

Van just stuck her head back in the cabinet to get the tea and change the subject. "Black or herbal—which would you prefer?"

"Oh, black, none of that froufrou stuff."

Jean made herself at home at the kitchen table, and they talked for a while about the weather and all the other safe little things that people discussed when getting to know each other. They liked each other immediately. Gradually, the conversation drifted off into private musings, with Van puttering over the tea and Jean staring out the window.

"What kind of mosaic are you?" Jean asked suddenly.

"Huh?"

"Your plaque," she said, nodding at the little wooden plaque over the stove. "'When the burdens of life shatter you into a million pieces, remake yourself into a beautiful mosaic.' What kind of mosaic are you?"

"Oh, you like?" When I was on vacation last year I bought it at an arts festival in Virginia. It was one of those feel-good-about-yourself summer days. Ten bucks that I could have used to drown my sorrows in the wine-tasting tent. Just another bad choice—God knows I've made enough of them. I don't know what kind," she said, sighing thoughtfully. "I'm still trying to figure out if all the pieces are still there and where they all go."

"Married?" asked Jean. "I don't see any husband pictures."

"Separated."

"Still talking?"

"Yep. Our life together is over, but he'll always be the only one for me."

"In that case, my advice is to get rid of him. I did a few years back. We've been fighting ever since. He's good at turning my daughter against me—just about ruined my relationship with her. I'm still trying to get that back on track. You're better off without a man complicating your life. They never listen to a word you say."

Van laughed. "I'll take that under advisement. Richard and I had a beautiful first life together."

"What happened?"

"He got a little too friendly with his executive assistant and started hitting the bottle pretty hard. I just couldn't trust him anymore."

"What a jerk. Like I said, take him to the curb and punt from there."

"I'm trying to move past it all. It was a difficult time for both of us."

"Not to change the subject, but nature calls. May I use your bathroom?"

Van pointed her down the hall as she put the dishes in the sink.

"What did you do to your bathroom, girl?" Jean yelled. "This is an oasis! I just *love* a tub with claw feet!"

Van could hear her giggling. She walked down the hall to the bathroom to find Jean on her knees, draped over the side of the tub.

"What are you doing on the floor?" Housecleaning hadn't been a top priority on Van's to-do list for quite a while, and she was relieved that she had cleaned yesterday. She got down on the floor and ran her hand lovingly along the edge of the tub.

"It's from my other grandparents' house. After they died, the house was sold and eventually burned down. To say good-bye, I drove past the yard one last time. Low and behold, the only thing left sitting in the middle of the yard was this old cast-iron tub. As a youngster, I had the hardest time hitching my leg up over the side to get in. My dad used to tell me how he would soap up the sides when he was little to see how fast he could swirl around the bottom. It's a heavy sucker. The owners were glad to get rid of it, and I felt like I saved an old friend. When I moved to Nevis, I brought it with me. I didn't want to change much in this house—too many fond memories of visiting my other grandparents here in the summer. But I love to take baths, so this is my one splurge. When I get bored or upset I come in here. I love to just soak and think. I've even eaten dinner in here. But, only when I'm really tired," she added with a laugh.

"Do you work?"

"Historian at the Smithsonian. I'm on a leave of absence. Teleconferences every so often, and a lot of planning documents to produce before I go back.

"You're impressive," Jean said, and they both found it funny. "No, I really am impressed," Jean said. She sat down flat on the floor and gave Van a smile. "I can see I'm really going to like living next door to you. Better get used to me."

"Oh, I already have." Van got to her feet. "Would you like a little red wine with that floor? I hear a good Chablis goes with any bathroom decor."

"Where did you learn the fine art of drinking?"

"College. Pays to go to a highbrow party school like Carolina. If you wanted to chug beer, you went to State."

FOUR

YANKEE DIMES AND WOODEN NICKELS

Van pulled out her music player and shuffled through her playlists until she got to the one called "Feeling a little Hamlet today." Even though it was a bad choice, she had to go there. The quiet strains of "Year of the Cat" began to fill her ears as she pushed open the screen door and headed for the boardwalk. It was one of her son's favorite songs. In fact, they all were his favorites, and they made her cry. Often she didn't make it to the end, but she had to go there—to validate him, to prove that once upon a time he really did exist. It was a reality check involving compulsion more than comfort.

Several songs into the playlist, Van sighed and pulled the buds from her ears, the pain of loss trumping over the warmth of memories. She sat down on her favorite boardwalk bench, stretched out, and closed her eyes to regroup and let the water wash the pain away. The swish of the water on the shore, and the water birds squabbling as they jockeyed for space on each piling, carried her to a calmer place. Footsteps on the boardwalk mellowed to a muted rhythm, and the conversations of passersby faded to patchy, muffled whisperings. She let her mind wander, sifting through all her mental detritus.

As had happened many times before, she was drawn toward the warmth of the shining sun, and there she found him. His baby voice, filled with quiet awe, whispered in her ear, and she felt his tiny arm crooked around her neck. "I want to fly, but not like a plane—like a bird," he whispered. He remained earthbound as the vision changed, and she saw him moving with grace, power, and speed as he took the ball toward the goal, the goalie crouching in anticipation. Without looking up, in a singularly unselfish act, he passed the ball to his wingman, who sailed it past the goalie and into the net. As the players high-fived at midfield, the roar of the crowd echoed and gradually changed to the sound of the surf. She mentally saw him there, too, catching a wave and barreling toward the shore. As he wiped out he laughed, then ran back into the water to catch another wave.

Tears spilled down the sides of Van's face, emptying out bottled-up emotions. She felt her chest tighten. The daydream shifted again as she heard a familiar voice yelling at her. "Hey, doodlebug, how 'bout a Yankee dime?" her grandfather called to the little girl as she came running across the lawn of the pickle boat house, laughing as she came. When she reached him he swept her up and swung her around in a circle before setting her on her feet again. Leaning down, he planted a kiss on her smiling upturned face. In spite of the tears, Van began to smile. It was a short-lived smile, though, as the sound of ringing in her pocket jarred her back to reality. Flustered, she pulled her cell phone out.

"Hello?"

"Hello? Regency Plaza?"

"No, I'm sorry. You must have the wrong number."

"Oh, I'm terribly sorry," the voice said.

Van opened her eyes and sighed as she put her cell phone away. She lived for daydreams like the one that had just been so abruptly interrupted. Disappointment turned to irritation, and she reddened as she saw a nearby man on the boardwalk blatantly ogling her.

"Careful—you're drooling," she muttered, turning away from his unwelcome stare. She hated when men gave her the once-over, although she had to admit, it had never been a frequent problem. She had never been one of those swish-and-sway types. Closing her eyes, she retreated back into her daydreams.

And the ringing began again. "What?" she shouted into the phone, and the voice on the other end began to laugh.

"Don't call me again," Van snarled as a flash of cold fear shot up her spine. "I have caller ID. I'll report you."

"Wait, don't hang up," said the voice. It chuckled devilishly again. "Say something else."

"What do you want?" Van yelled at the phone. She rolled into a sitting position, drawing the attention of others nearby, including Boardwalk Man.

She immediately transferred her ire to him. "Piss off. Go find someone else to stare at!"

But by this time, Boardwalk Man was almost doubled over with laughter, and Van could feel the heat from her anger rising in her face and igniting her eyes. As he began walking toward her like some kind of psycho stalker, her anger evaporated, and she dropped her hands into her lap and closed her mouth. Instinct was rapidly pushing her from fight to flight, but she was still incapable of moving.

"Am I ringing your phone? Are you five-five-five, four-five-one-seven?" The man heaved with laughter and continued to look directly at Van. "Don't you think that's funny?"

When Van continued to give no response his demeanor suddenly changed and the laughter froze on his lips. "I'm . . . so . . . I think we . . . your wrong number. I'm terribly sorry," he said.

She checked the phone in her hand, looked at him and back at the phone again. "This is *you?*" The improbability made her smile. "I do want you to know that I am on the 'do not call' list and that you can be fined a lot of money if you call me again," she said, half laughing.

"No, no, I promise, no more calls," the man said, holding his hands out in surrender. "I'm really sorry, but the look on your face was priceless." He gave a final awkward wave and walked off the boardwalk toward the parking lot. There was a last muffled laugh, and he was gone.

A little unnerved, Van took a deep breath to slow her pounding heart as a final shiver ran down her spine. Boardwalk Man was attractive, yet the adrenaline still coursing through her screamed a silent warning. She took another deep breath and tried to relax and stretch her long, slim legs out in front of her. A check of her watch assured her that she had about half an hour before she must head back to the house, her desk piled high with uncompleted work reports. She tried to pull herself back into her comfort zone, but her concentration was shot.

"Could I interest you in an ice cream?" said a familiar voice. Van jumped, startled. It was Boardwalk Man, standing in front of her with two ice-cream cones. "My feeble attempt at an apology for bothering you and making you mad?"

"That would be a really sweet gesture if you weren't standing in front of a 'No Eating on Boardwalk' sign." She tried not to laugh, but the corners of her mouth started to escape her control. If she didn't take a cone, he was going to be in trouble pretty quickly. As she looked at him closely, she saw something in his eyes that called to her in a primal way. Unmistakable attraction trumped any flight reflex she might have had.

"I can see you're enjoying this," he said, a little smile beginning to touch his eyes. "How about over on the street—can we go over there?" he said, gesturing with one of the cones he was holding.

"Maybe, though my mother told me never to accept sweets from strangers." Embarrassing him was like shooting fish in a barrel, and she was enjoying it. Boardwalk Man was actually pretty cute when he got embarrassed. She decided to let him dangle and twist for a while.

"Well, since you're already talking to a stranger, you must not listen to everything your mom taught you. Which way is it going to be: ice cream cone with a stranger, or the bench by yourself?"

"How could I be that cruel with you standing there and ice cream dribbling down your arm? But, I guess you already figured that, didn't you?"

"Yeah, I'm feeling very irresistible right now," he deadpanned. His eyes darkened as if he sensed her warming to him. "Can you take this before my fingers start sticking together?"

Van took the cone and quickly ran her tongue around the bottom of the ice cream to catch the drips. Not only was it chocolate, it was *good* chocolate.

"I'm sure your mother will give you a pass," he said.

"My mother is dead," she said coldly.

He froze in his tracks, and Van could almost see the wheels turning in his head. "I'm so sorry. That was so thoughtless of me. I really seem to be batting zero today—at least with you, anyway."

"It's okay," Van murmured. "It's been a while. Sorry I snapped at you. You just caught me off guard. She comes up so rarely in conversation anymore. I'm sure I would have gotten an etiquette lesson if I had left you to fend for yourself with two ice-cream cones."

They made their way over to one of the benches that lined a little grassy playing field. Van could feel his eyes on her, and she was beginning to like the way it felt. It was refreshing. There was a definite undercurrent of attraction between them as they sat in the sunshine, trying to keep ahead of the dripping cones. Her mother was probably doing barrel rolls in her grave.

"I would hope you're reading my T-shirt," Van said.

Boardwalk Man laughed as his eyes moved back up to her face. "Of course. So you're left-handed and the only one in your right brain?"

"Absolutely. It runs in my family. Everybody's a leftie. You have a problem with that?"

"No, I guess not. Everyone should be passionate about something."

"So . . . where are you from?"

He stopped in mid lick and chuckled. "Wow, you're direct. Is it that obvious that I'm not from around here?" He turned and smiled, and Van knew that she hadn't insulted him. It was a soft smile that made his eyes sparkle.

"You bought ice cream for someone you don't even know, and you're calling *me* direct? Pot or kettle? I think it's called the beauty of living in a small town. Everybody knows everybody. Of course, that applies to your personal business as well, but the trade-off is worth it. So unless you're the prodigal son returned, I figure you're either just passing through or a new resident.

Most people are trying to escape *from,* not *to,* Nevis. Nicely dressed—you don't look like you're escaping from anything."

He continued to look at Van for a moment, then let his gaze drift out across the field. He turned back to her and put out his hand. "Ryan Thomas. It's nice to meet you." He followed the outstretched hand with a smile that could calm the most skittish heart. It was hard to imagine someone with so dazzling a smile being unaware of its effect, especially on the opposite sex. "I was born and raised in Delaware; now I live in New York. I'm passing through, doing a little business, taking a holiday of sorts—getting the lay of the land, you might say."

"Do you work in New York?"

"I work in acquisitions with a firm there. Why? Do I scream 'New York' that loud?"

"Something like that. What do you acquisite?"

"I don't think that's the queen's English, but to answer your question, I acquire certain commodities for Hector Young and Associates, depending on what the specific needs are at any given time." He smirked. "I can see your eyes glazing over with eager interest. How about you?"

"I wasn't born here, but like most residents, I can trace my family back here to the founding fathers. Only the young people move away from Nevis, and if they do, they generally come back when they return to their senses. Guess you could say I've done that, too. I'm back here permanently now after years of quick trips on weekends."

"Do you work in Nevis?"

"No, D.C. I'm a historian at the Smithsonian; only right now I'm on a leave of absence—a working vacation of sorts. But that's okay; it's giving me time to exorcise my demons."

He tilted his head sideways and looked at her with soft, inquisitive eyes. "You have a few to exorcise?"

"Yeah, doesn't everybody?"

"Probably, if they're totally honest about it—which most of us aren't."

She hadn't expected that. It had been ever so long since she had someone understand what she was feeling, let alone pay attention to what she was saying. Van squeezed her eyes shut so he couldn't read her emotions. The silence that had felt at first like camaraderie now felt awkward. She got to her feet, and Ryan quickly followed. It felt like being back in high school on her first date.

Van forced herself to look up into Ryan's face. "Thank you for the ice cream. Consider us even—all forgiven."

He looked relieved. "Good. I didn't want to leave with that on my conscience."

"Could I leave you with one thought?"

"Sure." He hesitated, as if bracing himself for bad news.

"Next time you decide to pick up a girl by plying her with ice cream, order it in a cup."

"Sure. Next time." He snorted with relief and looked down at the ground. "I'd like there to be a next time," he said. He looked directly into her eyes, and there was that overwhelming smile again.

Van could feel herself melting. As a decent, sensitive human being, how could she say no to *that*? "I'd like that," she said softly. "I'd give you my name and number, but"—gesturing with her hands—"no paper, no pen." Van felt embarrassed again. She was actually *flirting* with this guy. She could feel the heat move up into her face.

"I only have a pen," he said, chuckling. "We may have to end this acquaintance right here. So great was my remorse, I deleted your number after I misdialed."

"Give me your pen," she said, and taking it, she took his hand, too, and began writing her name and phone number on the back. The hand was warm and strong, and she didn't want to give it back. Slowly she let go and held the pen out to him.

"No, you keep it. It was never totally happy with me. I think it was just a rebound relationship."

"Right." It was her turn to snort as she nodded and put the pen in her hip pocket.

"I'll never wash again," Ryan sighed as he looked down at his hand, and they both broke out in nervous laughter. "Why do I feel like I'm in the fifth grade again?"

"I hope you know I don't do that for just anybody," Van said.

He looked at her thoughtfully. "No, I didn't think so. Thanks. I'll call you. It may be a few days, though," he added. I'm heading south and then swinging back through on my way back to New York."

"That is the quickest kiss-off I ever got. You've had my number less than a minute, and you're already making excuses for not calling."

There was that magnetic smile again. "I promise I'll call you. Good-bye, Vanessa Hardy."

"Good-bye, Ryan Thomas. Take the Yankee dimes, but not the wooden nickels."

"What?"

She grinned at him, then turned and headed back to the boardwalk, resisting the urge to turn around.

✒

Ryan thought he could hear her begin to hum softly to herself, and it brought a quiet smile to his lips. He watched with admiration as she walked away. Even when women weren't trying to look sexy, there was still something magical about the way they moved. He looked toward the bay and caught sight of a tern diving expertly into the water. It was the ageless saga of the hunter and the hunted, and it never failed to fascinate him.

He reclaimed his seat on the bench and stretched out his six-foot frame. The slight breeze coming off the water was balmy. It was calm and quiet, with just the sound of bluebirds calling to each other in the surrounding trees. He closed his eyes and began planning step two, and a smile slowly spread across his upturned face. The day was beginning to go better than he could have expected.

He flipped open his cell phone. "Hey, just touching base. Think I'll be able to wrap this up a lot quicker than I thought. Just met someone who could be the answer to our prayers . . . No, totally clueless. You know my radar only picks up the cute ones." The smile abruptly disappeared from his face. "Wait— sending *who*? I don't need any help." Ryan got up and began to pace. "Tell 'em to fuck off . . . Shit, at least send someone else. Where's Earl? . . . How far?" His eyes darted around the park. "Never mind. I'll find the son of a bitch," he said. "Yeah, I'll return the favor sometime." He flipped the phone closed and slid it back into his pocket.

"I would have gone for a Yankee dime while I had the chance," a quiet voice whispered from behind him.

Ryan jumped. "Damn it, Hector! Don't creep up on me like that again."

The figure of a man stepped out from behind a nearby oak and approached. "Glad to see you can fit a little skirt chasing into the business day," he said, and chuckled.

"Screw you! Making a few contacts in the area will be helpful."

"Is that what that was? Could have sworn it was personal." Hector swung around the side of the bench and flopped down.

"And what the hell are *you* doing here? No, wait, scratch that. I don't care why you're here. Fuck off back to wherever the hell you came from. I don't need you breathing down my neck. Where's Earl?"

"No can do. Suits want to make sure this is all going to go down smoothly." Hector tossed his cigarette down and ground it out under his shoe. "Earl's taking care of business somewhere else. Gonna meet up with him later. Look, Ryan, my boy, I don't really care what you do on your own time. Screw this up and you'll be packing up your desk. Unless you want to admit that you just don't have it anymore?" He laughed again—a cold, spine-tingling sound. He lit another cigarette, took a long draw, and slowly exhaled smoke at Ryan as he gazed through narrowed eyes. "Don't make me hate this any more than I do already. I don't need you dragging me under—got my own problems. Just take care of business so we can get out of here. No loose ends."

"Have there ever been?"

"I'd hate to take it out of your hands."

Ryan looked at him with disgust. "Come on. Let's go find someone else for you to bullshit." Ryan got up and headed for the parking lot. Hector chuckled again as he got up and followed. He flicked the cigarette away but didn't bother to put it out.

"By the way, since you're such a smart-ass, what *is* a Yankee dime?" Ryan asked over his shoulder.

FIVE

BRING IT

Nevis demanded nothing. That was the appeal for Van: it let her go at her own pace. She had no desire to think about her estranged husband, and she couldn't think about her son. The memories were so painful that right now she could deal with them only by burying them beneath layers of neglect, guilt, and time and hoping they would just quietly fossilize there. So when she wasn't dedicating herself to work assignments she spent her time documenting and putting to paper all those who had come before her, ensuring that they were not forgotten, that they had left some trace. The thought that even one of them could slip into oblivion hurt her physically. The thought that the one forgotten could be her son was unbearable. And yet, she still couldn't bring herself to put his death date on the family tree.

Everything in her life seemed to have slipped away—everything, that is, except Nevis and the pickle boat house. They had a good old Southern feel, offering comforting memories and the illusion that life was slow, without any purpose other than its own. There was a healing strength here that even Van couldn't fully describe, and she kept waiting for the other shoe to drop.

Van and Jean spent lovely, lazy time on Van's front porch, listening to the Beach Boys and watching boats off in the distance ambling up and down the bay. They took turns bringing the booze or the iced tea (or both), depending on their mood that day. More importantly, neither ever failed to bring game or conversation. Just as they had predicted when they met, they became fast friends. It felt as if they had always been, and they could tell each other anything. Jean was a good listener, and even when she couldn't give advice she made Van laugh about her troubles. Van was laughing for the first time in years. Jean was a newfound ray of sunshine.

"I met the most interesting man on the boardwalk today." Van tried not to look directly at Jean, because she knew that since the divorce Jean had pretty much sworn off anything that smacked of romance. The moment Van said it she regretted it.

"What did he look like?"

Van felt suddenly flustered. "I don't know. Like a man . . . pants, a little stubble on the face, a callus or two . . ." She sank further down in her chair. "Jean, I should have known you'd be so superficial! I, uh, is that the best you can do?"

Jean locked her in her gaze and sucked her upper lip in. "Not once in all the time I've known you have you discussed a man with me—any man. With the exception of Charlie, of course, and he doesn't count. Men are not big on my list anymore, but there must have been something special about him for you to bring him up. Come on; come to Mama. How hot was he?"

Van gave her the most condescending look that she could manage, and then proceeded to melt under Jean's scorching gaze. "He was *so hot*," she wailed, hiding her red face in the crook of her arm.

"I knew it, knew it. Bingo!" Jean crowed, and giggled like a schoolgirl. She tried to pull Van's arm away from her face, all but tumbling them both onto the deck. Van had no hope of retreating from this physical assault, and she, too, began to giggle.

"Spill, before I have to go check the boardwalk for him myself," Jean demanded.

"Okay, okay, let me catch my breath," said Van. "It wasn't so much that he was hot. Don't get me wrong; he was good looking. But mostly, I was just so incredibly *drawn* to him. Can you believe it? I was actually flirting with him."

"Jeesh! You are a woman, remember, and a damn fine-looking one at that! Did he ask for your number? When are you going out? I want to know everything, starting with 'Hello, beautiful.'"

"Stop being a lunatic and slow down, Jean. He's coming back into town later this week, and he said he'd give me a call. It's nothing more exciting than that. Even then, I'll believe it when it happens. Wait! He gave me . . ." Van pulled the pen he gave her out of her pocket. ". . . *this*. See, I didn't make him up. He really does exist!"

Jean took the pen and flipped it over to read the inscription. "Hector Young and Associates. We should look this up and see if he's on the level."

Van burst out laughing. "What do you think he's going to do: rob me of my virtue and steal my inheritance?"

"Not while I'm here. He could be a serial killer, or something worse. Just leave it to Mama. I'll look him up and get back to you. Nobody gets through Mama Jean."

"Jean, you're letting your imagination run away with you. What could possibly be worse than a serial killer?"

Jean reached out and grabbed her arm. "Seriously, Van, stop laughing at me. It's been a while since you've been in the market. Don't jump in too fast. Go slow and don't overcommit. Think it through a little bit. If he seems too good to be true, he probably is. The devil's in the details."

Van rolled her eyes and took Jean's hand off her arm. "For jeesh sake, it'll be a cup of coffee and maybe a few smooches. Get a grip, girl. You act like there's something wrong with my BS detector. All I ever do is think things through. It's constantly one analysis after another. I need an interesting diversion. Besides, he didn't have that serial-killer personality. He didn't seem to have any ulterior motives." Van looked back out toward the bay to hide her grin as she remembered how his flirtation made her feel. It would be disappointing if he never called. She frowned as she caught sight of a red triangle fluttering in the distance.

"Small-craft warnings are out," Van mused.

"Really? But the weather seems so clear."

"As any sailor can tell you, calm as the bay seems, it can get you if you don't pay attention."

"Speaking of the devil being in the details, have you seen Charlie Sollars today?"

"No," Van replied, her eyes going back to Jean. "I can hear him clipping hedges around the back of the house. Why?"

"Cut his hair real short—looks like a porcupine."

"Charlie doesn't *have* enough hair to look like a porcupine," Van said, laughing.

"You know what I mean. It's sticking up all over where he has it. By the way, how much do you pay him to clip the hedges?"

"Nothing. You know Charlie—busy hands are happy hands. He won't take money for anything he does. I love that man

. . . reminds me of my dad. When I first moved down here Charlie and his wife, Debbie, took me under their wing. I think I filled a void. Their only daughter had run away from home as soon as she was old enough, never to be heard from again. He's been over here a lot since Debbie died—really took her passing hard. They were married forty years. Listening to them, you'd think they were oil and water, bickering all the time, but you could see the true love right below the surface. She died in his arms."

"Aww, that's sweet. He does have a kind look about him, as long as you stay out of his flower beds. Hey, did you hear about Charlie and the bikers?"

Van laughed and shook her head. This sounded good. All Charlie stories were good—even better if he was doing the telling.

"Well, you know the house down the street from Charlie's mom's house, the one that sold on Eighth Street?" The people that bought it are bikers. Seems they were driving people crazy, roaring up and down the street. Well, Charlie decided he was gonna set them straight on proper behavior. He went over one night and knocked on their door, all set to give them life's lecture. When he knocked on the door the biggest ass-fucking Diablos biker—

"Jean!" Van said, eyebrows raised in feigned shock. "Do you *eat* with that mouth?"

Jean chuckled. "As a fisherman's granddaughter, I would think you'd heard this all before."

"Oh, I have, but the first and last time I tried to repeat it, my grandmother washed my mouth out with soap—*Zest* soap! I think I was five!"

"Listen, do you want me to finish this or not? A big-ass Diablo answered the door and asked what he wanted. Charlie's no fool. He forgot all about the life lesson. He asked if they wanted to donate money to his church. The biker said sure, and now every time they see Charlie, they give him money. Isn't that hysterical?"

Van laughed. "Poor Charlie! It's a wonder they didn't beat him to a pulp. I don't know what I'd do without him around here. He fixes everything I ask him to fix, and things that I never even knew were broken. Such a sweetheart."

"Let's hope the two houses that just sold down that way haven't gone to any more Diablos. That'd be a little too much excitement. Those people scare me, especially that Rusty Clark fellow. I move to the other side of the street when I see them. I'm so relieved that Marla never got mixed up with that crowd."

Van gasped, straightening up in her chair and snapping her fingers. "I knew there was something I was forgetting to tell you. The last time I saw the Morgans they said they sold their place and were moving down near their kids."

"I'm sure the Morgans weren't one of the two I heard about. I think it's more likely the Jeffries and the Spencers. The Morgans are way over on the other side of town. There was a third house vacant over on Chestnut, but it burned down the other night."

"Not another arson?"

"Haven't heard yet," Jean replied. "Sure's hell hope not. That'd be the third in the last few months. You know, though, it's probably a good thing the Morgans are moving. They'll be closer to the kids . . . Did you know that old Mr. Morgan drives along the edge of the road so he can tell where he is? If the riding gets rough, he knows he's on the shoulder and he moves back over."

"No," said Van, laughing. "I did see him backing up the exit ramp on Route 261 near Owings a couple of months ago. But don't change the subject on me. Sure are a lot of home sales for such a sleepy town. I can't recall so many houses selling at once. Can't imagine why anyone would want to come here unless they were already connected. And then, on the other hand, there's Joe, the fella that helped me move in. That poor guy finally gets the jump on a house, and somebody burns it down! Odd."

"Noted," Jean said with a nod, and she immediately launched into a new story about the time she got locked in a bathroom stall and had to crawl underneath the door to escape. Normally, Van would be howling at her antics, but the breeze off the water had picked up, and she shook from the sudden chill. The pickle boat house creaked and groaned behind them.

SIX

CLOSURE

Van didn't have to wait long. Ryan called her several days later and arranged to swing by her house on his way back to New York.

It's no big deal; he's no big deal, she kept repeating to herself. But by the morning of his visit, she was a mass of nerves. She cleaned excessively, changed clothes three times, and was pacing as the time drew near. Something about Ryan really pulled her. She couldn't quite put it into words.

In ultimate surrender to nerves, she picked up the phone. "Jean, ah, could you come over for a minute?" Van was too embarrassed to explain why and was relieved when Jean didn't ask any questions.

"What's up?" Jean asked, coming in through the back door. She didn't knock anymore. No one in Nevis bothered to lock their doors. In fact, most residents still left their car keys in the ignition. Nevis would be a field day for the unscrupulous, if any should bother to notice.

Van sat at the kitchen table shuffling a deck of cards. "I feel like I've been neglecting you lately," she said. "Come play some rummy with me." She managed a smile despite the queasy sensation in the pit of her stomach.

"Sure," Jean said. "Dressed awfully fancy for rummy, aren't you? I only dress up for five hundred. Let me know next time; I'll come formal." She smirked as she walked around behind Van and gave her a little pat on the shoulder as she went. "Let's play till Ryan gets here. What time's he coming?"

For all her quirkiness, Jean was often right on the money. Van kept her head down and continued to shuffle. "Soon." Nothing more was said as the two friends began to play cards and wait.

❧

As he approached Van's front door, Ryan paused and looked down at the yellow flowers planted along the walkway. Yellow was his soft spot when it came to flowers. He reached down into the flower bed and picked the biggest blossom. When he arose again, he found himself looking straight into the disapproving face of Charlie Sollars.

"Oh. Hi, there. This one had a broken stem." Ryan grinned feebly, offering up the flower like exhibit A. The grin went unreciprocated. He cleared his throat, turned toward the porch, and bounded up the steps. Giving his clothes the once-over with his hands, he knocked on the door.

"Don't go anywhere," said Van, pleading with Jean as she bolted up out of her chair and headed for the door. She took a deep breath and pulled the door open to reveal a smiling Ryan. Van relaxed at once.

"Hi. Nice to see you again. Here, I brought you something." Ryan's eyes sparkled as he handed her the flower.

Van felt the blush rise on her face. "Oh, that's sweet! A marigold!" she said, laughing. "You shouldn't have. Can you give me just a minute? I'll put this in some water in the kitchen." Van started to turn away from Ryan when she suddenly whipped back around to face him. "Wait a minute. You just gave me that with your left hand. You're left-handed, you dog! Why'd you give me such grief over my shirt the other day?"

Ryan slowly began to smile. "You're cute when you're angry. I enjoy feisty."

Van could only answer his boldness with a deeper blush. "I'll be right back."

"I'll be right here," he replied.

Van darted back into the kitchen. "Go," she said, sweeping Jean out the back door with one hand and grabbing her arm and pulling her back inside with the other. "Wait! Do I look okay?"

Jean looked down at the marigold that Van was still holding. "You know he picked that out of your flower bed, don't you? And your face is just as red as a geranium."

"Yeah, I know," Van said, and giggled. "But he's still sweet."

"Let me know when you want me to smack that goofy smile off your face," Jean said, and the back door swung shut behind her.

When Van came back into the living room Ryan was studying the collection of pictures she had on the wall above her couch.

He turned as she entered. "Daguerreotypes. These are amazing and in good condition. Are they family? I really like this one," he said, pointing to the picture of a man and a woman, both dressed in black, gazing solemnly at the photographer.

"Yes. I love genealogy. I've done a lot of research, quite a few pictures, but these are my favorites, especially that one. It's my great-great-great-grandparents, William Seagle and Eliza Kline. They look so young! They were married in 1850. I've always wondered if this was their wedding picture."

"And the man in this one," Ryan said, picking a picture up off the table. "Who's this? He looks familiar. I think I know him from somewhere."

"Him? I don't think so. That's my husband, Richard."

"Oh, you're married? You never mentioned that little nugget of information. Perhaps I should go."

"No. Richard and I have been separated for a while. I just filed separation papers. When I have fulfilled legal separation requirements, I'm filing for divorce. Our life together is over and has been for a while." Van shifted uncomfortably on her feet and flipped her hair back behind her ear. "Look, I'm not in the habit of spilling my life story to men I meet on the boardwalk, even if they do buy me ice cream. Is that enough information for you?"

"Yeah. Sorry. I do appreciate your honesty. I just don't want to be the cause of any friction between you and your husband. As far as I know, I have never intentionally gotten involved with a married woman."

"I can assure you that won't be the case. I really just need a friend right now. Is that possible?"

"Sure," he said, with a little laugh, and set the frame back on the table. "I'm pretty certain I've met your husband before. Wait," he said, silencing Van with a finger to his lips and standing silently a moment. The blank, receptive look on his face gradually turned into a frown. "I wish I could say, but right now it escapes me. I'll think a while on it.

"And who's this?" he asked, turning his attention to the picture of a skydiver in free fall. "Awesome picture."

"That's my son. I love that picture. When he was a little boy he used to say he wanted to fly, but not like a plane, like a bird.

He always wanted to go skydiving. That was taken the day after he turned eighteen. We took him skydiving for his birthday. She laughed. "It could be anyone under those goggles and helmet."

"No, I can totally connect to this," Ryan said with a quizzical look on his face. "I get almost a vicarious rush just looking at the picture. How old?"

Van was momentarily at a loss for words and wished she could take back the ones she had already spoken. "He's gone. Six years after that picture was taken he was dead, killed in a freak accident right after law school."

The mood in the room changed as a note of awkwardness hung in the air. She looked up at him with pain in her eyes but no tears.

"I'm sorry. You must think I'm an insensitive lout. It seems like all I ever do is apologize to you. How long ago?"

"No, it's me. I should watch what I say. It makes it awkward. It's been two years."

"Still terribly hard, I imagine."

"Very much so. The guilt and the longing. There are so many things I'd like to go back and . . . It's overwhelming at times. I don't like to think of him as a memory, you know? I think of him as something I'm moving *toward,* not away from. It's not so much what he would have become or the potential he had; it's what he was. I miss the essence of him, most of all talking to him. Does that make any sense? He was such a smart, interesting, funny person. That's what I miss." Van walked over and took the picture frame from Ryan. "I miss all the times he would bring his guitar into my room and play for me something he was learning. I miss the way he laughed, and I miss the way he always gave me thoughtful opinions on what I was wearing when I asked. I miss . . ." Van closed her eyes and drew in a deep breath.

"You know what really hurts? I never got to say good-bye. When my mother died I sat and held her hand and watched her life slip away, her breathing slow down, and her heart stop. I told her I loved her, and I was able to let her go. Not my son. He slipped away without a good-bye, and there will forever be the last time together I didn't get, the last 'I love you' I didn't get to say. He died wet, cold, and alone."

Tears spilled down her cheeks as she blinked. "There is no closure. He haunts my daydreams and my nightmares. It's difficult talking about him, but at the same time it's hard to just dismiss him from my life." She put her head down. "I'm sorry. I shouldn't have said all that. I don't even know you." Van studied Ryan's face and smiled. "You are easy to talk to. Another time, maybe I'll tell you about him."

"So, let's say we change the subject," Ryan offered. His eyes lingered a moment longer on the photo as Van returned it to its proper place on the table. "This is a nice old house. I got a comfortable vibe as soon as I walked in the door. Lived here long?"

"Five generations of my family, every one adding character wrinkles, but no big changes over the years. It's a great old house full of memories. Like the teething marks my father left over there on the windowsill—just big enough to totter around and get into trouble. Or the scratch marks on the cast-iron spindles of the railing on the steps heading upstairs. Every kid who ever set foot in this house learned that they could slide the little round decoration up and down each spindle. And every one of 'em got yelled at for scratching the spindles. Or the hatch marks on the door frame in the bedroom to measure how fast everyone grew. It's all here.

"There have been a few unwanted changes, but not many. Had to cut down the big oak next to the house last year. That was hard. My son and his friend used to sneak out at night climbing down that tree. They thought we didn't know, but it's hard for kids to sneak around in a town this small—twenty sets of extra eyes keeping track of them. We always knew where they were and what they were up to. We let them think they got away with it. Why spoil a harmless childhood secret, right? Sneaking out is an ageless rite of passage."

Ryan chuckled. "I think it's a boy thing. Speaking of family, where do you find your genealogical information? Are there many records online?"

"People know I'm interested in genealogy, so they give me old things. Like those boxes over in the corner—Mrs. Morgan, my neighbor, gave them to me before she moved. I haven't even looked in them yet. Some records are online, some down at the courthouse. They say if you want to trace your family, just follow the land. I'm constantly in land records."

Ryan's interest piqued immediately. "Does your courthouse here have land records? Of course, that would be easier, having them close by," he added quickly.

"Yes. Just about all the records for this area are located right here. I've never had to leave Nevis to hunt down what I need."

Ryan looked away as something moving outside the window caught his attention. "Did you know half a dozen people are outside taking pictures of your house? Is there something I should know—be heading out the back door, maybe?"

Van walked over and flipped open the curtain. "Tourists. Today it's the oriental crowd. Relax. I don't think you have to bolt just yet. The county welcome center has my house listed on the summer house tour. You know, drumming up business—any business. If only there was something here for them to spend money on."

"No protection for the locals?" He chuckled.

"None," she deadpanned. "Total victims. Welcome to the human aquarium."

"What's so special about the house?"

Van stood there looking at him for a moment, trying to decide whether he really was interested or was merely being polite. "It's the last of the pickle boat houses. My great grand-father was a pickle boater, and he built and lived in this house. There used to be a lot of them strung out along the shoreline, but they've all since vanished, all but this one. Victims to time and progress. The residents of Nevis are proud, and their memories are long, and almost everyone in town has some memory or association wrapped up in this house. It's like a living symbol of our shared heritage. It's an everyman kind of house."

"Like I said, I can feel it. It has an odd way of making me feel right at home. But I have to ask, what's a pickle boater? I thought you *grew* pickles, not fished for 'em."

Van laughed and shook her head in disbelief. "That's right, I forgot. You're a city boy. Technically, you grow cucumbers and pickle them to make pickles. You can't actually grow a pickle." She laughed, and her mood began to lighten. "We're talking fish. Nevis wasn't always known for its breezes and boardwalk. They say years ago there were so many fish in the bay, you could almost walk across their backs to shore. Can you imagine the water teeming with them, all glittering silver in the sun? This little nothing town was once very well known for its pickled fleet. They brought up the rear, content just to provide a good life for their families. Do you know anything about fishing in this area?"

Ryan shook his head. "Nothing."

"Shad fishing was a thriving industry here. Fishermen lived in little bungalows, just like this one, plying their fishing trade. Farther up north, the bay narrows and the salt water mixes with fresh. In the spring, great schools of shad would come in from the sea and head north to spawn in the shallow fresh waters at the head of the bay. They say fishermen could go out with their little boats and gill nets and bring in enough profit in one season to tide them over for a year. Boats brought their hauls in and pickled them right here in Nevis. It was a good living for people . . . Unfortunately, success was also their undoing. They overfished and decimated the shad population until none of them could make a decent living. Progress wasn't a friend to this town.

"When I was little we spent summers here. Every Sunday, we'd get dressed up and march ourselves down to Granddaddy's pier, and he would take us to church by boat. The church sits back from the water, but there's a dock right out front. Beautiful church. All the stained-glass windows tell stories about the sea and sailing, like Jonah and the whale, and Noah and the ark.

"I was my granddad's favorite—followed him everywhere. If he was tuning up the car or working on the boat engine, my head was right in there beside his. My grandmother would call me into the house, yelling, 'Vannie off the pickle boat!' I was always bringing up the rear—the last to quit and come inside, too busy making mud pies on the front steps, chasing lizards in the rhododendron bushes, or tying the cat to one of the big porch posts. Me in my little jump suit, cowgirl boots, and a wild mass of dishwater-blond curls. I was the daydreamer, and I always dreamed that one day I would live in this house.

"So many good memories," she said with a faraway smile. "I like to think this house represents everything that's good and decent about people like my grandparents. They were honest, hardworking, and didn't ask for more than they needed. They were at peace—settled and content with their lives. That's how I would like my life to be." She paused, then said, "If you're up for a little field trip, I'll show you around Nevis."

"Madam, I am up for anything you suggest." He grinned. "Lead the way."

They headed out the back door to avoid the gaggle of tourists still photographing the house.

SEVEN

ONE MAN'S TRASH

Van and Ryan walked along the sunny boardwalk, admiring the town and the bay. Off to their right, the street ran parallel to the shore as far as they could see, before curving around a building and out away from the bay. Tall oaks lined the street and bordered a wide-open grassy space where a scampering herd of kids played tag. Every so often, a break in the curbing served as the sole reminder of an old driveway to a house long since disappeared. Pausing at one of the lookout points, forearms on the railing, Van and Ryan gazed out across the water. Haze lingered on the horizon as if in defiance of the beating sun, and the steel gray water looked like glass in the still air.

"Look, in the distance," said Van, pointing across the water. "See the opposite shoreline? That's Kent Island. Some days you can see trees. If you're ever back this way, I could take you sailing . . . if you'd like. We could go over that way. It's beautiful."

"No, no, I'll pass on that one," Ryan said, putting his hands up. "I have a healthy respect for the water. I don't even swim. You tell me about it while we're standing on dry land. Not that I'm averse to coming back," he added, quickly looking at Van. "Show me a pickle boat."

"Can't. They disappeared decades ago."

"Well, so what are these boats pulled up along the dock here?"

"Those are oyster boats. Come on, I'll show you what a pickle boat looked like."

Across a sandy parking lot sat a solitary building of faded yellow clapboard trimmed in rusty red. An old train station, it must have been quite a looker in its day. A mansard tile roof and traces of fish scale siding on the dormers hinted at its bygone glory. The big windows, and what looked like a little ticket window, had long been boarded up. Uneven paint suggested that a huge porch had once stretched across the entire front of the structure, though now only cinder blocks stacked against the foundation gave access to the front door.

Van pulled a jingling ring of keys out of her pocket and popped open the padlock on the door. "Watch your step," she said. "The porch was rotten and we had to pull it off."

The old red door groaned a little as it opened, and the smell and feel of old, dusty air hung heavy, greeting them the moment they walked across the threshold and onto the old narrow-planked floor.

"Wow, what is all this jun—er, stuff?" Ryan asked, stepping in behind Van and peering into the gloom. At one end, the space was stacked nearly to the ceiling with boxes and papers. Clothes were neatly organized in one corner; newspaper clippings hung in old frames on the walls; and in a far corner, a life-size carousel horse with muted red, white, and blue embellishments stood still attached to its faded barber-striped pole. The stallion's once fiery eyes now gazed back with a vacant, slightly dazed look—a sad reminder of a simpler, more innocent time. In between the more organized stacks were heaps of items piled haphazardly one upon another, their purpose and provenance indiscernible to the casual eye. An old-fashioned counter held flat trays of jewelry, and an antique cash register brooded under drapes of faded bunting.

"Welcome to the home of the future Nevis Historical Society," said Van, with a sweeping flourish of her hand. "Doesn't it just *breathe* history? I adore this old building."

"Right now it's the only thing breathing," Ryan said, inhaling through his mouth. "Where did all of this come from?"

"Collected, borrowed, salvaged. Some of it belonged to my grandparents. When I got old enough to appreciate Nevis I began collecting everything I could get my hands on. People bring me boxes of stuff. I'm not even sure what's here, but at least I know it's safe. Some people laugh at me, but I feel in my soul that one day things like this will matter. It's too important to let slip away. We should never let our past slip away." She turned and ran her hand lovingly along the top of a dusty box. "Boxes upon boxes I haven't even opened yet. Some of these might actually be old courthouse records. There was a fire years ago. One day researchers will be dying to get at these. Mark my words."

"Oh, I am," Ryan replied, resting his hand on a box of papers. He noted with disappointment that they were all taped shut.

"Come over here, and I'll show you a pickle boat," Van said, taking Ryan's hand and pulling him to the far end of the room. "Look," she said, pointing to an old framed photograph of a fisherman pulling a net aboard a wooden boat. The boat was long and low, not beautiful by any stretch—a work boat. "That's my great-granddad, and there's your pickle boat." She beamed with pride at the photo of the old man she obviously loved so well.

Ryan could see her becoming more animated with each piece of history she talked about. Clearly, this was her passion. Now she was pulling him in the opposite direction, to a display case with little cardboard buildings and miniature trees.

"Lovely," he said. "What is all this?"

"It's a model of Nevis in its heyday. I had someone I know build it from old descriptions, pictures, and drawings I'd found. To understand Nevis today, you have to understand what you *don't* see. I called this a 'nothing town,' but actually, Nevis has a pretty impressive history. After George Washington got done sleeping here and the fishing industry collapsed, the railroad moved in and recreated the town. Without air-conditioning, people in Washington were eager to escape the city. Summer there was stifling, and rich Washingtonians built summer houses at the north end of the rail line. The middle class, common folk like us"—she laughed—"came south by train to places like Nevis, along the shore of the bay. Nothing like a soft bay breeze and a cool dip in the water. Nevis was a jewel on the shore, blessed by the added attraction of an amusement park. It was Shangri-La for the common man.

"Here, next to my finger, running along the shore, is the boardwalk. It was over a thousand feet long. See the tiny steamboat? They used to bring vacationers from Baltimore. And over here, this is the end of the railway line, the Chesapeake Rail Express, which brought people out from Washington. That little building right there—that's where we are.

"These old postcards I collected," Van said, pulling a notebook off a stack of boxes, "give you a better sense of what was here. Nevis really began to grow when the railroad decided to develop the area as a resort. They laid out new streets in grid fashion. Streets running parallel to the shore are numbered. Perpendicular ones are arranged alphabetically after types of trees in the area. If you look across the parking lot, you are looking at Carr Avenue, named after one of the main planners of the community. The planned street grid from a hundred years ago is pretty much in place. I think that's pretty remarkable." Van looked quizzically at Ryan, waiting for some sort of affirmation.

"Well, you certainly have bits and pieces of a lot of things here," he said as he walked around the room peeking at this and picking up that. This was a side of Nevis that he had never stopped to consider in HYA's planning sessions. There were roots here that he didn't have, and he could almost feel them reaching out to him as if in response to an inner yearning that surprised him. And as he brushed against Van's shoulder, he could feel himself pulled down another, more dangerous path. He began to see Van in a different light—one tinged by an undeniable sexual attraction. Her small frame, looking even more petite amid the tall stacks of boxes and paraphernalia, was his type. In fact, everything about her was his type. He tended to admire strong, educated women and the tug-of-war they presented. They were the most challenging, but this made the conquest that much sweeter. Attraction—no, make that lusty, raw sex—was something he had never been one to avoid when the opportunity presented itself. His mind flashed rapidly through the memories of several encounters in unusual settings. Never a train depot, though. And suddenly, the dim, dusty atmosphere of the place began to stir his fantasies.

Out of the corner of his eye, he could see her looking at him. He turned and guided his hand up her back, leaning into her and taking her lip between his. She responded with a soft moan as her arms wound around him. Their tongues met as Ryan's hands slid down to the curve of her bottom and pulled her tighter to him. What he couldn't do to a woman like this! The thoughts were endlessly hypnotic . . .

"Ryan, are you with me? Earth to Ryan."

Jolted back to reality, he realized he was staring at the wall. Van was no longer standing next to him but had moved away and was flipping a tarpaulin up to expose an old oak cabinet sitting in the corner.

"Sorry, just taking it all in," Ryan said, thinking quickly and gesturing with his hand. Picking up an old newspaper, he moved toward her, the unexpected, always slightly alien emotion of guilt washed over him. "You were saying? Wow, this all original?" he asked, looking at the pressed-penny machine. "This must be worth a lot."

"All original, used right here in Nevis. And yes," she said, laughing, "it still makes very pretty pressed pennies showing a carousel. I think it dates from about 1900. Some of the postcards show a carousel from that era. If you have some change, I can press one for you."

"Sorry to disappoint, Ms. Hardy. Like most men, change is not one of the things I carry around in my pockets."

"Your loss, Mr. Man. Maybe you'll be more intrigued by this one." She pulled the tarp off another machine, much smaller than the first. "Care to guess?"

Ryan puzzled over it a moment, then said, "I have no idea . . . parking meter?"

"Penny arcade. This one's a mutoscope, an early type of motion-picture machine. It's like a flip book. Here, take a look. It works."

Ryan came close and put his eye up to the eyepiece while Van inserted a penny into the box and slowly began turning the side crank. As the pictures began to flip, Ryan chuckled, watching the old movie unfold.

"Wow," he said, straightening up with a twinkle in his eyes, and laughing. "Bathing suits have come a ways in the last hundred years. I'm assuming this would have been risqué for the era?"

"Oh, quite. No self-respecting woman would have even watched such frolicking on the beach. This was probably in a men's smoking area."

"These are terrific. Where on earth did you find them? They're in great shape."

"Oh, yeah, perfect running order. They were found in someone's attic in town. Her grandfather worked the arcade. When everything shut down suddenly, everything kind of went up for grabs. The locals probably carted off quite a bit more. How much of that survived is anyone's guess. Nevis is full of untapped potential just waiting to be discovered."

Ryan watched as Van lovingly replaced the tarps over the two arcade machines. "Van," he said gently, "what's your story? Somehow you seem out of place here in this little town that lives in its past."

"Do I? I was born in Washington, D.C., and grew up in the Maryland suburbs. My father was born and raised here. I was happily married for quite a while. When my son died, my marriage tanked. I hung in there like a good little wife until my mother died. That was the final straw, my last emotional connection with anyone. Have you ever been in a room full of people and felt alone—totally, achingly alone? I've felt that way for so long . . ." Van closed her eyes and took a breath before continuing in a quieter voice, "After we separated I came to live here. If I can't find peace here, then it isn't to be found. End of story." She looked at Ryan and shrugged.

Ryan looked at her with thoughtful eyes, and a little more guilt crept into his soul as he slammed the door on his momentary lapse into sexual fantasy. "I'm sorry about your son. I just can't imagine . . ." He shook his head.

"No, you could never imagine. Even in your worst imaginings, you couldn't. For months I cried every morning and every night in the car to and from work. Sometimes I just screamed. Friends would cheer me up, and as soon as I was out of sight the tears would flow once again. Have you ever suffered a deep loss?"

He shook his head. Unless, of course, he counted his entire life in general, but that wasn't something he would discuss with a stranger, no matter how comfortable he felt.

"The grief came in rolling, burning physical waves. Nothing was important—or unimportant, for that matter. For months I existed in a deep pit, and from sunup to sundown, Richard and I never stopped moving, because to stop meant time to feel, and we couldn't handle that. And all day and all night my mind just kept going, trying to rationalize the horror of it all. It consumed all my thoughts. I know what hell is like, and let me tell you, I never want to go back there."

"I honestly can't imagine. You know, when I first saw you daydreaming on the boardwalk I never would have thought you had such sadness in your life. I could tell you were a thoughtful person, but then later you were so happy."

"After I cussed you out."

"Right," he said, laughing. "After the sailor mouth. I never would have guessed."

"They tell me I look good for my age, but I'd gladly trade my smooth skin for a few laugh lines. Fate or happenstance—you never get over it. Some days you get through it, but you never get over it. Reminders come in the simplest ways: a song on the radio, a lookalike on the street, or, worst of all, a wedding invitation reminding you of what might have been. There are constant reminders of the wedding you will never see, the grandchild you will never hold, and the last hug you will never get. In the end, what it comes down to for me is faith and hope. I get through every day knowing that one day I will see him again. I know that without question. If I didn't believe that, I would have lain down a long time ago and not gotten up again."

Van reached up and clasped the small silver medal on the chain around her neck and closed her eyes, and still there were no tears.

"Religious medal?"

"James's confirmation saint. Do you know the story of St. Christopher? He ferried travelers across a dangerous stretch of river. One of them was the Christ child in disguise." She tucked her chin in and studied the figure on the medal. "I pray every night that St. Christopher recognized him and ferried him to safety on the other side."

They both sat in silence, she with nothing more to say and he with nothing that he *could* say. The thought of drowning filled Ryan with undeniable terror, and he began to sweat.

Van looked across the room at everything she had collected. "I love this place. Nevis represents everything my family has ever been. I have roots here. I'm not ready to let go of my past. I don't want it to be like names on a family tree, on a piece of paper, that have no story—just names, no longer real people."

"You know, Van, it's not always good to live in the past. Sometimes we have to let things go, and move on. That doesn't mean we forget. Memories can be beautiful. Everything we experience becomes a part of us, shapes us. But we also have to embrace the here and now of life and let it lead us into joyful things—maybe kicking and screaming, but getting us there nonetheless.

He sat down on an old steamer trunk. "Did you ever wish some new type of commerce would move into the area and revitalize Nevis? Instead of just scraping along, maybe these people should sell their land and move somewhere their families would have more of a future. I'm sure someone would come in and make offers if they knew locals would sell. In fact, people wouldn't even have to move away. Just imagine the jobs and employment a big project would bring into the area. It'd be like the railroad all over again—a renaissance."

Van drew back from Ryan until they were eye to eye. "Whoa, don't get carried away," she said. "People here don't want an influx of newcomers. They like their own ways, some of them handed down, father to son, since colonial times. They're happy here. It's slow and good. Opportunities here are different from those in cities like New York. Not everyone has to be a doctor or a lawyer or an investment banker to be somebody. When you grow up along the water you have an appreciation and respect for nature, and you see life a little differently. Only an outsider like you would see living in Nevis as a negative."

"'Whoa' is right. I surrender," Ryan said, backing away from her with his palms up. He laughed. "I didn't mean to get you all worked up, and I'm pretty sure I didn't say anything negative. Dang, you're feisty. It was just a passing thought. Peace, okay?

You're probably right: locals know best." Taken aback by Van's hostility, he decided to listen more and talk a little less. He could feel the conversation sliding off the tracks. Her blessing wasn't essential to getting his job done, but it would have made things a lot easier.

"You don't understand, but that's okay," she said. "I can't let go. It's all I value and all I have. I don't want my son to be just a memory. He existed and he still exists . . . somewhere." Her head was down, and she played with her fingers as she blinked back the tears that she could feel threatening to tumble down her face.

Ryan moved closer but did not go to her. He never quite knew what to do when a woman cried. And this time especially, it threw him for a loss. If all went as planned, as he hoped, Nevis would soon cease to exist. But he had never had to put a face on those plans until now. He didn't like what he was seeing or feeling, and that was a revelation. He didn't know Van well enough to reach out, hold and comfort her, even though he wanted that. He could only stand here awkwardly and wait out her emotions, hoping she could get herself together. He shoved his hands into his pockets, then just as quickly pulled a hand back out and reached out to Van, putting a small coin in her hand. "Here. You're religious."

Van picked the small guardian angel coin out of her palm.

"I, uh, always carry that in my pocket. I thought you could use it right now. Sorry, I've offended you."

She looked up with wide eyes that bored into his as if she were trying to read his soul. He flinched and looked away, embarrassed.

"I gave my son one of these," she said. "He had it in his pocket when he died. I found that so comforting. While I was searching for meaning in his death, I knew that he had found meaning in his life. He had faith. I must have bought a zillion of these after he died. I used to give them out to everyone. I can't tell you how many people told me that the angel coin came to them at a time in their life when they really needed it. This is such a special coin."

"I could impress you by saying my reason for having it was the same, but I have to admit, it was an impulse buy—just a lucky talisman."

"I don't think God would have a problem with that. You're not religious, I take it?"

"Not particularly. More superstitious than religious."

"Thank you, but you should take it back. I have a few. Maybe the day when you need it hasn't come yet. And then, hopefully, you'll see it more like I do."

Ryan shrugged and took it back. He had no idea why he had bought it. It just seemed to call to him.

They took their time walking back to Van's house. Their relationship was easy, and it would have been apparent to a casual observer that they were becoming close and falling fast. A casual step too close, and their hands bumped—and clasped. When neither let go, Van looked up at Ryan with a smile he couldn't resist, and he pulled her close to his side, where she remained for the rest of the walk back. It was a comforting embrace.

Ryan walked her up the steps of her porch, where he reluctantly released her. "Thank you for trusting me enough to share so much with me, Van," he said. "There *is* something irresistible about you." He hesitated and looked down at his shoes a moment. "I hope my saying that doesn't make you uncomfortable. I would give a penny for your thoughts, if I had one. But somehow, that feels like I'm shortchanging you, so what would you say to a Yankee dime?" And with that, he leaned in and kissed her lightly on the lips.

She pulled back in surprise, speechless.

"I looked up 'Yankee dime,'" he said, grinning. "That's ten times better than a penny!"

She laughed, and he could tell that she liked it. He stood staring at her for several seconds too long, then turned and walked away across the yard.

EIGHT

NO DEED GOES UNPUNISHED

Ryan met Hector at the courthouse to take care of business. They both were good at what they did, but not good together. It was always a game, a race, to see who could best the other and still come out looking pretty. Usually, it was Ryan, and Hector hated him for it. Hector always seemed to have Ryan's back, but as Ryan well knew, he usually had a knife in his hand.

Hector Young and Associates was the type of company that flew under the radar. For appearance's sake, it appeared to be a solid return on stockholder investments, if you could ever manage to invest. It was heavily controlled by an old-boy network, the kind that went to discreet, members-only places like the Dandy Club or Park House and never drew attention by its flashiness. HYA hired only the brightest, most qualified candidates, mostly lawyers. There were lawyers to steer the company around trouble as it cruised the shady side of corporate greed, and lawyers to get it out of trouble if someone screwed up. Lawyers screwed up only once at HYA. To the public eye, it was a pillar of the community, but this was just the gleaming white tip of the iceberg. Below the surface floated the dirty, bloated ice that could sink ships with utter indifference.

HYA usually got what it wanted, and what it wanted right now was land—*Nevis* land. Nevis was a rich resource, though not in the usual minerals, oil, or agriculture. Instead, it was rich in location. Strategically situated on the Chesapeake Bay, it had easy access to the sea—a sea too vast to be effectively monitored or patrolled by authorities.

Hector Young and Associates liked to do its own research, never accepting anything at face value. That was what made it so successful. One didn't achieve success like that by taking anything for granted, especially the competition. Killer instinct was key. HYA's first order of business was to find out whom it was dealing with—who owned the land.

Ryan and Hector spent the better part of the first afternoon scouring the land records for the surrounding area. Both were lawyers, and Ryan was particularly well schooled on land records in the region. The Nevis courthouse should have what they needed. The problem was that over the preceding 350 years, no one had developed a system to keep track of all the records. Shelves and boxes overflowed with liber and folio.

"Do you think we might get some help from Lilly Librarian over there?" Hector asked Ryan.

"Probably not," Ryan said. "She said land records could be anywhere in here. Any more info than that, and I suspect we're on our own. She's busy lining her pencils up straight." The librarian briefly looked in their direction and then, satisfied that all was well, went back to straightening the front desk.

Hector took a step back and ran his gaze up and down box upon box of all manner of written documents, each packed box an unlabeled surprise.

"No index for all this?" he muttered. "Shit, we could be here forever!"

"You could always go home and stay out of my way."

"I wouldn't give you the satisfaction," Hector said, pulling down a cardboard file box. The top slid off, and it began to rain papers down on his head and out across the little room, covering him in the musty smell of crackly old paper.

"Shit."

Ryan laughed. "Suit yourself," he muttered.

They spent the next few days pulling down and sifting through every box and piece of paper they could find, never quite sure what they were looking for, knowing only that they hadn't found it yet. Working at separate ends of the room seemed to work best, the distance between them lowering the aggravation factor. For all his faults, Hector was shrewd, sharp, and speedy, reviewing documents much faster than Ryan could get through them. And in that respect, Ryan was glad to have him helping. Hector, in turn, was happy as long as he knew where Ryan was and what he was doing.

Ryan couldn't concentrate, because his mind kept returning to Van. More than once he had to backtrack and remind himself of the task at hand. He had been with plenty of women. But this one was different: strong minded and smart. For once, the attraction wasn't entirely about lust. Not that she didn't have the whole package. He could get lost in those big brown eyes, and never mind how interested he was in the land—he found her topography far more intriguing. Still, she got under his skin. Ryan wiped his sweaty forehead and took a long breath to calm the guilty feeling beginning to roil in his stomach. Damn it, that woman! Nagging emotions and disconnected thoughts floated around in him, weightless and rootless. He didn't need any more conflict in his life than he already had. He should let Hector handle her.

He looked up to find Hector watching him, as if keenly fascinated by something in Ryan's demeanor. *Jesus help me,* Ryan thought as he turned his face away. This was a weakness he couldn't afford. He had to cut the bonds that were beginning to form between him and Vanessa Hardy.

On the fifth day of their search, a long, low, soft whistle drew Hector's attention back across the room. He looked up to see Ryan waving a piece of paper at him. Ryan Thomas was first, once again.

"Come have a look," Ryan said. "This is interesting—I think I've found something." He handed Hector a yellowed paper, edges in tatters but still clearly readable.

"What is it?"

"My friend, I think we just hit pay dirt, if you'll excuse the pun. That paper was shoved into the middle of this ledger volume. It doesn't seem to relate to anything else in the box so far. It's a colonial ground lease from the 1720s. I've seen these before. The owner of the property leased it to another party for ninety-nine years, renewable in perpetuity. These were pretty common in Maryland and Pennsylvania. In exchange for the lease, the lessee uses the land, builds on it, or whatever in exchange for a yearly payment to the lessor. Guess where this land is located?"

"Nassau?"

"Yeah, so you need to go book a flight. But no," Ryan said, proceeding past the sarcasm. "This is a lease agreement that looks like it's for the land that now makes up most of Nevis. Are you tracking with me?" he said, noting Hector's blank expression. "Damn, it means no one in Nevis owns the land they're living on. They're all *leasing* it." He grinned at Hector.

"Shit, I'll bet my firstborn that no one here even knows it. The yearly lease payments are probably rolled into the local tax bill. If we look hard enough, we can probably verify that in the tax ledgers for this time period."

Ryan continued to read down through the document, mumbling and musing as he went. "This script is murder to read. Okay," he said, drawing his finger halfway down the page, "there's a specific provision in here that prohibits the tenant from buying the land through any of the provisions of the document. That's very unusual. Original lessor was Jeremiah Harwell, blah, blah, blah, more legalese. You know, Hector," he said, pushing back in his chair, "if we can find out who this man's living descendants are, we can make it well worth their while to sell the land to us. Call the office and ask them to send someone down to trace the lineage."

Hector gave Ryan a sideways glance. "Oh, man, that's going to be like looking for a needle in a haystack. You realize how long that could take us?"

"Maybe not as long as you think. Van said something interesting the other day: People never move away from here—at least, not for good. Generation after generation remains in Nevis from cradle to grave. It shouldn't be too hard. I'll bet the records are all right here. Bet you a fiver the descendants are, too."

"What are you going to do when that chick finds out you didn't have the noblest of intentions?" Hector asked.

Ryan shrugged. "Not a problem. We'll be long gone by then. She's a looker; she'll find someone else to hold her hand soon enough." His stomach tightened as he spoke. It must be the meatloaf he had for lunch up the street.

"If I had a penny for every time we've been through this scenario, I'd be a rich man. You have no shame, Thomas. You need to find you a girl like Maggie. Now, *there's* a keeper."

"I haven't seen you with Maggie lately," Ryan replied. "Last I heard, you were taking her to the family estate for an afternoon of tea and meet the folks. What happened—pinkie not extend far enough?"

Hector immediately got up and looked down at his watch. "I need to head down and meet up with Earl just south of here. Later."

Ryan could have continued for another round, but he didn't. That subject required just the slightest twist of the knife to get the reaction he wanted. "I'll tag along. I haven't seen Earl in a while. There isn't a lot more I can do here. I'll go ahead and see if they can send down someone to pick up the genealogical search."

"Earl and I have business to attend to. Find something else to keep you occupied. I'll catch back up with you in a day or two."

There was no use arguing with Hector once his mind was made up. Although Ryan was curious about the business activity, he decided to cut his losses and focus on Van, find out a little more about her. No one—certainly not a woman—was going to break his stride. He was usually good at mixing in a little pleasure without letting it get in the way of business. In this case, he was going to push it to the limit.

NINE

I SAY YIN AND YOU SAY YANG

When dawn broke, it was obvious that there would be no ambling about and sitting on the boardwalk today. Dark clouds hung over the bay, almost kissing the tips of the chop. It was unusually cool for early September, and Van shivered a little as she peeked out the window. Most days, solitude was a treasure. It wasn't *aloneness*—just a gentle quiet that allowed her to hear and think all the little things that got lost in the usual chaos of noise. Once in a while, though, on days like this, she wished she still had a houseful of family. Sometimes, a little chaos could give birth to a revelation.

She didn't know how Ryan managed it, but he postponed going back to New York for a while. Van assumed he had enough pull in the company to schedule his own time. He certainly had the manner and dress of someone used to commanding people and attention. In a few short weeks, she and Ryan had managed to spend a lot of time together. Some evenings, they sat late into the night just talking and cuddling on her front porch. She was mesmerized by the way he looked at her, and he was the most attentive listener she had ever met. He never seemed to tire of asking questions about Nevis: who lived here, who their relatives were—endless questions about the land and how she followed it. They even went to the courthouse one day, and she showed him some of the genealogical sources she used. A smile crossed her lips at the thought of how they held hands. Actually, everything about Ryan made her smile . . . or blush.

Van hadn't seen Ryan for several days and wasn't holding out hope for today, either. Things had come up unexpectedly, he said, and he would be gone awhile. She felt caged and restless without him, pacing between rooms, trying to figure out what to do with herself. Maybe she was relying on him too much.

Finally, as if by instinct, she headed for the bathroom and started a bath. A bath was her failsafe when she was out of sorts, bored, or world-weary, so that the measure of a bad day could be tallied in the number of baths. She expected today to be more wearying than usual. Richard had insisted on coming to visit her, and she expected him late in the day. It would be difficult. Given her unchanging feelings about their relationship, there was no way the visit would turn out well.

She grabbed a tablet and pen in the study before undressing and climbing in the tub. Resisting the urge to add bubble bath, she sank down in the hot water and tilted her head back against the rim, eyes closed. The warmth of the water spread through body and bones, soothing both. She scooted down in the tub until the water touched the ends of her hair in the back. In the silence within, floating suspended in the water, she let her mind wander where it would.

Before long, she found herself dreaming about her favorite little boy again, all dressed in blue, his chubby little belly peeking out beneath the striped shirt. He reached up and handed her a little yellow flower, smiling with delight, his hand small, warm, and soft. Turning her mind's eye, she watched as he ran teetering back across the grass, laughing in his high little-boy voice, beckoning to her to chase him. Everything about him inspired the magic of the beautiful summer day surrounding them. "I love you," she whispered as she watched him go.

She sputtered as hot bathwater slid up over her face. With a start, she realized that she had fallen asleep. Pushing with her feet, she shoved herself farther up in the tub and dried her face off with a towel. With her body readjusted, she again closed her eyes. Sadly, she knew she wouldn't be able to rejoin the boy in the field, but perhaps she could find him somewhere else.

When the new vision finally appeared, it was nothing quite so lovely or comforting. They were arguing, a man and a woman on opposite sides of a room, neither looking at the other. "I can't take this anymore. I'm leaving," the woman sobbed as she began to unravel, turning away as if to spare herself the final indignity of having an audience present. But then, all at once, she seemed to pull herself together, as if drawing strength from some inner source. Pausing to take a deep breath, she stood up, straightened her shoulders, and turned to face the man across the room. "If I thought there was anything good and loving left to express and share between us, I would stay. But there isn't. There is finally nothing left to say. There's so much pain inside me, I don't see anything else when I look at you. Your eyes reflect only the pain—no love, no empathy, no shared purpose or burden." The woman hesitated. "I need someone to lean on, but I'm all alone. We're empty to each other. I don't blame you, and I don't blame me. We're just broken, and staying together isn't going to fix us. I would tell you I love you, but I don't think you'd hear me or that it would matter. Good-bye,

Richard. Take care of yourself." With that, the woman walked out of the room, slamming the door behind her. Van could feel the tears burning in her eyes as she watched her go. She slid down and completely submerged herself in the tub, becoming one with the humming swish, encased in her protective water-filled womb.

❧

Van's mood continued at a low ebb throughout the afternoon as she worked on her family trees and tried to keep the demons at bay. Today was a good day for it. She had been neglecting genealogy lately in favor of the nice weather and other distractions. The "other distractions" did make her smile again. Ryan was her black swan. She wasn't sure what she had done to deserve him. She knew with certainty only that she was smiling much more often and felt happy for the first time in a long while.

She flipped the computer on and pulled out the top three file folders from the desk. "Get off the papers, cat," she muttered, grabbing the bottom of the stack and trying to yank them out from under the well-nourished feline. It was like this every time she settled into a nice routine at the computer. She would immediately acquire a little furry friend. Sometimes a warm little purring head would settle itself gently onto her typing hand and doze until she had to use the computer mouse. Other times, she would have to bob and weave to evade the paw that kept flicking at her face, trying to catch her attention. Cats were great. They asked for so little, and that was just what she had to give.

As the time approached for Richard to arrive, she got into a rhythm of reading the wall clock, checking the window, and typing a little. Wall, clock, window, type. It shouldn't be this hard, she thought. Maybe she cared more about Richard than she was willing to admit. Maybe she did need him in her life. Her gaze wandered outside, and she found herself watching a pair of finches hopping in the limbs of the beech tree. She loved birds. Her grandfather had taught her that they were a symbol of the living soul. She liked that. They put her in a peaceful place, especially when they lined up like pearls on a string across the telephone lines outside her house.

She was so deep in thought and emotion that the knock on the door took her by surprise, and she jumped from the chair where she sat. When she reached the door it was hard to tell whether her heart was racing in anticipation or surprise.

She hugged Richard at the door and swept him into the room with a wave of her hand. He sat on the couch, and she crossed the room and sat near him in the easy chair, although sitting in it was anything but.

"You're looking good," she said.

"You, too." His smile was tight, and he tried to relax his clenched hands. "How've you been?"

"I've been good. Life is good here," Van said, nodding and smiling stiffly in return.

This set the tone for most of their conversation: soft topics that skimmed the surface of everyday life. Inevitably, the conversation began to slow and falter.

Richard got up from the couch. "I've missed you," he said as he closed the space between them. "We spent so much energy fighting when we were together. That's all we did. In the last months, I've been able to step back and get some perspective on our relationship. Van, I've really missed you."

"Richard, I really don't want to go down this road right now," she said, standing up face-to-face with him.

"I just feel like my days are so incomplete without you . . . Please," he whispered, and his voice began to break. "Come home." He timidly reached for Van's waist and tried to pull her close.

"Richard, please don't," she said, pulling back and turning away from him. "I'm not ready to have this conversation. I moved out so I could think things through. I still need time. I just can't continue the way we were going. I thought you understood that. The last thing I need is for you to pressure me."

"Van, I'm not trying to pressure you, but the longer we stay apart, the greater the risk that we'll let this part of our life slip away. We've already lost so much. We can weather this. If we go our separate ways, then everything we've ever worked for is gone. We'll have nothing to show for all those years. I'm truly sorry for what happened between us. I wasn't faithful. To the very bottom of my heart, I'm sorry. I needed someone, and I couldn't find you. As a grieving woman, you couldn't be there. I understand that. I can't take back what I did. If I could, I would."

There was nothing more that Van could say. She looked blankly at Richard, wondering how she could say it all differently so that he would understand. Her mind raced.

"Is there someone else?" he asked.

"Oh, no, no one," she said, and this was not a lie. Her growing feelings for Ryan had nothing to do with the alienation she felt from Richard.

"Can't you find it in your heart to forgive me?"

"No, I can't forgive you. You robbed me of two things I can never replace: trust and security. I'm sorry, I can't. After everything I've been through, I've lost the ability to forgive." Van leaned down and picked up Lulu. "I have a need that you just can't fill. I'm too old to have another baby. I don't have a grandchild. The only thing I can do is pick up Lulu and hold her close, feel her little heart beating against me, the way she warms and fills my arms. That's the only thing right now that comforts me."

"You seem to have tolerance for everyone but me, Van. It's a bit hypocritical," said Richard, his voice rising in frustration and irritation. "You talk about turning to God for comfort and how he answers you when you ask for his help, yet the Christian faith is all about forgiveness. Forgiving isn't an ability; it's a gift. Why don't you spend some time asking for that instead of asking only for what *you* need?"

Van looked at him, thunderstruck. "Wow. That hurts. It's not really about being forgiven, though, is it, Richard? Isn't it about you wanting not to fail at something?"

"It's not about failure. It's about us keeping together as a family."

"You know it was neither of our fault what happened to James. You don't have to judge everything in your life by whether it was a success or a failure. You quit telling me that you loved me, and you never hugged or even touched me. How come you could chat me all up when we were dating and then, when we got married, just ignore me? It's like false advertising, don't you think? The old bait and switch? No wonder women get bitchy. When I tried to talk to you it was like talking to a wall. No, I take it back. At least a wall will sometimes echo. With you, nothing. 'Love' is an active verb. You can't just love someone in your head."

"I do love you. I just have so much going on in my mind right now. It never stops. I can't sleep for hashing and rehashing everything that I can keep at bay during the day. You have no idea the turmoil I feel."

Van nodded in agreement. "I've had those days. Not as many now as in the beginning. Maybe you should go see someone," she said in a soft voice, putting her hand on his arm. "Maybe you're depressed. They can treat you for that."

"I can't, don't you understand that?" This time it was his turn to pull away. He put his hands on the back of the chair and hung his head.

"Look, I don't want to fight," he said.

She turned away from him. "Yeah, that's the problem. You never want to do anything."

"There you go again. Nice comment from someone who only wanted to have sex on New Year's and Memorial Day."

"Maybe if it felt more like a lovefest and less like a fuckfest, it might have been more often. I wanted to have more than just sex."

"It's a little hard when you just lie there like a stone maiden with 'please entertain me' written across your forehead."

"You took so long, I felt like drawing you a map with an arrow! I don't want to just give it away to someone who's just using me as a sexual release. Damn it, you have no idea how much I have loved you. But, I'm going to compartmentalize those feelings, just put them away like I have with Mom and James. I'm going to survive all of this. I'm going to flourish. And I want you to watch it happen!"

In the end, fighting was what they did best. By the time he left, Van felt as if she had gone through the wringer, and she watched in silence as he walked out to his car.

She thought most clearly when she wasn't with him—his visit only compounded her frustration and confusion. It was achingly lonely, wanting intimacy but knowing that the one you'd promised your love and your life to could not love you back. There was nowhere else to go. Van was in a prison of her own making. She had kept up her end of the "until death do us part" bargain but felt as if she had secretly made a pact with the devil and bartered away her soul. Life just couldn't continue that way. She had to ask herself whether love was enough to make her stay with Richard even when he couldn't make her happy. Her love didn't depend on whether *he* loved *her*. She would always love him. But she wondered if they would ever be whole enough people again to make each other happy. Somehow, the sum of their parts added up to less when they were together.

Exorcise the demons. She had been down this route before. She grabbed her car keys and took off out of town. She drove a long way in quiet thought before she started to scream, and she didn't stop screaming until she turned around and headed back into town.

❧

Day was rapidly giving way to night as she pulled back up to her house. She was too emotionally weary to get out of the car, and so she just sat there. And that was where Ryan found her, sitting in the front seat with a tear-stained face and a preoccupied stare.

"Van, what are you doing out here?" he said, his voice full of compassion as he gently tried to pull her out of the car. "What's wrong? Come inside, please."

But he could get her to go only as far as the porch before she refused to go any further. Van sat down on the top step, and Ryan found himself forced to sit down beside her. As he did she turned toward him, buried her face in his shoulder, and started to sob uncontrollably. This time it was so easy to wrap his arms around her and let her cry.

"It started with hang-up calls all the time. One day I hit the auto call-back. Imagine my surprise when I knew the voice on the other end! And e-mails—sexual, teasing, revealing an intimacy way beyond casual friends. He cheated on me, Ryan—the other half of my soul!" She babbled on, but her words drowned in the deluge of uncontrollable sobbing.

Ryan stroked her hair and whispered in a hushed voice as he tried gently to calm her down. For the first time that he could remember, he gave of himself without a thought to what he could get out of it, and it felt good and natural. And the two of them molded into each other like pieces of a puzzle, with neither one wanting to pull back. He held her a long time, even after she stopped crying and her breathing evened.

Finally, Van started to pull away. "I'm sorr—"

"Don't," he interrupted, and tightened his arms around her, pulling her closer to him and kissing her hair. She twisted around in his arms, wrapping her arms around his neck and closing her eyes as soft lips met in a gentle, tentative kiss. As the passion rose, the gentleness changed into desperate want, longing, and need.

"Stay," she implored.

"Yes," he answered at once. Taking him by the hand, she pulled him up from the steps, led him into the house, and closed the door.

❧

The next morning, they awoke to the sunlight peeking through the curtains. Ryan's leaving the house was obviously going to get more notice than his entrance last night. Certainly, Mr. Pickett would bear witness; that was a given. Jean, however, was another story. Van didn't want the endless stream of questions and scrutiny *that* would trigger.

"Do you think she's even home?" Ryan asked as he and Van stood giggling like two guilty children, peeking between the slats in the window blinds.

"She usually does her errands in the morning," said Van. "I think she might be gone. Quick—I think you should make a run for it now!"

Ryan bounced down the steps, a little more spring in his step than usual.

"Morning, Mr. Thomas. I see you're up early," Charlie said, coming around the side of the house. Caught dead to rights, Ryan could only nod and walk a little faster to his car without uttering a word. Van could hardly keep a straight face as Charlie turned his gaze on her, standing at the front door in her bathrobe.

Charlie approached her with an expression she had never seen on him before. "Van," he said, "you know I love you, and I know it's none of my damn business, but I just hate to see you get mixed up with that man. Something about him just doesn't sit right."

It wasn't as if she had to answer to him. "It'll be okay, Charlie, but thanks for your concern." She gave him a friendly pat on the shoulder before turning to go back into the house.

"Van," he said, lightly grabbing her arm. "Then at least think about taking it slow, okay? You're probably a little more vulnerable than you'd like to admit, and I'd hate to see someone take advantage of you. Okay?"

"Sure thing, Pop." And this time she gave him a peck on the cheek. She knew he had only her best interests at heart, but she was beginning to get a little annoyed with everyone telling her to take it slow. They all made her seem like a basket case or the village idiot. "Do me a favor and don't tell anyone, okay?"

❧

As Ryan drove away and reality returned, he came down from his emotional high. The smile slid off his face. "You dumb bastard, what are you doing and who the hell are you?" He was getting soft, getting in too deep with this woman. This wasn't like him at all. He ran his hand nervously through his hair. For God's sake, she was *consuming* him. When had he ever wanted to protect a woman instead of just sleeping with her and moving on? He was all over the place, as if the body snatchers had abducted him and replaced him with their own spawn. *The job couldn't be clearer, Thomas. Get the information, forget the woman, and get the hell out of this little burg before you totally lose yourself.*

TEN

EPISODIC NIGHTMARES

It was not a good night. Puzzling dreams and nightmares had come to Ryan before in the powerful moments just before dawn, when the spirit was vulnerable and weak like the light, and thoughts and meanings hid in murk and shadow. And the dreams about her were crazy, like out-of-body experiences that left him uneasy but unable to recall in detail what made them troubling—all interwoven with an oddly familiar classical music piece that his brain loved and insisted on playing over and over again. He sat bolt upright in the bed, awakened by the sound of his own screaming. Dripping wet, he peeled off his T-shirt and flung it at the foot of the bed, where the sheet and blanket already lay in disarray. It was two a.m.—his witching hour.

Ryan struggled out of bed and walked across the room to the balcony. He slid the door open and walked out into the night air as he summoned Beethoven's op 123 from the Web to his cell phone. The strains began to play, and just as he had suspected, they were the stuff of nightmares. He knew every musical nuance, yet he could remember no waking moment when he had heard it before, or how he even knew its name.

"Interesting scream. Rough night?" Hector asked.

Ryan whipped his head around toward the familiar smell of burning tobacco wafting from the balcony next door. The faint red glow of the cigarette gave a general indication of Hector's location. He sounded oddly peaceful in the darkness—a perfectly placed specter of negative dark energy.

"Where were you last night, Ryan?"

"Sorry, I didn't realize we were checking in. Your mother sends her best."

Hector cackled, sounded genuinely amused. "Mothers are fair game. Too bad yours isn't around to join in. It could have been a threesome." He cackled again.

"Fuck off."

"A little testy, are we? I seem to remember being out here first. Beethoven—interesting choice," he said, nodding and sending a smoke ring in Ryan's direction. "Another desperate play for depth and character?"

"It's keeping me calm so I don't act on impulse, jump this railing, and beat the shit out of you. I am impressed, though. How'd you know it was Beethoven?"

"Doesn't everyone grow up listening to classical music at supper? Opus One-twenty-three—Beethoven's search for spirituality. You're feeling suddenly religious. What's going on with you, Ryan?"

"You make conscience and spirituality sound like vices."

"We've done fine without 'em so far. Ryan, you're such a motherfucker—why don't you just sleep with her and get it over with?"

"Shut the hell up," Ryan hissed. "You just don't get it."

"You're the one that's not getting it, apparently. Today would be a good day to head back to New York. We have what we need. What time do you want to leave?"

"Tomorrow. I have loose ends to tie up." Ryan shut off the music, closed the door on the unwanted noise, and went back to bed. A flood of jumbled dreams had been plaguing him since he first arrived in Nevis. He needed to know what they meant. He knew he could piece them together. He just had to concentrate on the commonality. But in spite of all his efforts, he fell almost immediately into a deeper and more troubling sleep than before.

The National Aquarium—windows full of colorful fish floating lackadaisically in a calm blue world. It was peaceful, quiet, as Ryan put his finger up against the glass and watched, fascinated, while the lips of the huge orange fish with black stripes pushed up against the glass and kissed his fingertip. He watched as a tiny bead of water appeared near his finger and began to roll slowly down the wall of glass.

Intrigued, Ryan moved his finger to touch the bead, smearing the wetness around until it disappeared. And then a second bead appeared, and he moved his finger to touch that one, too. And a third appeared, and so on until the glass was trickling with drops of water down the length of the wall. The water began to seep through the pores in the glass and puddle at his feet.

The beautiful calm evaporated, and panic set in. As the water engulfed him, Ryan pounded helplessly on the glass, and excruciating pain shot through his body with the first breath of tepid water. Fighting the urge to breathe was useless, but just as he had resigned himself to breathe again, two strong hands seized him by the upper arms and pulled him to the water's surface. Relief and love swept over him as Van pulled him to her and hugged him tightly.

"Don't worry, son, I'm here. I'm here, James."

There was safety in her embrace, but she quickly pushed him back to arm's length and gave him the once-over. "You need a haircut, boy," she said, ruffling his hair. The boy ducked under her, tilting his head back in laughter as he began to run circles around her. Van stood motionless, absently twirling a yellow flower around in her fingers as she watched him run. Giggling and emboldened by her stillness, he darted too close and she quickly snatched him up into the air and twirled in a circle, with him laughing and squealing in childish delight until she returned him gently to his feet again.

"Do it again! Do it again!" the boy pleaded. "Mommy . . ."

Ryan bolted awake, screaming. "Van?"

ELEVEN

CUTTING THE MUSTARD

Never mind the Maine lobster and melted butter; no self-respecting Marylander would trade delicately flavored Bay crab steamed in red pepper and beer. Once a year, Van traded a couple of paychecks for bushels of blue crab and threw the biggest crab feast of the season. All she had to do was supply the crabs. The Natty Boh beer, potato salad, coleslaw, and other side dishes all came courtesy of friends.

Worshipping at the altar of the blue crab was like a religious experience, with all the pomp and circumstance of Sunday high mass. Only instead of fine altar cloth, ornamental stoups, and goblets crafted of precious metal, the tables were covered in plain brown paper, with disposable cups of vinegar and red pepper, and the beverage of choice served in pop-top cans. Jean and Van spent most of the morning dragging picnic tables around, hosing down lawn furniture, and equipping the tables with paring knives and every crab mallet they could find.

"Heard any more from Ryan?" Jean asked.

"Yeah, we talked last night." Van shot Jean a sideways glance to gauge whether she was baiting her. "He's coming today. Don't get all excited, though—he's bringing a business partner with him."

"Oh, I didn't know he was traveling with anyone. Don't even think about trying to set me up with him," Jean said, giving her a warning look. She was such a blowhard, but then, that was part of her appeal. Apparently, where Ryan spent the night was not going to be a major theme in their conversation.

"Relax; it was only a thought in passing!" Van replied. "Mea culpa. Now, help me bring the cooler and ice around. In fact, you're such a snow queen, you can take the ice."

"Don't think you're hurting my feelings—I'll wear the title proudly."

☙

It didn't matter that they weren't completely ready when the first guests showed up. They had been through this routine before. A crab feast was not something you rushed through. It required beer for the steamer pot, beer for the cook, and beer for your friends, not to mention mountains of potato salad and coleslaw.

Jean had decided to take Ryan under her wing and make him an honorary Marylander. She thought he was too much of a dandy to handle it, but Van was betting he would be able to cut the mustard.

"Ryan, I need your help," said Jean, grabbing him by the hand as soon as he arrived and dragging him toward the steamer pot. "Help me wrangle these loose crabs before they latch on to someone." As she spoke, she reached for the cooking tongs and sprayed the garden hose across the grass. Immediately, several hidden pairs of claws rose up out of the lawn and snapped at the air.

"Like *me,* you mean?" Ryan said, laughing as he tried to make his way over to Van "I don't think so. You go ahead; I'll observe your technique."

"Chicken," Jean said, using the tongs to toss each crab into the steamer pot. "What makes you think you can eat without working for it? Oh, right, you're a city boy. I guess we'll have to cut you some slack." She put the tongs back on the table and again grabbed Ryan by the hand. "Okay, I'm going to show you the proper way to eat crabs. Ready for Crab one-o-one?"

"I can watch someone else first." He shot Van a pleading look, but she gave him thumbs-up and promptly disappeared to mingle with her friends.

"Rule number one: never wipe your eyes. That's grade-A red pepper on those beauties—you'll think you just got Maced. See this?" she said, pointing at the goblet-shaped flap on the bottom of the shell. "This is the apron. Pull it up and off. Then pry the two halves of the shell apart with your thumbs. And watch the steam—these suckers are ho . . . hot!"

Ryan was a good sport and not squeamish. It was an untidy business, culminating in pepper-encrusted hands, and tiny crab-shell cuts burning with vinegar and red pepper. But it was worth it, and even Ryan, a lifelong lobster devotee, had to admit that the tender blue crab was a rare delicacy.

He was good at mingling, and soon everybody was a friend. Still, as he introduced himself to others, his eyes never strayed far from Van's every movement. He needed to talk to her alone, for he was coming to the realization that more than happenstance had brought them together.

"She's a very interesting woman."

Ryan's concentration broke, and he turned to acknowledge the young woman speaking to him, commanding his attention.

She was beautiful, with long, dark hair, laughing green eyes, and a killer smile. Ryan automatically returned the smile. It was a male reaction that the woman was clearly accustomed to.

"Hi, I'm Marla, Jean's daughter," she said, extending a well-manicured hand. She held on just a moment too long, forcing his eyes back up to hers. Again the beautiful smile. He glanced back in Van's direction, but she had disappeared from view. Reluctantly, he returned his attention to the dark-haired beauty.

"Nice to meet you. I didn't know Jean had a daughter. Do you live next door?"

"Oh, no. We do best with occasional visits. You're from New York. I'd give my right arm to live there—not a lot going on in a place like Nevis. I spent time here after my parents split up. It was either find some fun or go crazy. If you ever get too bored, you should give me a call."

"Van's done a pretty good job of showing me around, giving me the lay of the land," he said. "It's not such a bad place. It's all in what you appreciate. As you get older, it'll grow on you."

"I'm probably older than you think. How old do you think I am?"

He smiled. "Not old enough," he said, trying not to show his amusement. "You are a strikingly beautiful young woman, and it's been wonderful meeting y—"

"I'd bet there's the same age difference between us as between you and Vanessa," Marla said, with a tilt of her head as she curled a wisp of her hair around her finger.

Ryan didn't respond immediately but just studied her over the rim of his drink. A month ago, he might have taken her up on her unspoken offer. Still, he was a man who preferred to be the pursuer rather than the quarry, and a meaningless fling was of no real interest at the moment.

"Would you please excuse me?" he said. "I see someone I've been waiting to have a word with." And he backed away and melted into the crowd.

❧

"Cool your jets," said Jean, walking up behind Marla.

Marla turned and laughed. "What?"

"You know exactly what. Van is a friend of mine."

"I thought blood was thicker than water. Guess I was wrong, *Mom*."

"Don't be so obvious. It doesn't become you—in fact, it makes you look cheap."

❧

On the far side of the yard, after scanning the group for Ryan and finding him talking alone with Marla, Van had watched the whole flirtatious encounter. Red flags went up immediately as she saw the closeness of their stance, the way Marla leaned in and laughed while touching Ryan's arm, the way she flipped her hair behind her shoulder. No mixed signals there. As a woman, she had to admire the technique. But as a rival, she had to know how quickly a woman like that could spin a man's head. She started across the yard to limit the potential damage to her budding relationship with Ryan, but before she could close the distance she was relieved to see that he had disappeared and Jean was talking with Marla. She couldn't hear the conversation, but it didn't last long, and they dispersed into the crowd before she could join them.

Relieved, Van changed direction and approached a tall guy she didn't recognize, who was grabbing a beer out of the cooler.

"Hi, I'm Van," she said. "I don't believe we've been introduced."

"Hi, I work with Ryan."

"Are you Earl? Ryan has said so many nice things about you," she said, extending her hand. "So nice to meet you."

"No, I'm Hector Young," he said, shaking her hand. "I also work with Ryan."

"Oh, of course, Ryan works for your company."

"Actually, it's my father's company. I'm a junior. He still runs it, and I'm just one of the peons working there. Someday, hopefully, I'll get a chance to run it."

"It must be an amazing job to be able to travel around and see so many different places. I love listening to Ryan talk about it."

Hector laughed. "Yeah, Ryan's quite a talker. He could charm the hat off the pope. Although I'd say he's a little quieter since his accident."

"What accident?"

"Ryan didn't tell you? I'm surprised. A few years back, he was almost killed in a traffic accident—hit in a crosswalk by a city bus. Hospitalized for weeks. It was real touch and go for a while—they even had to resuscitate him once." Hector paused. "I guess I'm talking out of school. Well, I've already put my foot in my mouth, so I may as well finish. No one thought he had a ghost of a chance of making it, but he pulled through. He's the best that ever worked at Hector Young. In the boss's eyes, no one even comes close—makes the rest of us look like also-rans. But I know him better than anyone. The accident changed everything. It's subtle, but the edge is gone. Good for the also-rans, but I'd just as soon it didn't happen on my watch." Hector popped the top on his Natty Boh and leaned against one of the picnic tables. Like Ryan, he seemed to be a dab hand at meeting and dealing. "Just out of curiosity, has he told you why he's here?"

"He said he was in the area for some acquisitions work," said Van.

"Is that all he said? I guess I'm *not* surprised. Hector Young specializes in buying land. Ryan thinks, you being familiar with the area and all, you might make it easier for us to work out deals in Nevis. Play your cards right, and the people in this area can walk away with a chunk of change. He didn't tell you that? Ryan is good about seeking out helpful people to make business deals. Great instinct—at least, until the accident." Hector offered Van a sincere smile and put his hand on her shoulder. Van gave him a blank stare. "Ah, sorry, it looks like maybe I've gotten into the middle of something that I shouldn't have. Listen, I've known Ryan quite a while. The ladies all think he's very charming. Maybe you should take him with a little grain of salt. You wouldn't be the first woman who has misunderstood his intentions. I should know. I've had to come behind and clean up after him enough."

Van continued to look at him in silence, her shock gradually morphing into intense dislike. She shrugged her shoulder out from under his hand.

"Thanks for the info," she said. "If you'll excuse my saying so, I have a little trouble buying into all that. It doesn't sound like you and Ryan are very close."

"Listen, Ryan and I are tight; we often work as a team. Even when we aren't working together, we're watching out for each other. He and I have a lot riding on this venture of ours—a lot. He succeeds, I succeed. He doesn't succeed, we both lose. To be perfectly candid, everything was working fine until he met you. I sense a change in him I don't understand. I can't keep the guy focused, and everything is headed right down the tube. If you care about Ryan at all, then do what's best for him. Let him do what he needs to do here. We keep our jobs, and everyone's happy. What do you say?"

"I'd say I don't like you. You have the wrong impression about the people in this town—and Ryan, too. We don't take to big-time operators. It might be better if you left."

"Yeah, sure, no problem. I'll find my own way out. Nice meeting you, but think about what I said. It *is* a win-win."

Hector made his way across the yard, stopping for a brief moment to talk to Marla before he left. They both were passionate people who spoke effectively with their hands. Though Van couldn't hear a word, it was a short but sweet conversation, and both were smiling when they parted.

As much as Van disliked Hector, her gut feeling was there must be at least a kernel of truth in what he had said. It was Hector's motives that weren't entirely apparent. Clearly, he had an agenda, and he hadn't wasted any time getting to it. Van wasn't sure whether the win-win was for Ryan and her or Ryan and Hector.

She looked across the yard to where Ryan was talking to Jean and several of the neighborhood children. He looked calm and handsome as he laughed at something one of the kids said.

Van had always been a sucker for tall men. They had a way of making her feel both vulnerable and protected at the same time, so that she could concede control without feeling weak.

Right now she needed him to take control and make her feel safe and reassured after the onslaught of Hector's words.

Van didn't want to make a scene. She worked her way methodically across the yard, interjecting a comment or a laugh with each group, until she reached Jean. She took her by the elbow and directed her up the steps and into the house.

She said to Jean, "Remember that pen Ryan gave me?"

"Hector Young and Associates?"

"Yeah, did you ever look them up?"

Jean looked up, startled. "No, but I can get right on it."

"Would you, please? I'm going back out to talk to Ryan."

She worked her way back across the yard, saying good night and small-talking until she got around to Ryan. He greeted her with a smile.

"I just got done visiting with your friend."

Ryan looked puzzled. "What friend?"

"Hector."

Ryan scoffed. "*Friend?* He's strictly a business associate. We work together, period. What did he have to say?"

"I'm relieved to hear that. I'd hate to think a friend would talk so much trash about you."

Ryan's demeanor immediately became serious. "What did he say?"

"He says you're a lady's man and I should watch my heart."

"What the . . . Where is he?" he asked, turning toward the crowd, trying to find him.

"He's gone. I asked him to leave. I didn't like him talking about you that way behind your back."

"Thanks, but you don't have to protect me from Hector. We have a long history. I'm sure he didn't say anything behind my back that he hasn't said to my face. Ours is a complicated relationship. I apologize for bringing him." After a pause, he said, "You didn't believe his nonsense, did you?"

"No, should I?"

"No, of course not. Uh . . . what else did he say?"

"He told me about your bus accident. Said it's affected how you do your job. Is that true? He's obviously jealous of you, so I had a hard time reading between the lines."

"Yeah, he'd love to screw me over and work his way back into Hector Senior's good graces. Forget him. He loves to get under people's skin. In his case, it's not too hard."

Ryan paused a moment to think. "There is something I've wanted to talk to you about all day. Want to go sit on the porch? It's a little awkward with all these people."

So they headed around to the front porch and sat down in the two slat-backed rocking chairs. They rocked in silence for a while.

"I don't know why Hector would bring up my accident," Ryan said in a soft voice. "Maybe he's jealous of the time I'm spending with you. I don't know. I was lucky. The bus ran a stop sign and hit me in the crosswalk as it turned the corner, so I bounced off the side—just a glancing blow. The woman two feet in front of me wasn't so lucky. She got hit head-on and died at the scene. They rushed me to Our Lady of Mercy Hospital, where I got whisked right into surgery. At one point, they almost lost me. A few weeks later, I was back home.

"It's amazing what modern medicine can do now," he said. "What it can cure, and all that it still knows nothing about. A while back, you asked me if I had ever experienced a deep loss. I said no, but I wasn't completely honest. Van, my whole *life* is a deep loss. The fact is, I don't remember a whole lot about my life before the surgery. Without a memory, I came back to friends I didn't know, and a career I hated. They told me I had changed. I no longer had the drive and ambition to compete in a job I used to *own*. Doctors said it was anesthesia-induced amnesia and the effects would be temporary. They weren't. Then they decided it was a 'dissociative fugue,' but just a few of my memories have come back. I'm constantly struggling with what I am and what I feel that I should be." He paused and took a deep breath. "Hector and the rest of them have no idea of the extent of my memory loss. I should get an Oscar for the pretending I've had to do."

"Oh, Ryan. There are a lot of things I'd like to forget, but I can't imagine losing *everything*. At least I have a context for my life. That's terrible!"

"You're going to think I'm crazy when I say this. I should probably stop while you still have a good opinion of me." He laughed nervously, running his fingers around the inside of his collar. He paused a few more seconds, and then the thoughts began to tumble out of him as if it were a relief to give voice to them. "I remember the day of my surgery. In fact, I remember the surgery. I still see myself lying on the operating table with the doctors and attendants working over my body. I'm looking down at myself on the table. Incredible," he said shaking his head in disbelief.

"Oh, my word, you had an out-of-body experience?"

"Apparently." Ryan closed his eyes and continued to watch the memories unfold in his mind. "The memories in my head are so vivid: the hum of the lights as I hover near the ceiling . . . down below me, docs and nurses work frantically to save me; the shreds of my white dress shirt lie where they cut it off me. I can see my mother being comforted in the arms of my dad. Strange . . . I can't see their faces, but I know it's them. All these things are going on at the same time. I don't understand how I'm taking it all in at once. I can actually feel my parents' pain." He shook his head again.

"A real out-of-body experience! Incredible! Did you tell anyone? Your doctors?"

"No, no one. I was so shaken by what I couldn't remember, I was totally paranoid. I couldn't trust anyone, because I didn't know any of them. You've seen Hector. Can you imagine what would have happened if I had confided in *him*? He would have had a field day with that information.

"Fate must have been smiling a little on me. The one thing that never left me was my basic knowledge of the law—why, I'm not entirely sure. Sure, I'd slip with things here or there, but for the most part, my memory of the law is solid. It's bizarre," he said softly. "Lately, a lot of it has been coming back to me in dreams, as if my mind is working overtime to fill in the blanks. These dreams are trying to tell me something, and either I'm just not getting it or I don't *want* to know." He sighed and walked over to the porch railing and looked out toward the bay. His body trembled with anxiety, and Van could hear the anguish in his voice.

"In the last few weeks, I've begun to remember so much. I don't know what it is about being here. Nevis has been a real eye-opener for me. For the first time since the accident, I feel some real peace and belonging." Ryan became quiet and thoughtful but didn't turn around. "I think it's because of you."

Van was moved by the emotion radiating from him, but she made no attempt to close the space between the two of them.

"Van, are you a person who has faith in their instinct, their intuition?"

"Yes."

Ryan shook his head. "Well, I'm not. I trust my gut feelings to a certain extent, but in the end I need proof—the cold, hard facts. In this situation, they aren't there, but the nagging gut feeling remains. I don't know what to do with that," he said, turning to Van.

She gave a wistful shake of her head. "I can't help you, not knowing exactly what you're talking about."

"No, of course not. But, I'm sure you would agree that there are a lot of things that spin around in a person's mind that they would never give voice to. They just burrow deeper as they spin, slowly driving a person crazy."

At that moment, Jean came around and found Van on the front porch. From the look on her face and quickness of her pace, Van could see that something was wrong. She felt the pit of her stomach tighten.

"You look like a woman on a mission," Van said. "What's wrong?"

"I went right inside and looked up Ryan's employer from the pen he gave you—Hector Young and Associates." Jean glanced at Ryan out of the corner of her eye, then went on as if he weren't there. "His employer is a major land speculator. Buy cheap, sell high. If they can't get landholders to sell willingly, they pressure them into selling some other way. Right now they have their sights on Nevis." Jean handed Van a sheet of printer paper and then turned to scowl at Ryan. "Mr. Thomas, I think you have some explaining to do."

TWELVE

A BIGGER DOG

Before Ryan could utter a sound, Van stood up, stepped over to him, and slapped his face. "You Yankee son of a bitch! You thought you could buy me an ice cream, smile a little and tell me your sob story, and I would just give you enough information to sell out the town." She jabbed her finger into Ryan's chest. "Don't take us for a bunch of country bumpkins."

Ryan stood still throughout her tirade. His hand went instinctively to his face, but there the instinct stopped. He did not attempt to stop her. "What are you *talking* about?" he said. "Slow down. You're not making sense. You think I did what?" He turned on Jean. "Why are you checking up on my employer behind my back? All of a sudden, we're into trust issues here? I would have told you anything you wanted to know. All you had to do was ask."

"Don't try to deflect the issue," Van said. "I asked Jean to look up Hector Young. And from what I'm reading here, it's a good thing I did! Not exactly a stellar track record they have! You came here to cash in on the land. Buy cheap, sell high? Do you always use people to get what you want? I suppose you throw them away when you're done, too."

"Van, listen, it's not like that," he said, grabbing her arm. She took a step back, and he sighed and let go. He couldn't afford to drive her further away.

"Don't lie to me, and sure as hell don't touch me! Your wandering eye wasn't the only thing Hector clued me into. He said HYA was involved in a huge land deal in this area. He said you were using me to get insider information, to make the sales go smoother. Of course I didn't believe him. I thought too much of you and too little of him to think that could be true."

Ryan knew she had him. If she hadn't blindsided him, he could easily have talked his way out. He was good at that. Instead, he stood mute, horrified at the turn of events and at his lack of control over the situation. He had to give the two of them credit: they weren't quite as gullible as he had thought.

"I should have known! To think I *trusted* you . . ."

"You *can* trust me," he said, moving toward her again, but again she took a step back.

"It was no coincidence that you rang my phone on the boardwalk that day, was it?"

"No."

"How did you know my number?"

"I saw you earlier in the week. If you watch someone long enough, you can find out all kinds of things about them."

"That is so creepy and repulsive," Van said, turning her back to him. I've been such a sap."

"Look, Van, this doesn't have to be a negative thing. Look at the positive. Hector Young is a solid company. They can pay good money for Nevis land. I can influence how much they pay. People here can sell their properties for more money than they could ever dream of otherwise."

"I am looking at the positive," Van shot back, her eyes dark with fury. "I'm positive you're going to try to yank the land right out from under our feet. People's families have owned this land for generations, *centuries*. Roots go deep here. Did you ever stop to think what would happen to those who didn't want to sell? This will swallow them up! Come back in a year's time and see that all that we hold dear and special is gone. I can still look inside there and see where my great-grandfather struck matches on the stones of the fireplace to light his pipe. Do you really think I would let you take that away from me—let you bulldoze the pickle boat house? You sure as hell can try, but it will be over my dead body!"

She shot a look at Jean that froze her where she stood. "And don't lecture me. I'm not in the mood!" She stomped into the house without giving Ryan another look.

As the door slammed behind her Van could hear Jean's voice. "I couldn't have said it better. Why did you do that to her? You know, you're the first person she's opened up to in a long time. She trusted you. You brought something besides pain into her life . . . till now, anyway. Since she met you her eyes have begun to light up and just sparkle. Why did you have to turn out to be such a dick? Typical man. Get your sorry ass out of here before I turn the dog loose on you." And turning her back on Ryan, Jean went inside and slammed the door behind her.

Van was standing just inside the door, leaning her head against the wall. She turned, and Jean walked toward her.

"My BS detector is obviously broken," Van said weakly. "I think you can slap that smile off my face about now."

"I'm sorry."

"Yeah, me, too," Van said, sobbing, and she buried her face in Jean's shoulder.

"I've decided to give you a pass this time," said Jean, wrapping her arms around Van and just letting her cry. "I just wish we had a bigger dog."

❧

Ryan felt as if he had been run over by a freight train—a train with Hector as the engineer. For the life of him, he couldn't figure why Hector would sabotage everything they were doing in Nevis. Ryan knew he always had to watch his back with Hector, but the guy had never before put his own fortunes at risk to make Ryan look bad. Hector was no dummy, and he needed this to go right as much as Ryan did.

It didn't take Ryan long to find his faithless partner. He was down sitting on the boardwalk, as if expecting the coming wrath. He didn't bother to get up as he saw Ryan approaching.

Ryan walked up toe to toe with Hector, towering over him with both fists clenched.

"You asshole!" he growled. "What's your fucking problem? Jesus, Mary, and Joseph, can't you be discrete? Keep your damn mouth shut and your personal issues to yourself! She doesn't trust me anymore, which means you just pretty much destroyed everything we've been working for here."

"The only personal issues giving us any problems are yours," Hector replied. "From getting so personally involved with that woman. Find another piece of ass—one with less potential for problems."

Ryan grabbed Hector by the shirtfront and yanked him up inches away from his face. "I swear, if I didn't need you right now I'd kill you." He shoved him back against the bench and let go. Hector landed sitting up, but the bench toppled backward, dumping him on his back on the ground. Wisely, he didn't get up.

Ryan started to walk away, but suddenly he whirled around and pointed a finger at Hector. "Talk about her like that again, and I *will* kill you," he said. And then he turned and walked away past the gawking people on the boardwalk without another word or a backward glance.

⮞

Ryan took off down the boardwalk at a brisk walk. No amount of deep breathing or positive self-talk was going to calm him down right now. He knew he had just made a mistake, and not his first by any means. Losing his temper wasn't going to help the situation. He knew deep down—had known all along—that he had an intense attraction to Van and that it was getting in the way of what he needed to do. He just couldn't help himself. Now Hector was a big problem, much bigger than he would have been if Ryan had kept his head. He probably couldn't straighten it out with him. Hector had found the weakness he had always been searching for in Ryan, and Ryan had no doubt he would exploit it. One call to New York—that was all it would take.

Stop, slow down, and think it all through, Ryan said to himself. He was in it deep. There had to be a way to fix this. If he could noodle through it, there might be something he could salvage of the situation.

And then all the troubling thoughts that had been nagging at him suddenly coalesced. HYA and Van—they couldn't coexist in his life. He was at a point of no return. He would have to make a choice.

THIRTEEN

RECAPITULATION

The fire now burning in Van's gaze scared Jean. In Van's mind, Ryan was just one more lying cheat. She may have been gullible, but she didn't plan on sitting back and taking it. She immediately sat down with Jean and created a list, dividing up Nevis's residents according to whether they would sell or hold out. Inevitably, some would sell because of the obscene amount of money HYA was going to throw at them. But others would resent HYA in general, and especially for the way it was trying to buy its way into Nevis. And it was this second group that Van and Jean were going after.

"Why don't we meet with the more influential residents first?" Jean asked. "We can't do this all by ourselves."

"I agree. Once we get a few key people to agree not to sell, we can sway some of the others. We just have to stick together, help each other. I think we . . .

The doorbell interrupted her. "Be right back."

Van pulled the front door open and found herself face-to-face with Ryan.

"Go away," she hissed, and tried to slam the door in his face, but Ryan slipped his foot inside before she could get it closed.

"Van, wait, please," said Ryan. "I need to talk to you. Please. Look, I'll even just talk to you through the door. Just hear me out." Van opened the door, folded her arms across her chest, and waited.

"You were right last night," he said. "I owe you an apology, an explanation. Please hear me out. When I came to Nevis it was all just about business. Never in my wildest dreams did I ever expect to meet someone like you. It's true. When I spoke to you the first time on the boardwalk, I only saw you as an opportunity to help move along what I had to do here so I could get back to my life in New York. But you have to know, I've never used you. When it's been anyone else, yes, I've used them. I'm really good at using people. Getting what I want and need has never been a problem for me. But I never used you. I need for you to understand that. And when I kissed you the other night, my feelings for you were genuine." Ryan paused. "Are you going to deny that you felt something, too?" he whispered.

"Are you finished? The only reason you say you haven't used me is because your plan isn't far enough along. Look, you must have some good qualities, somewhere. I'm not usually wrong about people, and I'll admit I am—was—drawn to you. I'm baffled by that. But you see, Mr. Thomas, I'm not used to playing the victim, and I'm not going to start now. Any credibility you had with me is shot—zero, zip, gone. I don't have any need for someone I can't trust. So you can be on your way. I don't need a forwarding address. Don't bother me anymore." She unfolded her arms and grabbed the door.

"Wait," said Ryan, shoving his foot back in the door. "See, like you said, we have a connection; we're drawn to each other. I can tell you're as surprised by it as I am. You do things to me . . .

make my head spin. I tried to tell you before Jean interrupted us. I think I understand the connection. There's something deeper here than meets the eye, because we've met before."

"We never met before that day on the boardwalk."

At this moment, the little boy Ryan had been laughing with at the crab feast yesterday raced up the porch steps. "Mr. Ryan, Mr. Ryan, would you teach me the song you told Janet? She won't let me play."

Ryan sighed. "I'm sorry, Jason," he said. "Ms. Van and I are having a big-people discussion right now. Tell you what: I'll teach it to you once, but then you have to run along and play." He turned to the little girl standing nearby. "Janet, would you come here, please?" She came up the stairs with her head down, but he could see she was fighting to keep a grin from spreading across her little face. "Do you remember the song I taught you?"

She looked up at him, nodded her head, and began to sing in a clear soprano child's voice. "Birdies up in the trees, singing in the breeze, I like the birdies." When she was finished, she blushed and went back to studying the rubber toes of her sneakers.

Ryan smiled. "Janet, you have the voice of an angel. Now," he said to the little boy, "can you two run off and play?" She nodded with a huge grin, socked Jason on the arm, and fled down the steps with Jason close on her heels.

Ryan turned to Van and said, "You're pale. What's wrong?"

"Where did you learn that song?"

"It's just something that floats around in my head. Old memory, I would guess. Why?"

"My son made that song up." Van put her hand over her eyes. "How much digging into my personal life have you done,

Ryan? What game are you playing?" She turned and glared at him, her eyes burning with hurt and misery.

Ryan shook his head. "I don't know what you're talking about. I'm not trying to pull anything. I'm leveling with you. Ever since I came to Nevis, I've been having dreams, strange ones, over and over again. All this useless information that I've begun to accumulate in my head: names without faces, faces without names, dates . . . places I've never been."

Van continued to stare at Ryan, a series of emotions flitting across her face. She could feel her fingernails digging into the porch railing, and when she spoke again her voice was controlled and deliberate.

"Describe one of your dreams," she challenged.

"Most are about a young boy. I think it's me. And in many of them, there's a woman. The woman . . . honest, Van, she looks and feels like *you*."

"Dreams don't have to relate to reality. What on earth would make you think it was me?"

"I didn't say it was you, only that she *looked* like you."

Van swayed, and goose bumps rose on her arms, as if a cold breeze had sent an icy chill down her spine.

"Did your son die on May seventeenth?"

"Jesus! You have his death certificate? Is nothing sacred to you people?"

"Was your son treated by a Dr. Phillips?" Ryan asked.

"His medical records, too?"

Ryan continued with his interrogation. "On the day your son died, were you wearing a red dress?"

"Red plaid. Who have you been talking to?"

Beethoven's Opus One-twenty-three?"

"James's funeral mass. You're going to rot in hell, Mr. Thomas."

Ryan stopped. "I don't know how else to say this without being blunt." He paused. "I think I'm your son."

"Say what?"

"I may be standing here in the body of Ryan Thomas, but I am thinking with the body and soul of James Hardy. I know the specifics of James's life because that's who I am. The pieces in my memory are coming back. Drowning . . . an out-of-body experience . . . waking up in the hospital as Ryan Thomas—someone I didn't even know. There, I've said it. I'm pulling my elephant out into the center of the room."

Van's eyes never left Ryan's face, and she didn't even blink an eye at his bizarre statement.

"Van, say something. Anything."

And then she laughed. "No tunnel or bright light at the end?" she asked. "Write it all down. It's a prize winner. But you didn't do all your homework. My son was twenty-four when he died. How old are you—pushing thirty?"

"I'm thirty-five, but I don't think that matters."

"When you die you go to heaven, Mr. Thomas—or, in your case, somewhere a lot warmer. You don't come back as someone else! Not only are you an asshole, you are a thoroughgoing, greedy, good-for-nothing, *shameless* asshole. You would do anything to acquire Nevis land. I have no idea why you are having dreams about us unless it's because you're crazy! Now, get off my property before I call the police!"

Ryan ignored her and kept babbling. "I can't remember if there was a tunnel. I don't think I died. It doesn't seem like reincarnation—just switched into a different body. Maybe the real Ryan Thomas died and I came back into his body instead of mine. I sure as hell don't have a clue why God brought me back. Maybe I still had important things left to do." Ryan was quiet for a moment, frowning to himself. "The ring—did they give it back to you?"

"What ring?"

"The signet ring. I remember seeing Granddad's signet ring rolling around on the floor as the nurse dropped it in her haste in the emergency room when they treated me. Did they return it to you?"

"You talked to the emergency room staff?"

"Well?"

"Yes, damn it. They found it the next day on the emergency room floor."

Ryan smiled a big glorious, triumphant smile. "Good. Grandpa Diggy would've wanted that."

"Diggy?"

"I think that's what I always called him. I used to help him with his garden. Jeesh, where are these thoughts coming from?" Ryan rubbed his face. "I can't remember, though. Was he your father, or Dad's?"

"I can't listen to any more of this. Go!" Van yelled at him, doubling over and putting both hands over her ears.

"I can't go any more than you can turn around and go back into your house and leave me here. Go, prove me wrong," he challenged. "Leave me here, right now."

Van remained rooted to the spot where she stood.

"See? You can't walk away from me. From our very first meeting, I've felt a profound connection to you that I have never understood. I have felt closer to you, a stranger, than to anyone else in my life, and I've struggled to come to terms with you since the day I met you. It's love—lasting, eternal love—and it binds forever. I can't shake it, and you can't shake it. It's a tangible, living thing. It's just as strong whether we are mother and son, or lovers. Don't run away from me, Van. Acknowledge what you are feeling. Acknowledge *me*.

"I know this is a lot. I can see you don't believe me, but deep down, I think you know it might be true. If you don't believe, then tell me how I know all these things. Why is there such a deep connection between us that I am right now willing to throw away all that I have in this life to pursue a relationship with you? I have Hector all over my back, and I'm destroying my career. I'm torn between what I'm used to doing and what, deep down inside, seems the true course to take. Tell me, Van, why would I do and feel that?"

Van slumped into one of the porch chairs. It was a question that she couldn't begin to answer. She looked up at him, into his eyes. He looked nothing like her son, not even the expression in his eyes. And yet, he was right: she still couldn't walk away.

They looked at each other in total silence, and time ticked by, feeling like a powerful emotional bomb ready to explode. Van rocked in her chair, staring as if she might bore a hole through him, and he stood watching her eyes as she absorbed all that he had said.

Van knew that the human heart's deepest desires sometimes overrode what the mind thought impossible, and she wanted her son back more than anything else in heaven and earth. Rationality and need fought quietly within her for the son she couldn't be happy without. Her heart told her that her feelings for Ryan were real and deep. Like flip cards in a mutoscope, her memories began to flash by: recognizing Richard, skydiving, fear of water, the angel coin, left-handedness, a childhood song no one else knew, the signet ring . . . On and on they went. They were just snapshots in time, but viewed together in rapid succession, they created a moving story. And the story they created was her son James. She blinked, and Ryan could see that she had made the connection.

"James? You're telling me you're *James*? Oh, my God," she said, covering her face with her hands. "It's not possible. I'm having an affair with my son? Why did you lead me on?"

"Lead you on? I have *never* led you on," said Ryan. I'm just now seeing all these pieces fit into place. Every emotion I've expressed has been honest. I've told you, I was infatuated with you from the first moment I saw you. The longer I spend with you, the deeper the connection I feel. How could I possibly know . . . You think I planned . . . I'm happy about this—this sordid whatever you want to call it? I may be dating and fantasizing about my own mother! My life is screwed all to hell and back. I can't begin to tell you how many demons *I'm* trying to exorcise here! Since I met you . . ."

As the words refused to come out of his mouth he continued to try to talk with his hands, but they, too, were at a loss for words. Failing this, he dropped his hands and became still and silent. Without another word, he turned and walked off in the direction of his car.

Van watched him walk off and didn't try to stop him. She was without offense or defense on her lips—cold, alone, and empty.

FOURTEEN

CONSEQUENCES

Her son. *Alive.* Van turned their last conversation over and over in her mind. Ryan had given her so many details that would be almost impossible to dig up—things that only her son would know. But he couldn't be James. That was unfathomable. Still, every objection she silently raised, her gut instinct shot down with overwhelming force. The more she ignored the feeling, the stronger it grew.

She hadn't heard a peep out of him since they argued on her front porch. As minutes turned to hours, she could hardly sit still, but since he was the one to stalk off, she was not going to call him. Inside her gnawed the feeling that he would return to New York and she would never see or hear from him again. She wasn't sure she could handle that.

No matter what their relationship, Ryan was responsible for all the current evil in her little world of Nevis. She hated his duplicity. If he was at all sincere and who he claimed to be, he would have to fix things with HYA.

And so she went, around and around in mental and emotional turmoil. Finally, desperate to escape the torment of her own thoughts, she picked up the phone and dialed Jean. "Time to walk," she said.

"Yeah, sure. Meet you out front in about fifteen minutes."

If there was one constant that Van could rely on, it was that the beauty of Nevis grew with every change of day and season. Twilight had its own special quality. As the human world began to settle into silence, Mother Earth filled the sleepy coastal town with the sounds of croaking toad, piping bird, and rustling reed, with the soft breeze bringing in the warm scent of the bay. It was the time when Van and Jean could open their hearts to each other, whether rocking on Van's porch or taking their nightly walk along the big loop around the town.

Nevis was a safe little town, and Van didn't give the time of evening or the distance a second thought. People here still left doors unlocked and the keys in their car ignitions. As she and Jean met on the street, a quick glance at the sheer curtains in her neighbor's house told her that Mr. Pickett could probably attest to her whereabouts should anyone need to know. She felt a little twinge of pity that a person's life should be reduced to watching others live theirs. Everyone deserved the opportunity to live out their individual destiny. Mr. Pickett's life had shrunk considerably since the death of his wife, Alice, but he had managed to survive. Still, he deserved more than a life with a little white poodle and a paranoid outlook. Van had been thinking a lot about destiny lately. James had been taken much too soon.

It was a short quiet walk down around the main part of town. Darkness had chased most of the locals inside. Jean and Van compared notes on which neighbors seemed willing to go for HYA's jugular.

"I haven't seen any more of Ryan," Jean said as they walked past the darkened hardware store and Mac's Pharmacy. Did he return to New York, or did you hire someone to kill his sorry ass?"

Van gave Jean a quick glance and decided that being less than forthcoming about Ryan's latest personal revelations was the best way to handle her friend's overexuberance. "I neither know nor care where he is. And no, I didn't hire someone to put him out of my misery. For a minute there, I probably could have. I never saw that coming. He seemed so perfect."

"They all do. That's what makes them such insidiously evil creatures."

Van burst out laughing. "No, they aren't! Stop playing the woman scorned. You had a bad run of it, but they aren't all bad."

"Just remember what I said about a man complicating your life."

"Oh, I haven't forgotten. But Ryan is an opportunist, and what he did is unforgiveable. He says he wants to make things right. We'll see. There's no room for negotiation. It's my way or the highway out of town and back to New York." Van decided to change the course of the discussion into a less explosive area. "How's it going for you? Has Marla called?"

"Mmm. I left her a message the other day inviting her over, but she hasn't returned my call yet. So much resentment for one so young." Jean shook her head sadly. "I can't do anything right. Every time she blows me off, Pete wins—the bastard."

"It's not a game, Jean."

"Yeah, I know, but I'd at least like to feel like I'm winning *some* of the time. Her dad can do no wrong, yet she just refuses to have a relationship with me. Life is so short." Suddenly, Jean stopped and put her hand over her mouth. "Oh, Van, so sorry! I'm a thoughtless twit. Forgive me."

Van put her arm around Jean and gave her a gentle squeeze "It's okay. You don't ever have to bite your tongue for me.

Listening to you doesn't make me feel any worse than I usually do about James. You have a beautiful daughter. Of course you want a relationship with her!"

They walked a few more minutes in silence before Van spoke again. "I noticed that Marla can be quite charming when she wants to be."

Jean snorted. "I was hoping you weren't paying attention when she was coming on to all the guys at the picnic—especially Ryan. I don't understand why she has to act so cheap. I said something to her about it afterwards. Unless she sees a ring, she figures any guy is fair game. I will have to say, for all Ryan's faults, he did seem to be completely smitten with you. He sidestepped Marla's advances rather nicely—wasn't interested in her at all. Besides, what does Marla have that you don't have? Honestly, jaded as I am, I was almost rooting for him. He did make you happy."

Van looked at Jean and cracked up. "It's not working, but thanks anyway."

"You're welcome. You worry too much. You can't change fate. If it's meant to be, it'll happen. Maybe we haven't seen his true colors yet."

Van gave no reply as they turned down a short side street to begin the return trip back up along the boardwalk. This end of town was quiet and deserted, the only sound a yapping dog in the distance.

"Jean, did you ever wish really hard for something that you wanted, and then when you got it, it wasn't quite what you expected—and maybe you weren't prepared to pay the price?"

"Hah! Haven't we all?"

"I think it's happened to . . ." Van's voice trailed off, and she stopped walking. "What is all that commotion?"

They both stopped and peered around the corner. A hundred yards down the street, a crowd of people had gathered around two ambulances pulled up on the boardwalk, their lights firing the storefronts with an eerie, garish blue. There was a flurry of activity up and down the boardwalk. Gradually, as their eyes became accustomed to the pulsating lights, they could make out the form of a small white dog running frantically around the edge of the crowd.

Jean grabbed Van's arm. "Isn't that Susie, Ernest Pickett's dog?" She clapped and called until she caught the little dog's attention. The dog stopped momentarily before running straight for Jean, who grabbed the leash she was trailing, and scooped her up into her arms. "What are you doing out here alone, baby?" Where's Daddy, huh? Aw, look, her name is on her collar in a little heart."

"Don't let her go, Jean. I'm sure Mr. Pickett will see us coming long before we see him. Come on, I want to see what's going on up here."

As the women drew closer, they got a better look at the small crowd gathered around the ambulances, their faces illuminated in the flashing beacons. Van tried to inch closer, but the gawkers and response personnel were holding a tight perimeter.

"Oh, my, they're pulling a body out," Van whispered to Jean. "Who is it?"

An older man turned and addressed her. "We think it's one of those men down from New York."

Van buckled at the knees and grasped at Jean's sleeve to keep from going down. "Oh, dear God, is it Ryan? Not now, God! Don't do this to me again!" She tried to push her way through the crowd to get a glimpse of the figure on the stretcher, but it was no use. Feeling suddenly nauseated, she put her hands on her knees.

"I've got to call Ryan," she said. "Oh, God, please don't let it be him. Please. Jean, help me move away from here. Please?"

They backed out of the crowd as Van frantically dialed Ryan's cell phone. "Come on, answer!"

Ryan answered on the third ring.

"Ryan! Thank God you're okay!"

"I'm about as okay as can be expected. I wasn't sure we'd be talking again before I left. Van, I'm sorry I walked off like that, but I just don't know what else to say to you."

"Ryan, I had this horrible feeling . . ."

"What's wrong?" he asked.

"Where are you?" she asked him.

"At the motel. Tell me what's wrong, Van."

"Hector—where's Hector?"

"He's not here. Van! No more information from me. What is wrong?"

"I'm okay, I'm okay. *I'm* okay. Hector, he's . . . I think they just pulled his body out of the water near Betty's bakery. I think he's *dead,* Ryan."

Silence.

"Ryan? Hello? Are you still there?"

"That's impossible. He was alive and well when I last saw him. A little bruised, but otherwise healthy."

"What do you mean, bruised?"

More silence.

"Ryan, answer me. What did you do?"

"Relax. He mouthed off about you, and I hauled off and shoved him. That's it, nothing sinister. How do you know it was Hector? You're positive?"

"Well, no, not really. I, uh, actually, I was afraid it was you. They were pulling the body out of the water, and someone said it was one of the men from New York. I was so afraid it was you." She tried to keep her feelings in check, but her eyes were rapidly filling with tears.

"Are you at home?"

"No, I'm down near Betty's. Jean is with me. We went for a walk, and as we were coming back around the loop we saw all kinds of activity down at the water. Curiosity got the better of us, so we went closer to see what was going on."

"Van, listen to me and do exactly what I say. Go home. Don't come out or open your door to anyone you don't know. Not until I come get you. Do you understand?"

"No, I don't understand! What's going on? Tell me!"

"Look, just do as I say. Trust me. Can you trust me? I'll explain everything later, I promise. Now, hurry up and *go home*."

There was dead silence on the phone as Van weighed Ryan's urgent words against her need to know more.

"Damn it, Van! Please just trust me. Go!" At this point, he was shouting into the phone.

Van's feet and mind finally began to work in concert. "Okay, but you need to explain later. I have trust issues with you."

"I promise. I have to go." The phone went dead.

Jean gave Van a hug and said, "There's a fine line between love and hate. And you, hon, have got to pick a side."

Van pushed away from Jean and wiped her eyes and nose. "It'll be okay. Let's get home. This is too crazy a night to be out. Keep hold of Susie. We can drop her by Mr. Pickett's house. I can't imagine why she's running loose. He must be out of his mind with worry. He never goes anywhere without her."

Their repeated knocks on Pickett's door went unanswered despite the blaze of interior lights. They walked on to Van's house, where they wrote a note to leave on the screen door. They half expected to see him back home when they returned to leave the note, but still no Pickett, so Van had little choice but to take Susie home with her for the night.

FIFTEEN

A SHADE INSIDE

Ryan grabbed his wallet and keys on the fly and headed out the door. He was confused. It wasn't that he didn't believe Van; he just couldn't wrap his head around *why*. If it was Hector, it was probably not an accident, and definitely not a crime of opportunity. It had to be HYA related. Although rare, it wasn't unheard of for HYA to lose someone due to the dark nature of some of the business's dealings. The aftermath was always handled quietly and discreetly. Life went on, and the business went on. But *Hector*? If the boss's son was dead, then it was a safe bet that Ryan was next on the list. He took a few steps out the door and then returned to his room, pulled a small five-shot revolver out of the bottom of his dopp kit, and shoved it into his pants pocket.

Ryan didn't have to travel very far before he could see the lights of the emergency vehicles flashing at the far end of the boardwalk. No police tape yet—that was a plus. Experience had taught him that if he acted as though he belonged there, he could likely get as close as he needed. He put his head down and pushed his way through the crowd of bystanders, toward the nearer ambulance, where an EMT stood talking on his cell phone.

"... getting ready to transport one white male, deceased, tentatively identified from wallet found on the body as one Hector Young, age thirty-two, resident New York City."

Ryan grabbed the EMT by the arm and pulled the phone away. "Did you say Hector Young?" I know him. He's my business partner. Where is he? Is he all right?"

The EMT yanked his arm away from Ryan's grasp and put the phone back up to his ear. "We'll call on our way . . . Understood. Later." He shifted his attention on Ryan. "No, not all right. You're an acquaintance of the deceased? You can ID the body? Come with me." Ryan was pushed and pulled through the tight crowd to a stretcher with a body on it, covered by a sheet.

The EMT said to the policeman standing guard over the body, "Give us a look, McCall. This is a business associate," he said, nodding in Ryan's direction. "He may be able to make a positive ID."

"I don't know how much more you need. He had identification on him," the policeman said, pulling the sheet back from the face of the corpse.

Ryan leaned forward, then quickly looked away. "Yes, that's Hector Young," he said. "What happened?"

"Don't know. We were responding to another emergency here earlier in the evening when we were alerted to a body in the water. When was the last time you saw or spoke to Mr. Young?" asked the policeman.

"I was talking to him down here, oh, I don't know, maybe four o'clock yesterday. I can't imagine what happened."

"There is some bruising on the body, so right now we aren't ruling out foul play. Don't worry, in a town this small, we'll have it solved soon enough. Isn't too much that's a secret around here." Officer McCall gave Ryan a long, thoughtful stare that brought goose bumps to Ryan's arms. McCall pulled a notebook out of his pocket. A little too late, Ryan decided that the less he said, the better.

"I need to get your name and phone number in case we have any questions for you later," the cop said. "And hey, with that accent, don't plan on leaving town right now. New York is just a little bit far to have a friendly talk—know what I mean?"

Officer McCall straightened and turned at the call of his name from across the boardwalk. "Okay, let's get this body out of here," he said. "I'd like to have my supper before midnight."

First chance he got, Ryan moved quickly back to his car. He wasn't sure what he had walked into, but it wasn't good, and he seemed to have placed himself squarely in the middle of it. Maybe he shouldn't have made himself so visible. *Shit.* He checked his rearview mirror, but he was alone on the road. Maybe he had a little time. He headed for Van's house, where he could think things through. He had never prepared himself for anything like this.

He didn't see anything unusual on the street as he pulled slightly past the driveway and parked. Van opened the door before he even knocked.

"Ryan, thank God, I was so worried," she said, throwing her arms around him and pulling him inside. Then she remembered that she was still angry with him, and she drew away and locked the door behind him. "You're as white as a sheet. What happened?"

"I just got done identifying the body."

"Poor Hector," she said. "I can't say we hit it off, but I would never wish this on him or anyone else."

"Things are a little more complicated than I expected. Once they begin interviewing witnesses I think they're going to come looking for me."

"Ryan, you didn't . . ."

"*Kill* him? Heavens no—much as I would have liked to—but I did threaten to, in front of witnesses, on the boardwalk earlier tonight."

"Why on earth would you do something that stupid?"

"I know, I know," Ryan said, shaking his head. "Hector knew exactly how to push my buttons." He hesitated and then let out a sigh of resignation. "I threatened to kill him if he spouted off about you anymore." He looked at Van and then quickly looked away.

"Oh . . . I see."

"Look, would it be okay if I crashed here tonight? This isn't the first place anyone would think to look for me. I need some time to think before anyone knows where I am."

"Yes, of course," she said, leading him into the living room. "But you could just tell the police the truth: that you were angry. That's what honest people do. Once they find out what kind of jerk Hector was I'm sure they'll understand. There must be any number of people he rubbed the wrong way. It's better to have the authorities on your side than to be working at odds with them." She paused, as if considering this. "But then again, you do seem to have things to hide. You have to tell me something."

Sitting down beside her on the couch, he said, "As you may have figured out by now, Hector and I are in a very dirty business. When you work just inside the law, you try very hard to keep the authorities out of your daily activities. I don't know what is going on right now, except that I'm in way over my head. And if I want to live to see my grandkids, I've got to figure out who killed Hector, and why. I can't just spill my guts to the police. HYA doesn't tolerate screw-ups, or anything or anybody that gives them unwanted attention. They're very good and they're subtle.

"Van, there are a lot of things I should tell you, but the less you know right now, the better. I don't want to get you any more involved than you are already. That's the only way I can protect you. I know there are problems between us, and I'm sorry about the way I left you the other night. But right now I don't have anyone I can trust but you. If it matters at all, my feelings for you haven't changed."

Van didn't try to hide any of the animosity that she was feeling toward Ryan. It was a coldness that she usually reserved for Richard. "If you are being honest with me, Ryan, and you really care about me and about Nevis, I'll help you . . . if you help me. Help me stop these people from buying Nevis and turning it into a yuppie parking lot. Then we can talk about feelings."

"Van, it's too late. You and all these people in town, you don't have clear title to the property in Nevis. The original land deed is set up as a colonial lease. Your families have been renting for hundreds of years and probably didn't even realize it. Even if Hector Young can't buy properties outright, all HYA has to do is find the descendant who legally owns the land and throw more money at him than he could ever dream of. He'll sell. Van, it's not a level playing field. They have an unlimited supply of money."

"That doesn't make sense. My grandparents owned this house free and clear. If they had been paying, it would have shown up somewhere."

"Not necessarily. The amount was very small, and the payments have probably been hidden in something like a yearly tax bill."

"Look, Ryan. It's not that I don't have sympathy for the predicament you're in, but I expect you to do right by Nevis if you want any sort of relationship with me. You can't have it both ways. You want me to protect you, but I don't see you protecting me and mine. I don't care how you fix it—just do it. Then maybe I can believe in you again. Are we clear about that?"

"I understand. I know you don't trust me. But everything I've told you is true, and I *am* doing my best to protect you. I won't leave you high and dry. I promise."

Those were Ryan's final words to Van. By the time she got up early the next morning, he was gone. No note, no nothing. She should have realized she couldn't trust him.

SIXTEEN

EXPENDABLES

Ryan left Van's house early in the morning and walked down to the isolated far end of the boardwalk, where he sat down on one of the benches. Rolled up in his hand was the land deed to the town of Nevis. Success was literally at his trembling fingertips. With the deed, the buyout was a fait accompli, his place at the firm assured. This would be the biggest land buyout in the history of the company. He could already feel the congratulatory pats on the back, already taste the partnership and all the perks that came with it. He took a deep breath, closed his eyes, and wished it were that simple. How the hell was he going to get out of the mess he was in? He was an impostor, a few steps ahead of the law, and an object of contempt to the only person who really knew and cared about him.

There could be no going back to HYA. He was beginning to loathe everything it stood for. These were nice people in Nevis, who had welcomed him with open, trusting arms. And he had abused that trust while smiling to their faces. His actions were despicable. He wanted to be the man who Van thought he was—the kind of man who, he now realized, he had been in his previous life—and, God willing, might possibly be again.

If he stayed in Nevis, it would be only a matter of time before the police came looking for him with more questions than he could safely answer. By the time they got done with him, jail time was a real possibility. And all things considered, jail might not be such a bad fate, he mused darkly. It might be preferable to the swift, murderous wrath of HYA once he started singing.

Ryan reached into his pocket and pulled out the angel coin that Van had given back to him. He ran his fingernail across the high-relief angel. The coin made him feel like a hypocrite. "Heads you win, tails I lose," he whispered as he flipped the coin high in the air.

"Heads," Hector said as he snatched the coin out of the air, balancing it on Ryan's shoulder as he placed his other hand on Ryan's other shoulder. "Greetings from the other side," he said, and flounced down on the bench with a laugh.

"I should've known you wouldn't have the good sense to stay dead after they pulled you out of the bay," Ryan said. "What happened to Earl?"

"Too bad about Earl. Him, I really liked. He had the good sense to keep his head down and his nose out of trouble—up until last night, that is. Good worker bee."

"Yeah, well, now I'm in hot water for falsely identifying his body. Who killed him?"

"He got a little too pushy with the Diablos, on the other side of town. They have a mentality you can't push—know what I mean?"

"Yeah. You pushed too hard, and Earl took it for the team."

Hector looked at Ryan and laughed. "Exactly! I kind of thought it would go down like that, so I asked him to hold on to my wallet while I took one last dip in the bay for old time's sake. Poor bastard. Diablos are vindicated; I'm happy; life is good. Now, back to you. The golden boy is oh, so troubled. Look, man, all's forgiven. I spoke out of turn. If you want to work something out with this woman, fine. But let's be realistic here. We have a lot riding on this. Can't you keep your . . . that is, slow things down a little bit until we're done here? Give me the deed, and I'll go back to New York and make our report. Even though I still have unfinished work here, I'll close this out and then come back. That frees you up to do whatever you want to pursue personally here. Huh?"

Ryan just looked at him. Did Hector really think he was going to buy it? Right now he actually hated Hector more than himself, and that was saying something. Hector had no conscience. All was fair in business as long as he was on the winning side. In fact, Ryan couldn't remember a single time that he could ever stand Hector. He had always been a revolting human being.

"Sorry—cold day in hell," said Ryan.

"Did you know that the courthouse has scanned a lot of documents that it hasn't catalogued yet?" Hector said. "I understand it saves wear and tear on the old paper. Whatcha wanna bet there's a scan of the deed in there somewhere? Shouldn't take too long to find, even with Lilly Librarian's help. Whatcha think?"

Ryan didn't reply. He pulled the coin off his shoulder and began rubbing the angel again, this time with his thumbnail.

"Ryan, why are you running yourself through the wringer like this? With that deed in hand, it's all smooth sailing for us. We got what we wanted. The boss is happy; we look good. Like I said, life is good." When Ryan didn't respond he said, "It's pretty clear, isn't it? Even if we can't find the heir to the land, we're doing all these people a favor. Where else could they ever realize the kind of profit they'll see if they get an offer from us? These aren't big players, Ryan; they're the expendables, the *little* people. They'll be happy with whatever money gets thrown at them. We have bigger fish to fry at home."

Ryan blew air out between his lips and got up from the bench. He hesitated a moment, head down, looking at his shoes. Shifting his eyes to Hector's face, he held his gaze. What was the measure of a man? Suddenly, without uttering a word, he took the deed, crunched it around the coin, and hurled it with all his strength out into the bay.

"What the hell?" Hector leaped to his feet, mouth open in amazement. "What the hell are you *doing,* you asshole?" He shoved Ryan back a few feet and came at him a second time, fists raised. "You son of a bitch, what have you done? What *have* you done?"

Ryan took a couple of steps back and raised his hands, palms toward Hector. "I'll take that bet. There is no scan, Hector. Let's face it: little people can only do little things. But you know," he said, shaking his head and chuckling, "sometimes that's more than enough. There are some things you just can't put a price on. I'm sure you can finish cleaning up here. You don't have to babysit me anymore. Good-bye, Hector." And with that, he turned his back on him and began walking away in the direction of Van's house.

"Come back here, you son of a bitch!" Hector yelled. "We're not done yet."

Ryan never turned, but responded with his middle finger as he kept walking. Ryan Thomas could rot in hell, too. But James Hardy had other plans.

SEVENTEEN

ONE FOR THE TEAM

Ryan didn't plan on staying long at Van's house, but he had left some things unsaid. Perhaps it would have been better to leave it in a note this morning. His reception from Van was chilly. No sooner was he sitting at her table than she excused herself, only to return a minute later with something in her hand.

Van put the jewelry box down in front of him and flipped it open to reveal a gold signet ring. "I thought you might like to have your grandfather's ring back."

Ryan looked from the box to Van but didn't say anything for a moment. His eyes returned to the small box sitting on the table. "You're testing me," he said, nodding slowly. Then he shrugged. "I guess that's to be expected. You still haven't come to terms with me yet. Were you expecting it to fit? You do realize it probably doesn't fit me anymore, right?"

"There's an engraving on the inside—"

"If I know what it is, you'll believe me," he said interrupting her, "and if I don't tell you what it says, I'm a liar?"

"Maybe."

There was a long pause as Ryan studied Van. "Maybe I should go, Van. I've given you more than enough reasons to believe

I'm your son. If by now your gut instinct isn't telling you who I am, you'll never accept it. Whether you do or not changes nothing. In fact, it's probably better not to have you involved with me at this point anyway."

Van reached over and snapped the box shut. "Thanks, Ryan. You've more than answered my question. Now, get out!" She started for the front door.

"Carl, you are my forever. Estelle."

Van froze in mid step.

"I know we're in a situation that defies logic and rationality here, but still, I wish you had believed without me saying that. There's a part of me that wants the mother in you to recognize the son in me. Otherwise, I could go crazy here . . . alone . . . wondering if I'm hallucinating or something."

Van shook her head no but didn't turn around. "Out of all the grieving mothers on this earth, why did God send *you* back to *me*?" she said, crumpling to her knees. And putting her hands to her face, she began to sob.

Ryan crossed the room in two long strides and pulled his mother up and wrapped his arms around her. Van turned in his arms and buried her face against his chest as he kissed the top of her head and held her tight, fighting back tears of his own.

"I need to leave Nevis for a while and go back to New York. I'm cutting all ties with HYA," Ryan whispered.

"No! Absolutely not!" Van pulled back to look him in the face and clung even tighter to his arms. "Ryan, please, don't go. Don't do this to me! They are never going to let you walk away! Are you *crazy*? What makes you think you can do that?" She looked at him with eyes of desperation.

"Because I know too much, that's why. Or at least, they *think* I know too much. I need to go back to New York and call their bluff *before* they bluff. They don't know how much memory loss I actually have. If they think information will come out if something happens to me, then they'll be more hesitant to mess with me. When I feel as though I can safely come back to Nevis I will. I just can't leave things the way they are right now. The longer I wait, the greater the danger for me and anyone associated with me. But before I go there are a couple of things you need to know. Hector is still alive."

"But you identified his body."

"I identified a body, but it wasn't Hector's. It was Earl."

"Why on earth . . . ?"

"Because as soon as I saw it was Earl with Hector's ID on him I knew something was horribly wrong. Going along with the charade buys me time to protect myself and figure out what's really going on. HYA is running more than one game in Nevis. That's why Hector was willing to sabotage everything I was working on here. He was squaring away illicit drug activities with the Diablos. Controlling the drug trade flowing up and down the coast is becoming a very profitable side venture for HYA. Apparently, HYA and the bikers haven't reached a deal considered fair to both parties. Earl unknowingly took one for the team—and especially for Hector."

"That's disgusting. Poor Earl. What kind of evil have you brought here, Ryan? I'm afraid—for me, for you . . . everyone here in town. We don't need this here. You're making enemies everywhere—playing games with HYA, giving false statements to the police. They're going to come looking for you when they put it all together. What are you going to tell the police then?"

Ryan shook his head. "I won't deny it's bad. I'm trying to rectify some of the damage I've done. "I'll tell the police that I made a mistake. I was in a state of shock—anything that will satisfy them."

"You know that isn't going to satisfy the police. Once they find out you're lying they'll take you in and wring you for every bit of information they can get out of you. They'll want to know why. These small-town cops see the law a little differently."

"Honestly, the police are the least of my problems. Hector found me this morning on the boardwalk. Something I didn't tell you last night: Hector and I found a deed in the courthouse that proves the land in Nevis is only being *leased* by its current residents. Hector desperately wants to take the proof back to HYA—preferably alone, so he can take credit."

"Did you give it to him?"

"Of course not. Have some faith. Hector only cares about Hector. I threw it into the bay. That's the end of it unless he can find a scanned copy in the courthouse. I'm sure he's been in touch with New York. If he does find a copy, and HYA finds the Harwell descendants and buys them out, you can kiss Nevis good-bye."

"I'm a Harwell."

"*You're* a Harwell?" Ryan repeated, and then he frowned. "I should know that. That makes me a Harwell. How long has our family been living in this area?"

"Forever. My ancestors were some of the area's earliest settlers." Letting go of Ryan just long enough to grasp one of his hands, she drew him over to the bookcase, where she pulled out a notebook. "Look. Here's the beginning of my tree in this area," she said, leafing through the different tabs in the book. "Jeremiah Harwell—he would have been the first," she said, pointing.

Ryan took a step backward and began to laugh. "You're related to Jeremiah Harwell? I can't believe what I'm hearing! His direct descendants are the ones HYA will be looking for. They legally own the land! Shit! How well is all this documented?" He grabbed Van and hugged her almost breathless.

"Stop! I can't breathe, and you're making me dizzy," Van said, gasping for air as she pried herself loose. "I don't include anything that I can't trace back to an original source." She ran her finger across the footnotes at the bottom of the page. "With this individual, there *is* one missing link. I have a shaky connection here between Jeremiah and his son William. I've always intended to search some more but just haven't gotten back to it."

"Hector and I have spent a lot of time in the courthouse trying to track the ancestry. He insinuated that the courthouse had scanned the lease agreement, but I'm not sure whether that was bravado or truth. I'm sure he'll try to find it. If you can prove that Jeremiah Harwell is your direct ancestor, then the land may belong to you through inheritance. We can put an end to this. But if your lineage can't be proved, then you're still in an uphill fight here. Hector Young will move right in and strong-arm you and the rest of the town right out of here. You don't have the resources to compete with them. They'll run you ragged until you give up."

Van put her hands on her hips, and her entire demeanor changed. "So that's why you appeared to be so interested in the courthouse and my records. It wasn't me you were interested in. You *were* using me, you bastard."

Ryan immediately looked contrite. "Yes, I'm sorry. Guilty, guilty, and guilty. I have been a bastard, and other words that you probably don't even know. But I'm trying to help you now and set things right. We need to work together. Can you set your anger aside just for now? I don't have a lot of time here."

Van put her hands in her hair and ruffled it around on her head. "Okay, but I don't know. I've run into a brick wall with Jeremiah Harwell. I don't have any other leads to follow."

"Have you exhausted all the courthouse documents? What about the boxes you showed me, stored in the railroad museum? If court records are in there, maybe we can find something. I need you to go through them—all of them. Everything you can find."

"It will take me *forever* to sort through all that stuff. The boxes aren't even labeled."

"You've got to look for any documentation that connects your family to Jeremiah Harwell. We have to prove that you're related, in case they find the scan. If something happens to me, I want you to keep on digging until you find it, okay? Even if you run out of leads, do whatever it takes to make a connection, even if you have to hire someone to prove it for you. But don't discuss what you're doing any more than you have to. Keep it on the down low. If the land lease ceases to become an issue, HYA will piece together land purchases until they make it impossible for the holdouts to live here anymore. One way or another, they'll try to get what they want."

"Ryan, what are you expecting to happen to you?"

"Right now I'm not sure. It's probably not good. All I can do is go back to New York and try to talk us out of trouble."

A knock at the door made both of them jump. Ryan backed away from the door as Van opened it to a Nevis policeman.

Officer McCall immediately began sizing up the white teacup

poodle that had trailed Van to the door. "Good evening, ma'am. Is that Ernest Pickett's dog?"

"Yes, Officer, it is," said Van. "We found her running loose out on the boardwalk last night. Mr. Pickett never lets her wander, and she was dragging her leash. He didn't answer his door last night, so I brought her home with me. Mr. Pickett has got to be sick with worry. He never goes anywhere without that dog. We left a note . . ."

"Ms. Hardy," the policeman said, "Ernest Pickett was found unconscious out on the boardwalk last night."

"Oh, my God, what happened?"

"We're not entirely sure. Possibly some kind of altercation with the drowning victim; maybe he was just a witness. He's in critical condition under police protection at St. Leonard Hospital. Once he's stable, we'll interview him."

Officer McCall's eyes returned to the poodle. "Does Pickett have any family that you know of who can care for the dog?"

"No, he was alone. If it's all right, Susie can stay here. She's used to me from living next door, and I don't mind taking care of her."

"That would be fine, I suppose. Mr. Thomas," he said, turning and addressing Ryan. "How convenient. We have information from several witnesses that you had a heated exchange with Mr. Young yesterday evening on the boardwalk and that you were heard to threaten him. I need you to come down to the station and give a full statement on that incident. I also need to ask you some other questions, regarding your relationship and activities with Mr. Young."

"I would like to call an attorney," Ryan said. "I don't want to answer any questions without legal counsel."

"You need to come with us down to the station. You can call counsel from there. However, at this point in time, we only want a statement from you, and answers to some very basic questions. If at some point you want to call a lawyer, we can stop and accommodate that."

"Are you going to hold me?"

"That depends on what you tell us, Mr. Thomas. If you have nothing to hide, well, then there's nothing to worry about, is there? Let's just keep it informal and friendly right now." Officer McCall turned to Van. "Sorry for the inconvenience. We'll let you know about the dog."

Van nodded and focused all her attention on Ryan, trying to will her feelings into him so that he could see how scared she was and how much she cared about him.

"I'll see you, Van," he said. "Keep busy while I'm gone, okay? You are so close to having it all tied together." He reached out and pulled her to him, enveloping her in a tight embrace. "It'll all be okay," he whispered. Then he kissed her cheek and stepped out the door with the police officer.

She watched as they got into the police car and disappeared down the road. Closing the door, she sat down on the couch, drew herself up into a little ball, and pulled her grandmother's afghan up around her—and wept. If it hurt this bad when she was angry at him, she had to seriously rethink their relationship. One by one, the two little dogs jumped up to comfort her, and late evening found all three still snuggled close.

EIGHTEEN

AN AFTERTHOUGHT

Ryan walked out and got into the backseat of the police car. As long as he could keep his cool he was okay. After all, Hector wasn't dead, so the altercation would become inconsequential. He only had to answer for misidentifying Earl's body. Shock, the body's appearance, darkness—any would serve as an adequate defense. Whatever worked to get him back on the road to New York as soon as possible.

"Mr. Thomas? Mr. Thomas, please exit the vehicle."

"What?" Ryan snapped out of his reverie to see the officer holding the car door open, talking at him.

He automatically climbed out, although he wasn't sure exactly what the officer had said. He accompanied McCall into the town hall and upstairs into the tiny police office, eyeing the place as he went. Every head was obscured by a computer screen, and the tapping cadence of typing fingers punctuated the otherwise quiet bullpen. He had expected an interrogation room with metal furniture, bare walls, and a one-way mirror. Instead, the room had a homier feel: attractive table, padded chairs, and some cheap artwork on the walls. Still, his anxiety was running rampant. All his experience as a hotshot New

York lawyer had never prepared him for a possible murder rap in some coastal backwater.

"Mr. Thomas, as I said earlier, I need to document your interaction with Mr. Young and your whereabouts on the night of the twenty-seventh. Unless you have objections, this conversation will be recorded to ensure that the information you are providing is documented accurately."

Ryan knew that speaking without a lawyer was a bad move, but insisting on one made him look guilty as hell. He would just have to represent himself and hope he didn't have a fool for a client. "No objections. Get on with it."

For the next half an hour or so, Ryan gave a blow-by-blow of his relationship with Hector, and their altercation on the boardwalk before "Hector's" sudden death. Officer McCall did little interrupting, occasionally repeating a time, name, or place for clarity's sake. Ryan hoped he could stay consistent in his stories and provide just enough information about his personal and professional background to keep suspicion off himself and HYA.

"Hector Young and I have worked as attorneys for Hector Young and Associates for about eight years. We often work as a team on company business. That's why we were in Nevis. For proprietary reasons, I would prefer not to discuss the specifics of our business. During the course of my time here, I have become acquainted with Vanessa Hardy. On the day in question, I attended a gathering at Ms. Hardy's house. Hector Young came as a guest of mine, and we mixed and mingled during the afternoon. Mr. Young left before I did. I met up with him later in the afternoon, down on the boardwalk. I figured he would be down there since it's such a beautiful area and we had spent a lot of free time down there. I was right and did find him there, sitting on a bench.

"He made several insulting remarks about Ms. Hardy, and in defense of her honor, I grabbed him by the shirt collar and exchanged some heated words with him. I ended up shoving him back down on a bench, which tipped over with him still on it. At that point, I walked away. I didn't see him again until the emergency team pulled him from the water, and I did a tentative identification."

Ryan paused and looked McCall in the eyes. "It's true, I did threaten to kill him, but only if he continued to impugn Ms. Hardy's character. She's a nice lady, and I didn't think she deserved that. I did lose my temper. I regret what I said, but I didn't mean it. Had we gotten into it again, I might well have hit him a couple of times with a fist, but murder, hardly. I knew there were other people on the boardwalk when I said what I did. Why would I say something so incriminating in front of witnesses if I really meant it?"

"I don't know, Mr. Thomas. Why would you? Considering that Mr. Young is dead, it's a pretty damning admission you've made here."

"Listen, Hector Young is—*was*—a self-serving ass, but I didn't kill him. We've had a working relationship for eight years. He's been an ass ever since I met him. Why would I suddenly kill him now?"

"I don't know a lot, Mr. Thomas, but one thing I do know is that a man will do strange things for a woman—things he may not normally think he's capable of." Officer McCall paused and looked at Ryan, but Ryan didn't bite.

"I'll miss him. He was good competition—kept me on edge. I can't believe he's gone." Ryan sighed and ran his hand through his hair.

"Would you like to take a brief break, Mr. Thomas?"

"No, I'm fine. It's just, I was so upset that night, and it was so dark . . . What if it wasn't Hector? That isn't possible, is it? There are counterchecks to make sure there was no mistake. Someone in the family has identified the body?" He looked at Officer McCall with the most distraught face he could muster.

"Currently, no one from the family has come forward to identify the body. As a coworker, your identification of the body was considered sufficient and spares the family the trauma of viewing the body. You aren't recanting that identification, are you?"

"It was such a shock. What if I made a mistake? You'd put the wrong man in the grave," he said, his voice rising. He put his head in his hands.

"Mr. Thomas. That just wouldn't happen. Do you need a break to pull yourself together? If it would make you feel better, more sure, I can arrange for you to view the body again."

Ryan pulled his head up from his hands. "Yes, yes. Could you do that? I'm going to have nightmares over this. Poor Hector." He put his head back in his hands.

Officer McCall sighed and pulled out his cell phone. "Arrange a viewing of the Young body by a Mr. Ryan Thomas, as soon as possible . . . I'll hold . . ." He checked his watch. "Yes, twenty minutes . . . Right. Thanks." He flipped his phone shut. "Let's go, Mr. Thomas."

Ryan took a couple of deep breaths and got up. "I need to use the bathroom first—do you mind?" He shuffled down the hall to the men's room. Once inside, he leaned against the sink and checked his e-mails for a while before leaning over and flushing the toilet. After washing his hands, he walked out to find Officer McCall leaning against the wall, waiting.

A short car ride took them to the morgue. Even with death the one absolute certainty in life, the morgue looked like an afterthought. Located to the rear of a commercial building in the downtown area, it was marked by a small green striped awning and a row of parking spaces designated "Morgue Customers Only."

The small, sterile parlor, adorned with pictures of pleasant streams and mountains, did little to make either man feel comfortable, and a pall immediately fell over their mood. Elmer Dyson, a young man with freckles and a shock of red hair, was waiting for them and had already pulled the drawer open. A sheet covered the body of the deceased.

Ryan scanned the rest of the rows and columns of drawers, and a shiver ran down his spine. Hopefully, they were all empty. There was a disturbing smell. Whether it was death, mortuary chemicals, or both, he didn't know, but it immediately brought to mind funeral parlors. This would be a quick business.

Ryan and Officer McCall approached the body, and the attendant pulled back the sheet from the face with a theatrical flourish. "Ta da," he said.

Ryan did a double take. Officer McCall gave the attendant a look that could kill, and moved him out of the way with the sheer mass of his body.

"Sorry," the attendant mumbled, his face red. "I'm the only one here—well, sort of," he added, looking back over his shoulder.

Ryan took one look and quickly walked out of the room.

McCall signaled the attendant to cover the body again and followed Ryan out into the hall. "Good. See, Mr. Thomas, you can rest easy now. Mr. Young is in good ha—"

"That's not Hector," Ryan blurted. "It's Earl Jackson, my other coworker. That's the same body I looked at last night?" He turned to McCall. "Where's Hector's body? *Both* my coworkers are dead?"

"This is the *only* body. You're telling me this isn't Hector Young? You identified him. He had ID on him, and you confirmed his identity. You aren't playing games with me, are you, Mr. Thomas? It's a punishable offense to make false statements to the police."

"No, no games. It was such a shock," Ryan stammered. "You had his wallet . . . It was dark, and I didn't look but for an instant—dead bodies give me the creeps . . . I obviously wasn't thinking clearly. I didn't mean to deceive or hinder your investigation. It's Earl. I'm sure, one hundred percent sure. He was in town. Hector said so."

McCall approached Ryan, who instinctively stiffened. The officer grabbed him by the shirtsleeve and pulled him closer. "I'm gonna say this one time, so listen close. Nevis is a nice little town—good people. We don't go out of our way to tell other folks how to live their lives, and we take care of our own. It doesn't take a lot to see that you and yours are bad news for our town. I don't know much about you or your New York friend, Mr. Thomas, but I aim to find out. In the meantime, I'm gonna suggest you leave Nevis and don't come back unless we send for you. I see you around here again screwing with my town, things could get uncomfortable."

His hot breath stirred the contents of Ryan's stomach.

"It wouldn't be too smart to put your hands on a New York lawyer," said Ryan, wondering if the morgue attendant was still within earshot. "Now, am I free to go?"

McCall released his grip and straightened Ryan's shirt. "I think we're good."

McCall drove him as far as the boardwalk and made him get out—not fast enough, as far as Ryan was concerned. Ryan power walked to the motel, packed his bags, and was driving north to New York within the half hour.

NINETEEN

A WILL, A WAY, AND SOME MONEY

The new identification of the boardwalk drowning victim forced the Nevis police into a whole new theory. An initial investigation that seemed to be an open-and-shut case incriminating Ryan Thomas fell apart with a resounding thud. Not to be burned a second time, the police summoned Earl Jackson's parents to Nevis to identify their son's remains. Once again Elmer Dyson found himself standing at the head of the sheet-covered corpse, waiting to unveil the victim's face.

"Okay, Dyson, please pull the sheet back so Mr. and Mrs. Jackson can see. Easy does it," McCall said, with a withering look.

Elmer pulled the sheet back with no flourish or commentary of any kind and stepped back from the body with his head down.

"Yes, that's him. That's my baby," Mrs. Jackson said, and she pressed her face into the chest of her silent, stone-faced husband. Her sobs filled the little building as Mr. Jackson escorted her from the room.

The bigger question of why the deceased was carrying the identification of a coworker, Hector Young, and the current whereabouts of that coworker began to consume and overwhelm the finite resources of Nevis's little police force. But what the Nevis police lacked in size and finesse, it more than made up for with the determination of Officer McCall.

McCall sat at his desk, drumming with his pencil eraser on his mouse pad. He was a big man, but he was not a *happy* big man. With a pit bull's tenacity, he was not one to let a case go until he was satisfied with the answers to every question.

"McCall, how 'bout another cup?" Officer Little asked, holding up a mug.

"Bug off, Mike. I can't think with you waving that around."

"Why don't you just call this an accident and let it go."

"Nah, that sounds like something you would do. Me . . . something isn't right here. What am I missing?" He absent-mindedly picked up the phone ringing at his elbow.

"McCall . . . Yes! How long ago did he regain consciousness? . . . On my way. Mike," he said, turning to his partner, who was still at the coffeemaker, "I'm off to the hospital. Ernest Pickett just regained consciousness, but he's still in critical condition. I'm going to try and get a statement from him."

The Nevis police had placed around-the-clock protection at the hospital as soon as they realized Pickett might be a potential witness in the drowning case. His awakening was the first opportunity to determine what he might have seen or heard. Officer McCall wasted no time in getting to the hospital to see him.

"I'll take it from here," he said to the officer standing guard at the door to Pickett's hospital room. "Come back in about fifteen minutes."

"Officer, before you go in may I have a word with you, please?" asked a petite nurse at the nurses' station. "Just a word of caution.

We need Mr. Pickett to remain calm. You might want to avoid mentioning Susie. He keeps asking for her. We keep trying to tell him his wife is deceased, but he just gets terribly angry. It's not what he needs."

"Ma'am," McCall said, taking his hat off as he leaned down toward her. "Ms. Stewart," he said, reading her name tag but trying not to offend her by staring at her chest too long, "I don't believe Mr. Pickett's wife's name was Susie. It was Alice. His *dog* is Susie, and she's safe and sound. A neighbor found her running loose on the boardwalk." He gave her a shy, boyish smile and put his hat back on.

"Lord Almighty, I guess he would be upset, then, wouldn't he?" Nurse Stewart said. "All right, then," she said, and she smiled back at him in her own shy way. "I think it's all right for you to go in, then. Just don't tire him out—he needs his rest."

McCall entered the hospital room to find Pickett hooked up to a skein of tubes and monitor wires. Hospitals freaked him out. He and his partner put their lives on the line every day, even in a small town like Nevis, and this was one place he wanted to stay the hell away from. He slowly approached the bed where the patient lay under a sheet not much whiter than his face. The old man didn't move or acknowledge his visitor in any way.

"Mr. Pickett, I'm Officer McCall. I'd like to ask you a few questions about the night you got hurt, if you don't mind."

The old man opened his eyes and looked at the officer but didn't say a word. He just frowned and continued to stare.

"May I have your full name, Mr. Pickett?" McCall asked.

"You just addressed me by name, you jackass. Get on with your questions," Pickett growled through his clenched jaw. His dentures still floated in a glass beside the bed. His blazing eyes assured McCall that he was lucid enough to continue.

"Mr. Pickett, what were you doing the night of your attack?"

"I took Susie for a walk along the boardwalk, just like I do every night. Damn people walk their dogs along my property in front and ruin the grass. I don't let my dog do that. Where's Susie?"

"Susie's fine. She is with your next-door neighbor, Ms. Hardy."

For an instant, almost imperceptibly, the corners of Pickett's mouth crept up. "She'd better take good care of her until I come and get her." He struggled to sit up amid the tubes and wires but soon gave it up. "I'll sue—"

"Yes, sir," McCall interrupted. "I'll tell her. Everything's fine; Susie's fine. Now, can you tell me what happened on the boardwalk when you were walking Susie? Did you see Earl Jackson, the man from New York?"

"I saw two men on the boardwalk . . . arguing. They were standing in the middle, blocking the way, 'specially the big guy. I was getting ready to give them a piece of my mind. Bastards, scaring my Susie! I pay taxes! I should be allowed to walk in town without having to walk around people. Sue all their asses! Yeah, I saw 'em. They were arguing. Big one cussing the little one out. The son of a bitch stabbed him and pushed him into the water. I tried to yell for help, but the pain in my chest . . . . I couldn't help the man. Oh, my God, the pain in my chest . . ." His hand went to his chest, and he began to gasp for air.

McCall grabbed his hand and drew in close to him. "Mr. Pickett," he whispered, "who stabbed him?" Was it Ryan Thomas? Hector Young?"

"No, damn fool," Picket whispered. "The biker—big guy, red beard . . . Rusty . . ."

Pickett's hand went limp, his body gave a jerk, and the monitor at his bedside began to flash and beep. Suddenly, nurses, a crash cart, and emergency personnel materialized from nowhere, buzzing into the room like bees from a hive.

McCall found himself shoved out of the room and forced to stand in the corridor. His mind raced. A biker, and not just any biker. Rusty Clark, the biggest, meanest enforcer the Diablo biker gang ever had. More questions. Was this a chance encounter—wrong place, wrong time—or was there a connection between the New York man and the Diablos? McCall paced impatiently, drumming his fingers on his notepad, waiting for his chance to reenter the room. He approached the first nurse who came out the door: the same little nurse he had spoken with earlier.

"Excuse me, ma'am, Ms. Stewart," he said. "It's important that I finish up my conversation with Mr. Pickett. Will that be possible tonight?"

She looked up with her big brown eyes. I'm sorry, Officer, but I'm afraid Mr. Pickett just passed. He didn't make it." She gave a little half-stifled sob.

McCall's eyes bulged as Ms. Stewart scurried on down the corridor. He watched her for a moment, then left the hospital, hat in hand and with no plan in mind.

❧

For all McCall's professionalism and thoroughness in investigating the case, he was smart enough to weigh the bang for the buck and consider calling it quits when the costs outweighed the benefits—especially the benefits to him personally. The Diablos and Rusty Clark were too much to chew without a live witness. Still, McCall was taken aback when, one afternoon, he received a call about the case.

"Meet me at Tenth and Walnut at two p.m. I have information about the Earl Jackson case. My client doesn't like publicity."

At Tenth and Walnut, a man of small build approached McCall and handed him a large envelope. "I think this will be enough to complete your investigation. The evidence inside exonerates Hector Young and supports a finding of accidental drowning."

Officer McCall took the envelope and thumbed through the contents. Just as the man had predicted, the stack of crisp hundred-dollar bills attested to Mr. Young's innocence and pointed instead to an accidental tumble into the cold waters of the Chesapeake Bay. "Looks just about right," said McCall without missing a beat. "Pleasure doing business with you."

TWENTY

DADDY ISSUES

Van and Jean wasted no time searching for the missing descendants of Jeremiah Harwell. Van knew the documents housed in the courthouse well enough, but sharing the librarian's limited expertise and time with other patrons made the search unproductive, especially when one voracious researcher kept the librarian in constant motion.

Van put her head down on the stack of books and crossed her arms over her head. "Jean, I have run out of options," she said. "I don't even know where else to look. Maybe I should try to hire someone to pick up the trail. I'm thinking . . . See the lady at that front table over there? Nice clothes, expensive jewelry?"

"Yeah, I've been hating on her a while, too."

Van laughed quietly. "Besides that. Dressed like that, she's obviously not from around here. She's kept the librarian hoofing, using some of the same resources that we have. Some documents haven't even been filed back before she has them at her table. She's doing genealogical research, too."

Jean watched the woman for a moment, then whispered, "Maybe we—meaning *you,* of course—should strike up a conversation with her."

"I love the way you think," said Van, and she got up from their table and walked over to where the stranger sat.

"Excuse me, I hate to bother you," she said. "I couldn't help but notice some of the references you're using. Are you a genealogist?"

The woman looked up and laughed. "I am. May I help you with something?" Her voice was quiet and polished, and she exuded a confidence and authority that was a bit intimidating. Van took an instant liking to her.

"May I sit?" Van asked. The woman nodded. "I promise I won't keep you; I can tell you're very busy. I've been working on a difficult area in my family tree, and I've hit a brick wall. I need to make a connection between two individuals, and I just can't find *anything*. I've been through all the wills and land records that I can think to search, used every online genealogical site I can find, and still nothing. I couldn't help but notice, you look so good at it. I thought maybe you could suggest what else I might do before I break down and hire a pro. I apologize for being so bold. Normally I'm not at all forward with strangers, but this is so important, and genealogy seems to be a sharing sort of hobby." She trailed off into a whisper and a nervous, hopeful smile.

The woman laughed again. "Well, I wouldn't call it a sharing hobby for me. It's how I make my living. I'm a professional researcher." She extended a beautifully manicured hand. "Margaret Douglas."

Van shook her hand. "Vanessa Hardy. Everybody calls me Van. Nice to meet you."

"In what time frame are you running into problems? It's local history?"

"First, if you're a professional researcher, then time is money to you. Can I pay you for your time?"

"No, that's all right. I can't help you too much, anyway. I'm working for a client right now. But I could use a short break. So what do you have?"

Van heard the sharp intake of Peggy's breath as Van spread her extensive Ahnentafel chart across the table and traced down through the names, explaining as she went. She felt a surge of pride in all that she had found and documented on her family.

"I'm trying to make a connection between a Jeremiah Harwell and William Harwell. They both lived and died in the Nevis area in the seventeen hundreds. I can trace my line back to William but can find nothing to support his being the son of Jeremiah. There wasn't a huge population in Nevis back then, but William just seems to come out of nowhere, like he's from outer space."

Leaning forward on her elbows, Peggy studied the chart for a while before she spoke again. "This is so extensive, I'm afraid . . . it might take me a little bit longer than I thought, just to take this all in. Forgive, me, I really underestimated you. You're much better at this than the average researcher." She gave another smile that could light up a room. "Would you be willing to let me take a copy of these and study them before I give you any advice?"

"I would be absolutely thrilled to give you a copy and let you do that. I really do appreciate your help, and as I said, I'm more than willing to pay you."

"Oh, no, not necessary. Your tree looks very interesting. I'm in the middle of something, but I'll see if I can help you. Give me a couple of days."

Van copied all her documents and gave them to Peggy with her phone number. She gave Jean a smug little look as they left for home. This was going to pan out. She just knew it.

❧

Peggy spread Van's documents out again on the table in front of her and started circling names and dates. After a while, she began nodding in agreement with a remembered conversation, and a slow smile spread across her face. She grabbed her phone from her purse and autodialed. It was a short, efficient conversation in whispery tones.

Peggy made a series of notes before requesting additional references from the front desk, backtracking over some of the reference materials used by Van and Jean. She worked another couple of hours before packing everything up and leaving the courthouse. Outside, she paused and surveyed the parking lot. He was late. No sooner had she settled on one of the benches than she caught sight of a small blue sports car zipping up to the building. The car came to an abrupt halt at the bottom of the steps. Peggy got in on the passenger side. But then she slid all the way across the seat, wrapped her arms around the driver's neck, and smacked him full on the lips.

"Hey, sweetie. When I didn't see your car I thought maybe you might not be coming." She looked up tentatively at her boyfriend.

"Leave you sitting here all alone? Not a chance. You know that by now, Maggie, baby. Missed you so much." The driver leaned in and gave her a long, lingering kiss.

Peggy pulled back and giggled, her lips quivering around the kiss. "I love you, too," she said, caressing his cheek with her hand. She dropped her hand to his, where it remained for the rest of the drive.

"You realize you're the only one who calls me Maggie?"

"Because I'm the only one who truly appreciates how wonderful you are."

She laughed. "Where are we going for dinner?"

"Anywhere my baby wants. Fasten your seat belt," said Hector, and he floored the gas pedal, spewing gravel and dust in his wake as he headed out Route 261 away from Nevis.

They chose an out-of-the-way restaurant in a small strip mall a short distance out of town. Choosing a table away from the door, Hector seated her first and then took her hand in his as he sat.

"How've you been?" he said. "Like I said, I've missed you."

"I'm having the best time in this little courthouse. The same names keep popping up over and over again: births, marriages, children, land sales, death, wills, estate inventories. I feel like I know them personally. You can trace a person's entire life three hundred years ago. It's fascinating! I think I'll find what I'm looking for—I'm flying through records."

"You know, don't you, that the longer it takes you, the longer we can be together? I can't see you when we get back to New York. Nothing's changed. I should already be back there, but I think I can juggle that for a little while, before anyone starts looking for me."

"He still won't change his mind?"

"Nope."

"If he hates me so much, why doesn't he fire me?"

Hector began to sneer. "Oh, you're good enough to work for the company—just not good enough to date his son."

"You could defy him."

Hector laughed. "He'd disown me, and then you wouldn't want me. I'd be a penniless nobody."

Peggy gave him a disgusted look. "You know that isn't true, and I don't care about the money. I'll always love you. You're the most wonderful person I've ever met." She began playing with the straw in her water glass. "We could just disappear and start a life somewhere else." She looked up at him with earnest eyes, full of hope.

"Maggie, seriously, we could never run far enough."

"You really think he'd find us?"

"I know he would. My father never loses. It's the whole point to his life."

"I don't mean to hurt your feelings with this," she said. "So don't get mad, okay? Why don't you stand up to him? Are you so afraid of him?"

"Absolutely. I'm not ashamed to admit that I'm terrified of the bastard, of what he could do to me—and to you—if he knew we were still together. You have no idea."

They sat in silence—he in anger and pain, she unable to understand or empathize.

"Ah, Maggie, Maggie," Hector said, taking her hand, "let's talk about something else. I don't want to talk about anything but us. Live in the now with me, lovely Maggie," he teased, trailing kisses up her hand.

Maggie smiled but automatically withdrew her hand as the waiter approached to take their order. Hector ordered rack of lamb for each of them, to be followed by Smith Island cake for dessert. Waiting for the meal was a pleasure as they got lost in the private bubble of their relationship. It seemed too short a time when the waiter returned bearing a plate of lamb.

"Shall I bring you a second plate, to make it easier to share?" he asked.

Hector's eyes narrowed. "Where's the second rack of lamb? We ordered two."

"Uh, no, sir, I placed an order for only one."

Hector threw his napkin down on the table. "What is wrong with you people? Do you see two people sitting here?" He got out of his chair.

"Hector, please," said Maggie. She tried to grab his hand, but it had already come off the table, in a fist.

"No. They should be able to get this right. Go get your manager, now!"

"Hector, please, you're embarrassing me. Please sit down," Maggie pleaded. She reached again and managed to grab his hand and squeeze it. He didn't respond. She squeezed again and ran her thumb across the top of his hand. Hector's eyes darted to hers and held her gaze for a few seconds before she saw the fire in his eyes begin to dim. His eyes flicked back to the waiter.

"Bring us a second plate." Hector sat down, wiped the back of his hand across his brow, and turned his attention back to Maggie. "Forgive me. It's been a long day." The fire in his eyes went out.

"Are you all right? I've never seen you so upset."

"I'm fine. Forget it—bad day."

He abruptly changed the subject. "Your research—you know this is vitally important, right? Any real progress?"

Maggie's smile began to return. "Actually, there is. Someone is researching exactly the same family line that I am. What a coincidence, huh?"

Hector sat up a little straighter. "How do you know that?"

"The lady came over and introduced herself and asked for my help. She was really nice. She noticed we were using some of the same references."

"Who?"

"She wrote her information down for me," Maggie said, fishing the piece of paper out of her purse and handing it to Hector.

He read the name and crunched the paper up in his fist. "Vanessa Hardy. Did she say why she was researching this?"

"It's her line, and she has a brick wall she can't work through. She's in a hurry to make the connection, but she didn't say why." Maggie stopped and cocked her head to one side as she studied the tension in Hector's face for a moment. "What's the matter? She couldn't have been nicer."

"I know all about her. She might have seemed nice, but she's actually the single biggest obstacle to HYA in Nevis. Bad, bad news for our business. Stay away from her."

"Hector, I can't. I promised her I would help her. I even have a copy of the research she's done so far."

"Lose it. Distract her. Or better yet, mislead her. Keep her from completing the documentation on her line until after you complete yours and the company can act on it. Think of it as corporate competition. Don't give up our advantage, Maggie. Okay? I know it's hard for you to be tough, baby, but we're talking business here—my family business. Can you do that for me?"

Maggie hesitated. Hector very rarely asked her for anything. "I don't know. What's the harm? She was really nice."

"I can't get into company business; you know that. You just have to trust me, baby. I've never been false to you." He reached over and took her hand, and she felt her hesitation melt away. It was true; he had never done her wrong.

"Okay, I'll try, but I'm not going to lie to her," she said, shaking her head. "I'm not good at that." She thought for a moment and then began nodding. "I'll avoid her."

Hector smiled and patted her hand. It was a smile that few besides Maggie ever saw. "That's my girl."

They finished their dinner and headed back to Maggie's place, where they spent several more hours together as he flirted and she blushed. Laughing and joking was easy for them—the easy way of a close couple—and they shared what they would do when they no longer had anyone to answer to but themselves. Hector left not long after midnight.

TWENTY-ONE

BIRDS OF A FEATHER

Ryan knew that in the corporate world, where worth was often measured by the ability to size up an opponent and beat him at his own game, success need not always be associated with monetary gain. It was sometimes better to beat an opponent without any regard to who ended up with the most in his pile. That was Ryan's only hope in going to New York. Without a doubt, Hector had communicated to his father everything that happened in Nevis—with his own slant on it, of course. Hector was a "payback's a bitch" kind of guy. By now, management was not happy.

Ryan couldn't outman or outplan HYA. He could only hope to have the upper hand by working quickly, with the inside information he did have, to create an uncomfortable atmosphere for HYA—one that would convince them that there were better uses for their resources than hunting him down as an example to other potentially wayward employees. Some might call it blackmail. Ryan thought of it more as a sensible meeting of the minds.

As he drove to New York, the hum of his tires on the road drone on like a generator powering his churning, racing mind.

He would be direct and target the heartbeat of HYA: its founder and CEO and his own personal mentor, Hector Young Senior. It was his only hope of salvaging the compromised position he had put himself in. He drove with a white line fever up Interstate 95, through the Holland Tunnel, and into Manhattan. His preference would have been to swing by his brownstone, but he couldn't chance running into someone watching for him there. Hell, he couldn't even risk using his cell phone. So he checked into the New Yorker under an assumed name and spent the night protecting his assets—shifting money between various private accounts, downloading and e-mailing documents, and refining his strategy.

ʖ

The next morning, Ryan was up and out early. Leaving the hotel, he made a series of turns and backtracks to make sure he was still alone, then pulled into a midtown parking garage. With tires squealing, he raced up to the top level, pulled quickly into a space near the elevator, and got out, inhaling deeply that familiar dry, dusty smell of New York. When the elevator arrived it was empty. Ryan took a key from his pocket, inserted it into the floor button panel, and punched a code.

The elevator lurched upward and opened at the penthouse level, onto a well-appointed lobby filled with bright light, dark wood, and soft, elegant classical music. He nodded to the secretary at the desk and proceeded through the wood-paneled double doors beyond her desk. She smiled briefly in acknowledgment and went back to whatever she was doing.

Classical music played softly against a backdrop of water trickling across polished rock surfaces. Rich brocade fabric in shades of gold and cream harmonized with sheer curtains as, across the room, a flight of origami cranes took wing.

"I could say I'm surprised to see you, Ryan, but then, you always were a ballsy guy," said the distinguished-looking gray-haired man who looked up as he entered. "Since I can assume you're not here to do anything for me, what can I do for you?"

"I'm here to ask you to accept my resignation from HYA. And because, if I didn't come back, I'd be dead inside a week."

"What makes you think you still won't be?" The man didn't smile or blink.

"I'm here to talk to you man to man, Hector."

The man laughed quietly. "I've always enjoyed our discussions. Go ahead, I'm listening. Would you like to sit while you're here?" Hector got up and moved over to a leather couch and directed Ryan to a chair nearby. As the older man sat he picked up a piece of black origami paper and began folding it as he spoke. "If I may start the conversation, is it true that you destroyed the one document that would have all but guaranteed our acquisition of the Nevis property?"

Ryan walked forward and put his hands on the back of the chair but didn't sit. "That isn't true. That deed would have guaranteed nothing. One descendant, possibly the only heir to Jeremiah Harwell, will never sell, not for any price." Ryan took a breath and continued. "I have never betrayed you. I would call it a difference of opinion. We don't need Nevis. The acquisition just doesn't seem right. Pick another place along the coast. Nevis can't be the only one."

Hector gave a deep, hearty, amused laugh. "Son, that's a pretty expensive difference of opinion. There is no right or wrong in the real world, only shades of gray. Someone is going to develop that land someday. It's ripe for the picking. We have to have vision and seize our opportunities where they lie. It's a race, the spoils go to the swiftest, and all that other rubbish you need to hear to feel good about all this," he said, dismissing the thought with a wave of the hand holding the half-finished crane. He sighed and then fixed Ryan with his keen, cold eyes. "What bothers me most is that you defied the company, and when you do that you defy me. How can I ever trust you again? I don't understand the betrayal on either a company or a personal level. The world was at your feet, waiting, Ryan. You stood to inherit everything I have. Everything I have was going to be yours," he said, shaking his head. "I thought of you as a son, treated you like a son—certainly more of a son than that imbecile who bears my name. You've made the mistake, possibly a fatal one, of getting personally involved. Is it the woman?"

"Maybe."

Hector got up from the couch and walked over to the window. He spent a moment looking out at the pedestrians two hundred feet below before turning around to glare at Ryan. "You're giving up a lucrative career, not to mention playing with your life, for a *maybe*?"

Ryan didn't respond.

"Victim to the feminine wiles, huh? There have been so many—why her, Ryan?"

"If I told you she was different, would you believe or even understand me?"

Hector Young shrugged his shoulders.

"It's difficult for me to explain. I feel a connection to her in a way that I've never felt with anyone else in my life."

"Ah, sex is cheap; connection, not so much. And you can't walk away from her, even knowing that unless you do, you're destroying your life?"

"No, I won't walk away."

Hector walked back over to his desk and sat down. Neither man said a word. They just studied each other, Hector with the pads of his two index fingers pressed together forming a triangle that rested lightly against his lips; Ryan just watching, trying to gather from the elder man's face some clue to his thoughts and feelings. Ryan recognized the intimidation tactic. He had seen it used a hundred times, but he wasn't sure whether, at this moment, he was seeing a tactical choice or just natural instinct.

"Ryan, you know too much. I can't let you just walk away. It's nothing personal; I think you know the high esteem I hold you in. But I'd be a fool to let you go, and I haven't reached this position in life by being foolish."

"See, that's the thing," Ryan said. "I know just enough to get *me* into trouble, but not as much as you think when it comes to getting HYA in trouble."

"You know entirely too much," Hector said dismissively.

"It's not my intention to try to bring HYA or any of its activities to its knees. I want to cut all ties. I, uh, wouldn't want to be forced into a position of using what I *do* know to guarantee that. But for argument's sake, I could go that route. I'm not so stupid as to walk in here without first taking certain, um, precautions to ensure that I walk back out again."

"You could be lying."

"Could be, but you yourself have said I know too much. Put yourself in my shoes. What would you do if you were in my position? That should help you with how to respond to my request and what I've said. Are you willing to take the risk?"

"Ryan, you are so refreshing!" Hector said, chuckling in a paternal sort of way. "We need you here at HYA. Others should be so clever." He paused, as if mulling over Ryan's offer. "Very well," he said as he rose and walked around the desk to Ryan, who was still standing behind the chair. "I'm not concerned about the damage you could do to HYA, and I have no intention of harming you, especially considering that the person you care the most about, you left alone in Nevis. It's the principle of the situation. I can't just let employees run amok, screwing over the company. I'm willing to let bygones be bygones on two conditions. One, obviously, is that you keep your mouth shut about HYA's past, present, and future business."

"I understand, and I can live with that. The second?"

"At some point in the future, I may need your assistance— nothing you can't handle. I would expect your full assistance at that time."

"And in return, no further interference?"

"None."

The room was silent but for the muted strains of Verdi and the soft trickle of the stone fountain.

"I accept, with one condition of my own. I need a liquor license in Nevis."

Hector looked over the rims of his glasses. "Liquor license? I think I can arrange that. What are you going to do with a liquor license? HYA could use a—"

"No, no strings. The license has to be totally independent of HYA."

"Done," Hector said, sliding the black origami crane into Ryan's shirt pocket and gently tapping it with his fingertips. "Such a magnificent bird. Did you know that cranes mate for life?" The two men held each other's gaze for several seconds.

Hector walked over to the office door but paused before opening it. "When you grow jaded with this new life—which I fully expect to happen—come back. HYA always strives to keep its brightest people." Opening the door, he leaned out toward the receptionist. "Carol, would you please ask Oliver to escort Mr. Thomas down to the parking garage?" He turned to Ryan and extended his hand. "I wish I could say it was a pleasure doing business with you today, Ryan. Please leave your elevator key at the desk on your way out."

Ryan shook Hector's hand and followed Oliver out to the parking garage. The escort was, of course, more about keeping him out of other HYA offices than about keeping him safe. He also wasn't surprised that someone had been snooping around in his car while he was inside. HYA was always on the ball and thorough.

He had never considered that the company would threaten Van's security to get his cooperation. He could not get back to Nevis fast enough.

TWENTY-TWO

CRYPT KEEPERS

Van saw meeting with Margaret Douglas last night as an act of providence. Meeting someone with her expertise was pure serendipity. She couldn't wait to tell Ryan, but she had no idea where he was.

To help pass the time, Van latched on to the most mindless activity she could find: watching Charlie edge her flower bed. He worked on his own clock, and it didn't matter if a chore was finished today or stretched into tomorrow. All that he seemed to care about was that it kept him busy and that it would look right when he was done. What Charlie didn't care so much for was anyone looking over his shoulder while he worked. He was just about to change chores and move out of Van's sight when suddenly she spoke and broke the tension.

"Come sit with me, Charlie, and rest a minute. You look all kinds of tense. We haven't talked in a while."

He joined her on the porch, and they rocked for a while in silence.

"Charlie, you know how they say to be careful what you wish for, because you just might get it? Do you ever wish you could talk to your wife, even if it was just for a couple of minutes?"

"Sure, all the time. She wasn't gone five minutes before I had a million questions I wanted to ask her, and things I wanted to tell her." He nodded thoughtfully. "Yep."

"I've often thought how wonderful it would be to pick up the phone one day, and there'd be James on the other end." Van laughed. "Like a call from the hereafter. Oh, just to hear his voice again." She sighed and looked at kindly old Charlie. "I'm not crazy, then?"

"You know, I'm starting to lose a lot of my dear friends," he said. "I'm at that age. We old-timers kinda share and cope together. Naw, that's pretty normal," he said, and he reached out and put a suntanned hand over hers and gave it a squeeze. Ageless strength seemed to flow from the gnarled old hand.

"What if you could have her back, but just not in the way you would have expected? Like, what if she came back, but not as your wife? Suppose . . . she was just someone you bumped into down at the bakery one day? And you knew it was her? Of course, we know that isn't possible, but what if it was? How would you handle that?"

Charlie's serious face broke out into a huge grin. "Land sakes, girl, what are you talking about?"

"Wait, now, I'm being serious. Really, what would you do?"

"Well," he said, pulling his lower lip up tight against the upper one and nodding slowly, "I expect I'd love her the same way I do right now, because true love, it lasts forever. It's so real you can reach out and touch it when you meet the right person." He stopped and mused a moment. "Yeah," he said, shaking his head, "lasts forever."

"Do you think it's possible ever to meet them again—here on earth, that is?"

"Naw. I say a prayer that I can be with her a little in my dreams or just being thoughtful, but I don't ask for any more than that. You take what the big man gives you." Charlie got up and hugged Van. "It's hard, isn't it?" He went on down the steps in his familiar slow shuffle and headed around back, pulling out his handkerchief as he went.

❧

Van rocked a little longer, and when she couldn't think of a good reason to put it off any longer she got in her car and drove out to the cemetery. Trudging up the hill, she immediately started searching for the spot. There was no point of reference for finding her son's grave—no big, beautiful archangel statue or little lamb perched on the top of a child's gravestone. In fact, there was no point of reference for his death at all. She hated modern cemeteries—just acre after acre of dead people. No beautifully crafted headstones saying something about the lives of those who lay there and those they left behind. Just cold metal markers sunken in the ground like those they named.

She didn't visit often. So many conflicting feelings: duty, love, loneliness. This was the memory place for her. She had always believed that the essence of James, his soul, was with God; all that remained here were bones. But sometimes she needed a place to focus, and in those moments, she came here. Today she needed soul-searching and advice to solve the newest wrinkle in her already complicated life.

When she finally found James's grave she knelt and started right in on the task at hand: pulling grass runners away from the edge of the marker. Taking a tissue from her pocket, she gently wiped the dirt and debris from the face of the stone. There was a coldness to it that even the bright sunshine of a summer's day couldn't warm. Satisfied, she pulled a pink pebble out of her pocket and placed it between the first and last name. Then she sat down at the head of the grave to stare at the stone engraving. James Hardy. Teary eyes traced the beading of the rosary along the top. This marker had a story, a story about a little boy who kept a rosary tucked into his pillowcase at night because no harm could come to someone in prayer. The Celtic cross to the left told another story. It resembled the one James always wanted to have tattooed on his arm. It was the kind of tattoo that some good Catholic boys dreamed about and that others, like Sam, wore in remembrance of a childhood friend.

Her hands tried to brush away the tears continuously rolling down her cheeks. She appeared to sit alone in her grief—the silent figure of a slight woman sitting cross-legged at a grave, head down, so immersed in sorrow that her surroundings had no substance. And yet, she was anything but quiet or alone. She sat in deep conversation with those she held closest. She beseeched her God to help her and asked her son to forgive her.

"Oh, James, you don't know how much I wish I could have a conversation with you right now. You always gave me the best advice. No matter what, you were always honest. I need you. I can put my life back together . . . with him. But I'm not deserting you. I don't want to hurt you. He can't be you. It's not possible. I know you're with God, and I know I'll see you again."

Off in the distance, she watched the slow, almost regal strut of a peacock moving warily past her. As she fought to control her emotions, she watched swallows fighting the stiff breeze and noted how the blue of the sky deepened as her eyes followed it from the horizon upward to its zenith. It was always breezy here, and the cold went right through her. She pulled herself together, lowered her eyes to the ground, and began again.

"There is a part of me that wants to move on, with him, but I feel that I'm betraying you . . . forgetting you, deserting you. You're not a memory. Every day brings me a step, not away from you, but closer. Who's going to come and remember you—love you? I don't want to hurt you or forget you."

She put her hands to her eyes and burst into tears. "God, help me to bear this. I don't know what to do. How can you possibly be both people? I can't be with both of you. Which one of you do I give up? I can't choose. Please, can't you give me a sign? Talk to me, please. God, don't desert me."

She put her head down and listened with all her heart, and all was still quiet. She looked toward the Christ figure standing in the green, with his arms outstretched, embracing the world with his love. She felt his embrace, and it comforted her. When she needed him, he wiped her clean of troubled thoughts and overwhelmed emotions. She silently beseeched him.

All remained quiet except an internal feeling that spoke to her. It wasn't like the voice she had heard so long ago, but it was reasonable, and it still spoke to her with authority. Even though she could not hear His voice, she could feel His presence, and it calmed her. And when He was finished with her she was able to dry her tears and get to her feet.

"Take care of my son, wherever he is," she said. "And if this is a mistake, please forgive me and guide me. You know that I love you. I can't handle this without you. Please help me."

She walked quickly back to her car. As she pulled out she stopped for the peacocks while they slowly strutted across the road. Peacocks. Visitors complained about them all the time—that they were incessant pests who pulled flowers out of the grave vases, impeded traffic, and keened their eerie calls. Jean hated them—said they reminded her of "crypt keepers." But for Van, they reminded her that there was a life better than this one and that God was seeing even when she couldn't. With them, she knew James wasn't alone here. And neither was she.

❧

Van drove back to town and circled the block a couple of times before it occurred to her that this was farmers' market day—she could do this all day and still not find a close parking space.

Reluctantly, she parked in a vacant lot close by and started to walk. She liked this section of town with its quaint old buildings and storefronts. *Sweet to the eye,* she thought as she gazed along the street. Even in its faded glory, it still called to her. She made a mental note to come back and just take it all in, write about it, maybe even sketch it.

TWENTY-THREE

FAMILIARITY BREEDS CONTEMPT

Ryan had never seen so many cars in Nevis, bumper to bumper along the curb, leaving him nowhere to park. When he finally found a space, he hit the sidewalk at a pace just under a run. Every other breath was a little prayer that he would find Van all right. Ahead, he could see several side streets converging into the main town circle.

At the traffic circle, he looked down the street to his right. Their eyes met at the same instant: the bulky shape of Officer McCall pushing away from the car he had been leaning against.

"Thomas," the officer yelled. He was not in uniform, though nothing else about him was casual. Every step toward Ryan reeked of tough-guy attitude.

"Fuck a duck! He's all the trouble I need right now," Ryan said to himself. McCall's approach forced him to choose the middle street, and he whipped around and started across, freezing in his tracks as he recognized the approaching figure of Hector Young Jr.

"Ryan!"

"Make it *two* ducks," Ryan said to himself. And he turned to the left side street only to recognize the figure of Van approaching in the distance. The sight of her, obviously alive and well, was a blessed relief, but she was so far down the street that Hector would reach him long before he got to her. Hector called to him again and accelerated his pace. Ryan took a couple of steps forward until he could no longer see Van, then stayed there in the pending vortex of forces bearing down on him.

"How was New York?" Hector asked as he drew close.

"What do you want?"

"Oh, nothing from you. Talked to the boss—laissez-faire. I'm looking for your girlfriend. I have a proposition for her."

"Stay away from her; she's not interested."

"Guess I'll find out. What woman could resist a proposition from me once she sees what I have to offer, eh?" Hector laughed.

"I'm not going to let you hurt her. Stay away from her," Ryan repeated, and he stepped forward to check Hector's advance. From the corner of his eye, Ryan could also see McCall approaching. While Ryan's body moved in apparent slow motion, his mind raced through a number of options for keeping his body in one piece. He braced himself as the hulking cop closed in on him. He didn't have to wait long.

"What part of 'I don't want to see your face again' did you not understand, Mr. Thomas?"

Ryan turned to face him. "Why, Officer McCall! Imagine us running into each other here! I was just headed to your office to let you know that unavoidable business has brought me back to Nevis. I was going to give you the courtesy of check—"

McCall stepped in front of Hector, grabbed Ryan by the shirt front, and drew him in close. "You dumb little shit. I don't like having my instructions ignored."

The smell of onions, garlic, and kielbasa was overpowering, and the tight grip of the cop's fist on Ryan's shirt pressed uncomfortably against his windpipe. Ryan was standing on his toes, but in another moment he could be dangling in the air.

"What the hell," said Hector, regaining his balance and coming back at McCall with raised fists.

It was as if Hector had not existed until that moment. Officer McCall instantly dropped Ryan and whirled to defend himself against the new and unknown threat. Ryan regained his footing and slowly backed up.

"Officer McCall, I'd like you to meet the temporarily drowned, no longer dead Hector Young. Hector, this is Officer McCall."

Hector immediately dropped his fists. "Officer . . . as in *police*?"

McCall uncocked the fist he was about to launch at Hector's face. "Hector Young? *The* Hector Young? Son of a bitch, I can't tell you how much I've wanted to talk to you! How 'bout you and I have a little chat about your recent death?" As he spoke, McCall grabbed a fistful of shirt and pulled Hector in the direction of his car. "You can come, too, Mr. Smart-Ass," he said, talking over his shoulder to Ryan. But by now Ryan was almost out of earshot. After making the formal introduction, he had wasted no time in sprinting across the circle and down the third street, toward Van.

"We're not finished, Thomas!" McCall yelled after him.

TWENTY-FOUR

DARK AND DIRTY

Van stopped walking as the figure of a man appeared at the end of the street. She could swear it was Ryan, but before she could call to him, he disappeared. No, she thought, if he was back in town, he would surely have called. She quickened her pace, but before she could close the distance to the corner the man reappeared. This time he was running full speed, straight for her, jacket flapping in the breeze and hair flying. It was a desperate, scrambling kind of run in which the body was trying to do too many things at once, none of them well. Relief swept over her as she recognized that it was indeed Ryan.

She began to run toward him.

Ryan was breathless when he reached her. She tried to wrap her arms around his neck, but he peeled them off none too gently in one sweeping motion. Without stopping, he grabbed her by the elbow and rushed her back around the corner she had just come from.

"Keep walking," he said. "Let me catch my breath. Where's your car?"

"It's HYA? They're after you?"

"Not exactly. Just keep walking."

Van quickly led him to her car, and they jumped in and took off, away from the downtown area.

"Who are you running from?"

"Let's just say that when I left Nevis a few days ago I wasn't invited back. Don't take us straight back to the house. Can you drive somewhere close so we can talk, but not where we would be isolated?"

"Sure," said Van. "Then you're going to tell me what's going on. You're scaring me!"

"Promise. Drive," he said, sliding down in the car seat.

Van drove to the north part of town and parked near the boardwalk, a short walk from her house.

"All right," she said. "What's going on? Who told you not to come back?"

Ryan ignored the question. "Good to see you again," he said, giving her a long, lingering squeeze. "Come on. Get out of the car and walk with me."

"Ryan, I was so worried when you didn't come back after giving your police statement. What happened? Did you go to New York?"

He said nothing until they were some distance away from the car. "I reidentified the body as Earl, and the police let me go, though I didn't make any friends there. New York—well, it is what it is. We've reached a compromise, for the time being. And Nevis—let's just say Officer McCall and I will never be close friends. I was trying to avoid him when I saw you there on the street. We're good right now. He's otherwise occupied.

"Van, Hector's been looking for you," he went on. "I was afraid he was going to find you before I got back. Don't let him anywhere near you. I don't think he'd touch you—bullying is more his style. But that wouldn't stop him from having a third party do his dirty work. Earl is proof of that. What have you found in the courthouse?"

"*Nada.* Jean and I exhausted ourselves. The good news is, we met someone at the courthouse who's going to help us."

"What kind of someone?"

"Later. Don't change the subject. I'm safe in the courthouse, but with you it looks like I need protection. Talk to me. Life's been nothing but drama since I met you: dead bodies floating in the bay, reincarnated sons, hide-and-seek with the local constabulary, not to mention that crazy, uncouth Hector. I didn't sign up for this. You need to tell me everything."

"There isn't much more to tell. I'm not Ryan Thomas. That cold son of a bitch dedicated his life to a business full of illegal endeavors designed to please investors. I'm not him. Memories are coming back. I'm surviving this strange cosmic game, although I'm not entirely sure what the rules are—or how you win. Now I've been able to shift the game, but beyond that, I don't know.

"Look, Van," he continued, "when I brought up my suspicions that I might be your son, that didn't mean I wanted to resume my life as your son. It would be naive to think I could do that. But, it wouldn't have been fair to either of us never to have brought it up. If I wanted to torpedo our relationship, I couldn't have made up anything worse than what I've already told you."

Ryan nervously put his hands in his pockets and jingled his keys around. "I know the way you look at me, and I know the way I feel when I look at you. Nothing you or I say will change that. I'd like to stay in Nevis and try to work out a relationship with you. I'm just not sure right now what that relationship is. Obviously, I have feelings for you that aren't exactly familial. I can't deny that, and I don't want to lie about it. Those feelings are intense, but at the same time, what do I do with that?"

Van walked over and leaned up against the back of one of the benches. "When I first came to Nevis I was going to make my life simple, try to put myself and my life back together. I'm still one of the walking wounded, Ryan. I'm not sure I'm ready for a serious, deep relationship. I've made a point of making my life shallow—a superficial existence with few ties, the better to avoid the pain. There is healing, but there will always be the pain, too. But if there's one thing I've learned, it's that God puts people in your life to help you heal, and I think that's why you're here. Your being my son goes against everything I have faith in and hope for. I want to believe that my son is with God and I will see him again. That hope has gotten me through every hour of every day since James died. I buried James, and that is where he's going to stay. On the other hand, I've prayed so many times to have him back, even if only for a minute. I find it hard to believe that you could know so much without being my son. That's my dilemma.

"I understand why you shared what you did with me, Ryan. But you're right. It doesn't matter anymore. We can't go back to the way life used to be. Your bombshell doesn't feel threatening anymore, and maybe I can move past it. I think the loving bond that existed for us in your previous life is eternal and has transformed into something else—something just as intense and pure. I want to have a relationship with you," she said in a whisper. "I have deep and abiding feelings for you, and I can't pretend they are maternal. I ache to be near you, emotionally and physically, and I haven't felt like that in a long, long time. But I don't want to carry on any long-distance relationship with me here and you in New York. I am not moving to New York, and I would not ask you to give up everything and live here." She spoke with an air of finality in her voice. "I know that you would never be satisfied living in a small place like this." She looked at Ryan and waited.

Ryan joined her leaning up against the bench. "Can't we let this scenario play out?" he said staring at his shoes. "Spend some time together? Try to figure out just what our relationship is? If it doesn't survive time or both our scrutiny, I'll walk away. Walk away completely, I promise. Won't you at least give it a chance? We both deserve a shot at happiness. Maybe that happiness dictates that we should be together as something other than mother and son. Can't you let time tell us whether that's possible? I'm not going back to New York to the life I've had these last couple of years. That isn't the person I am or want to be. How would you feel . . . about me staying? I could open a business here. Would you be opposed to that?"

"What on earth would you do here in this little two-bit place?" she asked.

She watched a broad smile grow until his whole face was alight.

"Ryan, what have you done?" she said, an edge of alarm creeping into her voice.

"Problem solved. I just purchased, by proxy, the old tomato warehouse that was a part of the auctions this afternoon. I'm thinking of opening a tavern, like an English pub, with good food—the kind of place that can be the heart of a little town. After some renovations, you'll be looking at the proprietor of the brand-new Nevis Tavern."

Van laughed at the prospect. "What on earth? You never . . . You amaze me! When did this little nugget pop into your head?"

"I've actually been thinking about it for a while, daydreaming about what I would do with my life if I ever had the opportunity. Disillusionment'll do that to you."

"The Tomato Tavern—there's old stenciling of tomatoes on the side, right?"

The very one. Would you like a job? I'll need good-looking barmaids."

"No, I'll pass on that one, thank you," she said, feeling a little embarrassed. "Need a bookkeeper, by any chance?" she asked, rolling a pebble around with her foot. "That's what Jean does."

"That might work. I obviously need someone I can trust. I'll have several positions I need to fill, but I can worry about those later."

Van stopped abruptly. "Oh, liquor license? Aren't those kind of doled out according to who you know?"

"Yep, and I know who, so not a problem."

"Who do—?"

Ryan put his finger on her lips to shush her. "Not a problem, okay?"

She smiled around his finger. "Okay."

They walked on, their long-legged shadows moving across the storefronts and bungalows.

"Ryan, what about HYA? You were so worried about them before. How could you have solved everything with them so easily? They aren't going to come after you?"

"Nope, they let me walk away."

Van stopped and narrowed her eyes. "I thought you said they would never let you walk away."

"I guess I wasn't as big a fish as I thought." He grabbed Van's elbow and started guiding her forward.

"Wait. Stop."

"Oh, I'm sorry," Ryan said, letting go of her arm.

"No, not that." Van put her hand on her hip. "Stop brushing me off like that. What are you not telling me? I don't believe they just let you go. You made it clear they wouldn't let you do that. Did you threaten them? Make a deal? I want specifics."

When Ryan didn't react, Van lost her patience with him. She turned and walked away from him.

❧

Ryan silently stood his ground. HYA was a subject that he would never be able to discuss fully with her. There were too many things he wasn't proud of, and many others that he must protect her from. She had to be able to trust him, and maybe, after all she had been through, it wasn't something she could do.

"I can't discuss HYA with you. You have to trust me."

She stopped but didn't turn around. "I always need to be able to trust you. Without trust, there's nothing. A relationship cannot exist without trust. I never want to doubt you."

"I know," he said. "And I will never do that to you. I'm not lying to you now. There were no strings attached to my departure from HYA. Hector Senior looks on me as the son he never had. As a good businessman, he didn't want to lose me. But as a better businessman, he realized I could do a lot of damage to the company if they threatened me. That's the truth. Letting me go was a win-win solution."

Van turned and looked at him, weighing his words and his expression. Ryan stood his ground, trying to look sincere and hoping she would accept what he was telling her. If she didn't cooperate, things were not going to work out. He exhaled and took a breath when he realized he had stopped breathing. Maybe she hadn't noticed. A moment passed, and still they stood weighing each other's emotions.

"We've been through the win-win situation before," Van finally said, breaking the tension between them. "I don't find it reassuring. Okay . . . for now. But as God is my witness, if you're not telling me the truth, I won't be responsible." She walked back and put her arm through his. "Where'd you learn to run a bar?"

"I didn't, but I don't really have to know—I just have to hire the right people. They're the ones that have to know."

"Oh, yeah? Like who?"

"Like Bennie, the best barman I ever met. He can mix a martini and solve all your problems and never break a sweat. He'll be perfect for Nevis.

"Where is Bennie now?"

"In Boston—Bennie from Boston."

Van cracked up. "You're pulling my leg, right? There is no Bennie from Boston, is there?"

"There most certainly is. I'm hurt that you would ever suggest I'm lying."

He gave her his most sincere face, but she didn't take the bait. "Well, I can't wait for the day when I get to meet this Bennie from Boston."

"You'll be the first one I introduce him to, I promise. It'll be right after I introduce you to Peggy from Poughkeepsie."

"You are the biggest liar," she said, smacking him on the arm.

Ryan laughed and ducked away from further physical attack. "You'll have to get a whole lot stronger if you want to do any lasting damage," he said, and he pulled her to him and kissed her on the lips before she could protest. But there was no protest. The kiss deepened, and they broke it only when they reached an unspoken line that neither was ready to cross.

"If you want to get physical, I'll win every time, said Ryan, chuckling. "And enjoy every minute of it, I might add."

Van laughed, too, but took his hand as she blushed at his brazenness. She stopped as the boardwalk turned away from town and headed back towards the shore. She seemed reluctant to continue in that direction.

"Let's go back to your house," Ryan said, tucking her arm in his. "By now McCall should have figured out that I'm not there."

They walked quietly for a while, just enjoying the closeness.

"There really is a Peggy, but not from Poughkeepsie," Ryan said, with an impish smile. "I've known her for quite a while. But don't get the wrong idea," he added quickly. "Strictly platonic. She's one of the best researchers I've ever known."

"I see. Maybe I should recommend people for your staff, just to keep you honest. I, too, know someone who's a researcher. She does genealogy. By the way, what do you need a researcher for in a bar?"

"Not a bar—tavern. Don't make it sound dark and dirty. It'll be a nice place. Good food, nice music—more of a family place than a bar. Why do I need a researcher? Because the tavern is going to serve a dual purpose. It'll be a legitimate business, and it will serve as a front for my other little endeavor, as an investigator. It would be a good fit with my skills."

"And where are you going to get the capital to underwrite all these fabulous plans?"

"Money isn't a problem. HYA is really good about compensating its employees, especially the good ones."

"And you have no guilt about spending your ill-gotten gains?"

"Ill-gotten?" He thought about it. "I guess you could categorize some of them like that, but not all. Not everything HYA does is below the belt. They have quite a few very profitable, worthy ventures. And no, no guilt, because I intend to use what I have for good things."

TWENTY-FIVE

ALL THE WRONG BUTTONS

Nevis was too small a place to avoid people for any length of time. Margaret Douglas had promised Hector that she wouldn't help Van, but she could dodge her for only so long. They met several times at the courthouse before Margaret told her she couldn't help her.

"I was so hoping you could knock down the brick wall," Van said. "Nothing new at all?"

Margaret shook her head. "No, nothing. I'm sorry, Van. I've never seen such a difficult tree. I really thought I could help."

"No, that's okay. I know you tried. You're heading back to New York soon?"

"Yep, done here. I'm heading out in the next day or so."

Van put her notebooks down on the porch retaining wall. "Want to grab a bite to eat? My treat—just a thank-you for all the help."

"I'd love to," Margaret said, glancing at her buzzing cell phone, "but I have plans. "You know, I think I left that last document on the copy machine—all that work and then I just leave it. Be right back." She headed back into the building, talking into the phone as she went. "Yeah, right here . . . No, leave it alone. Don't come . . . please. Listen to me."

❧

Van made herself comfortable sitting on the low porch wall, watching the cars come and go in the parking lot and on the street, guessing at which ride or car matched up with each person leaving the courthouse. Then came a stumper: a blue sports car, moving fast when it hit the parking lot, flinging gravel and dust in all directions. It didn't belong, and when the driver got out, Van froze. Hector Young. She was all alone, and Margaret nowhere in sight. As he approached, she silently prayed for it to be a brief encounter.

"Ms. Hardy! What a pleasant surprise! I trust you've been well? I've been asking after you. We have some business to discuss."

"We don't have any business," Van said, trying not to stare at the bruise under his eye.

"Are you waiting for Ryan? If so, maybe I'll hang. We have some catching up to do, too."

"Ryan doesn't work for HYA anymore. He walked away."

A broad smile spread across Hector's face, and he laughed. "No one walks away from HYA, doll. If that's what Ryan told you, then he only told you half the story. The only way he *walked* away was if he cut a deal for his firstborn. Must have paid a pretty hefty price, too, since he hasn't told you. Better find out before you're in too deep to walk away. That's the most sincere advice I can give you."

"You haven't had a sincere thought in your life, Hector. You just want to see how much of a wedge you can drive between Ryan and me. But you know, you're a little late."

"I'm not trying to drive you apart. Ryan'll do that all by himself. You think you really *know* him? Can you really have a relationship with someone who can't tell you about his past, because you'd be so revolted you'd bolt for the nearest exit?" Hector sidled closer.

"Fuck off, Hector," Van said as she caught sight of a scowling Ryan coming up the sidewalk.

"Get away from her. Why are you here, Hector?"

Hector turned and smiled at Ryan as if they were long-lost pals. "Officer McCall asked me to give you a message. Gentleman that I am, however, I will save that till later, because we are in mixed company. Van, on the other hand," he said, turning and nodding in her direction, "was telling me about your change in employment. Come on, Ryan. You need to come clean with her. We both know there are still strings attached to HYA. My dad may be a bastard, but he's not a *dumb* bastard. What did you promise him to let you walk away, hmm?" He leaned against the wall, comfortable in his smugness. "Whatever it was, when I become CEO after dear old Dad, it won't be enough."

His guard was down, and Van and Ryan could see hatred for Ryan spilling out of him. He could no longer keep up the pretext of civility. "I'll make sure someone puts you six feet under before I let you walk away. You'd better hope my dad has a long and prosperous life."

"Hector!"

Hector whirled around to find Margaret standing behind him.

"What's . . . You *know* him?" Van gasped as she jumped down off the wall.

"Maggie, baby, I didn't know you were behind me."

Hector took a step toward her, but she backed away, freezing him in place. Confusion rolled across his face. "Baby, what's wrong?"

"I can't believe you said that," Margaret replied. "What kind of person would say something . . . God, you're out of control. You're like someone I don't even *know*."

"You know me better than anyone, Maggie. Sweetie, you know me." Hector's voice was silky smooth. "I love you. Ryan just pushes all the wrong buttons in me, that's all."

"I guess the waiter the other day pushed all the wrong buttons, too, huh? Lot of difficult people in this world, I guess. I've never heard such hatred come out of someone's mouth." She shook her head as if she were trying to shake the words back out of her ears. Maggie looked at Hector and then flung herself at Ryan, who wrapped his arms protectively around her and pulled her close. It wasn't clear who was more surprised: Van, Ryan, or Hector. Ryan hid his shock well, remaining stone faced, but both Hector and Van looked gob-smacked.

"Hector, Peggy is going to catch a ride back with us," said Ryan. "Maybe you should talk later. Van, Peggy, please go wait for me in the car. Hector and I have some business to discuss. It'll only take a couple of minutes." He handed his keys to Van as she pried the shaken Peggy loose from him, put her arm around her, and walked her toward Ryan's car.

"Baby, we'll talk later," Hector called after her, his face flushed scarlet.

She made no attempt to acknowledge him.

❧

When Van and Peggy were safely at the car and out of earshot Hector turned on Ryan.

"Straight to you—she went straight to you," he said, incredulous. How long's *that* been fucking going on, you son of a bitch? Not content to mess up just one woman's life at a time? You could've had anything you wanted: the company, my father . . . and now *Maggie*? I should have guessed you'd turn her against me. Don't you respect anything?" He started toward the parking lot.

Ryan stepped in front of him, effectively blocking his path down the steps. The two men met eye to glaring eye, with a hostility that would have terrified the women if they had been close enough to witness it.

"Stay away from all three of us," Ryan said through gritted teeth.

"Better make a will, Thomas," Hector replied. "She's the one thing in my life I won't lose. I may not be able to fight the old man, but you, you're a different story." He moved past Ryan but made no attempt to head in the direction of the women. Down the steps he went, into his car, and out of the parking lot like a demon on fire.

Ryan breathed a silent sigh of relief as he tried to slow his racing heart. He had expected blows. He knew better than to take Hector lightly, especially where Peggy was concerned. Ryan's newfound sense of security evaporated. Obviously, Peggy was here to complete research on the deed for HYA, and the search was still ongoing. Hector Senior hadn't pulled in any of his dogs. None of them was safe.

The women hurried back across the parking lot. Peggy grabbed Ryan by the shirtsleeve and buried her tear-stained face against his chest.

"I'm sorry, Peggy," he said, his mind in a whirl, trying to determine whether he could trust her. "It's okay. He's gone." She continued to sob, getting his shirt all wet. "I'm surprised to see you. How long have you been in town?"

"Not long," said Peggy, hedging.

Ryan looked over her head to give a reassuring look to Van, who stood dumbstruck, overwhelmed by the whole situation. "Let's go get a cup of coffee and talk. Is that okay with you, Van?" Ryan asked, trying to get her to focus on him. She shifted her eyes toward him and nodded. Her expression gave nothing away, and that worried him almost as much as his former business associates did.

TWENTY-SIX

KEEPING FRIENDS CLOSE

Not a word was said as the three drove to the diner in Nevis. Ryan was thoughtful, Van livid, and Peggy collected. Peggy sat in the backseat and made no further attempt to approach or touch Ryan.

"Are you working on a project with Hector?" Ryan asked as soon as they were seated.

"No. Hector's working in New York. I'm on my own."

"So you aren't involved in researching the land deal for Nevis?"

"I don't know anything about a land deal," she lied. "Ellen Kenzie and I are here researching genealogy. HYA didn't say what it was for." Peggy hated lying, but Hector had said Van was a threat. "It's confidential information . . ."

"You can speak freely in front of Van," Ryan interjected. "She knows everything."

"No, Ryan, I'm not. I've been tracing wills here in Nevis. I wasn't given a—"

"Margaret, Peggy, Maggie, or whatever the hell your name is in this moment, what's your relationship to Hector?" Van asked. "What kind of wills?"

"I'm sorry, Van. I'm Margaret Douglas," Peggy said, reaching across the table, but Van drew her hand back and put it in her lap. "Most people call me Peggy. Hector is the only one who has ever called me Maggie. It always made me feel special when he said that." She sniffed, and her eyes welled up, but they didn't overflow. "Ryan and I—we've worked together off and on for years. I do freelance work for HYA," Peggy said without elaborating. "I had no idea you knew Ryan."

"What kind of wills are you researching," Ryan asked, repeating Van's unanswered question.

Peggy kept her eyes down to avoid his intense gaze. "Ellen and I developed a list of prominent Nevis citizens. She was working on their trees, and I've been reviewing wills. Honest, Ryan, that's all I know."

"And where is Ellen?"

"She left yesterday. I'm heading home tomorrow."

"Did your work benefit from any of the genealogical information that Van gave you?"

"No. Like I told Van, the information dead-ended. I did pass it all on to Ellen, though."

"Great," said Van, rolling her eyes.

Ryan was silent but continued to stare thoughtfully at Peggy.

"What's going on?" Peggy said. "Tell me. If I did something wrong, I'm sorry. And, Ryan, I'm sorry I grabbed you and cried all over your shirt. What Hector said was shocking, and you were the first thing I saw. I don't mean to cause any trouble between you and Van, or with you and Hector. I'm really making a mess of things here. I should go." She rose to leave, but Van caught her by the sleeve.

"No, *Peggy*," Van said, shaking her head as she looked directly at Ryan. "Please sit back down. We need to finish. You shouldn't go wandering around by yourself right now, either. I don't trust Hector."

"Oh, he wouldn't hurt me. But I've never seen him that mad before. I felt like I was looking at a complete stranger." She turned to Ryan. "Have you ever seen him behave like that before?"

"There has almost never been a time when I *haven't* seen him acting like an ass. He's a twisted person whom everyone else has to deal with daily. Hector struggles to be different from his father, but his bitterness makes him just like him: cold, calculating, vengeful." You've been his only redeeming feature. You're good for him, Peggy, but in the long run, he's not good for you."

Peggy changed the subject. "You've changed, Ryan, from when I first met you. I thought you were insufferable. But now you're entirely different."

Ryan and Van exchanged a look but said nothing. Peggy's eyes began to redden again. "I've always thought there was no one like him. If it weren't for his father, we'd probably be married by now."

"Ryan, he really worries me," said Van. "I saw the look on Hector's face when Peggy ran to you. He's never going to forgive you for that. You're going to be constantly looking over your shoulder."

"I *am* concerned about Hector," Ryan confessed. "But I've always had to watch my back with him. It's nothing new." He settled back in the booth. "One of my main concerns now is that he leave you and Peggy alone. Peggy, what do you want to do now? How can I help you?"

Peggy looked gratefully at Ryan. "Thanks, you've done enough. I'm afraid to have you any more involved. I just want to steer clear of Hector right now."

"I don't want you going back to where you were staying. Hector knows where it is, right? There's no way he won't be waiting for you. Van, could she stay with you tonight?"

"Absolutely. "We need to stick together."

As they left the diner, Ryan leaned in to Van and whispered, "Don't let her out of your sight. She's lying through her teeth. We need to find out how much she really knows and what she's passed on to others."

TWENTY-SEVEN

DIGGING UP DETAILS

Van reluctantly left Peggy to settle into the small upstairs bedroom in the pickle boat house. What was she supposed to do with her? If not for Ryan, Van would sooner have sent her packing. She had little tolerance for dishonesty and collusion. Peggy, on the other hand, sighed with relief as Van retreated to the other side of the house. Van's body language made her feelings loud and clear.

When Peggy finally came looking for Van she found her sitting in the window seat, daydreaming. She hesitated to intrude on her reverie. Van looked fragile—perfectly still, with her hands folded gently in her lap and her hair tossed behind her shoulders.

"Van," Peggy whispered. No response. "Vanessa," she repeated, and this time Van turned at the sound of her name. "I need to talk to you, to apologize." She paused. "I, ah, it's, ah . . . about our friendship. I don't deserve it. I've been false to you."

Van shrugged her shoulders and shook her head. "What are you talking about?"

Peggy slid into the little chair next to Van. "I haven't been helping you. You and Ryan have been incredibly kind to me. I can't handle this anymore. I've been unfair and deceitful. Even tonight I didn't level with you. I haven't had any plans to help you. Your interests are competing with HYA's interests. They're paying me to trace the descendants of Jeremiah Harwell—the whole tree, not just Nevis wills. When you came to me that day in the courthouse, working on the same family tree, I was floored. It was like winning the lottery. Your tree was so much more complete than what I had yet come up with, and all of it with citations. You can't believe the amount of time you saved me." She laughed. "All I had to do was retrace and verify. I'm so ashamed."

Van sighed. Ryan was right. Peggy was just one more dishonest person. She shuddered to think what kind of damage Peggy had done—or could still do—to Nevis. "I really opened up to you," she said. "I trusted you. You've been friends with Ryan for years. Why would you do that?"

"That first night, I had every intention of helping you. But then I met Hector for dinner, and he convinced me that your research was working against the interests of HYA—and, by extension, against Hector and me. I agreed to befriend you with empty promises of helping you trace your family line. I know that was wrong," she said, wringing her hands. "Every time you confided in me and I responded like a friend I felt guilty. The responses were genuine, but the underlying intent wasn't. I've let my feelings for Hector color the kind of person I am: a false friend and a liar. Ryan was right last night: Hector isn't good for me—and I haven't been good for you."

Van abruptly stood up, all her fear bubbling over into anger. "Get out. Now, before I do something I regret."

"I understand," said Peggy. "I knew you wouldn't want me here when I told you the truth. I'm still packed, and someone's coming to pick me up. I'll just go get my bags and be out of your way."

As Peggy headed up the stairs Van got her phone out of her purse. She hit speed dial for Ryan and walked out onto the deck to calm herself. "You were right, Ryan. She just spilled her guts."

"I'm not surprised," he said. "Keep her talking. I'm on my way."

"Hurry. I just told her to get out."

Ryan let loose with a string of profanity. "Van, why the hell would . . . ! Run her down, for God's sake! This might be our only peek at HYA's hand."

But Van was too late. Her stomach tightened as she caught a glimpse of Peggy's ride disappearing down the street, leaving her alone with Ryan's oaths still ringing in her ears. She had let her anger screw up everything. There was nothing to do now but wait for Ryan. His frustration and disappointment in her wouldn't even come close to what she was already feeling. As she entered the kitchen her eye was immediately drawn to an envelope propped up against the vase in the center of the table. It was addressed "Van" in beautiful, strong script. With her heart thumping like a trip-hammer, Van sat down in the window seat and pulled out the carefully folded sheets of paper. The inner page, written in the same strong script, read:

Dear Van,

Again, I'm very sorry for the pain and betrayal you are feeling over my unforgivable behavior. Unfortunately, we don't get redos in life, do we? I would if I could. Enclosed you will find copies of the research that I finished on the Harwell line. I'm sure you will be pleased to see the connection between you and the Harwells, although maybe not quite in the way that you were expecting.

I could find no evidence that Jeremiah Harwell had any direct descendants. From early court documents, it appears that Jeremiah's wife, Abigail, gave birth to a son, William, after his death, but failed to establish in court that Jeremiah was the father. Whether this makes a statement about her social reputation in general, I do not know. Being unmarried with a child of questionable birth, she faced the scorn of the town and quickly married a man named Alexander Hill to limit the damage to her reputation. Who the actual father was remains unclear. Regardless, the child carried the last name Harwell. By court decree, he was not recognized as legitimate offspring of Jeremiah or entitled to inherit any of his estate. Thus ends the direct line of Jeremiah Harwell, without apparent issue. Citations are enclosed.

What is surprising is that your husband, Richard Hardy, is also of this Harwell line, through Jeremiah's siblings. A younger sister, Bess Harwell, married Lemuel Hardy at the age of 14. She relocated with her husband to Northumberland County, Virginia, taking her brother, Coleman, with her. It is in her will that I found documentation that she inherited "worldly goods of her loving and goodly brother Jeremiah Harwell, late of Nevis, in the province of Maryland, to be conveyed, upon her death, to her brother Coleman Harwell, (alias Hardy), youngest brother to Jeremiah." Young Coleman Harwell, being very young, takes the last name of his sister's husband. Upon Bess's death, he comes into his full inheritance under the last will and testament bequeathing Bess's estate. Coleman Harwell Hardy's line can be traced direct and intact from him and his wife, Elizabeth, of Virginia, down to your husband, Richard Hardy, also of Virginia. It appears that Richard may be the only living or dead direct descendant of these two individuals and would be the only descendant with a claim to any inheritable "goods or property," should such exist. Again, all citations and copies are here, including copies of Bess Harwell Hardy's will as well as the document establishing Lemuel Hardy as Coleman Harwell's legal guardian.

I wouldn't be so gauche as to presume at this time what your relationship with Richard would be—whether amicable or not. The best advice I can give you is to have Richard's Y-DNA tested. Should a showdown with HYA ever occur, you can request exhumation of Jeremiah Harwell's body from St John's churchyard for the purpose of testing his Y-DNA. A match between the two Y-DNA samples would bolster the claim of your husband's descendancy and right to inheritance.

I have some things to sort out in my life, in particular with Hector. When I have settled these matters, I will contact Ryan, if he will ever talk to me again. I can tell by the way you look at Ryan and talk about him that there is something deep and special about your relationship with him. It's the same way Hector and I have looked at each other—that is, until now. If I find a chance to rectify any of the damage I have done, I'll be in touch.

All my best, Van,

Peggy

Van's flesh began to crawl. Richard was Jeremiah Harwell's legitimate heir? Selling Nevis to HYA would be the perfect retaliation for her leaving him. Would she ever be able to sever their connection?

The slam of the front door broke her reverie. Her lecture had arrived. She shoved the letter back into the envelope.

"Where is she?"

"Ryan, she's gone. I'm sorry. I tried to catch her. She was working against Nevis, researching Jeremiah Harwell's heirs. She used all the information that I gave her to complete her own charts, and I think she forwarded it all to HYA. She left me a letter and copies of all her charts. Here, read it." She shoved the envelope at Ryan.

"No, I believe you."

"You really need to read all of it."

Ryan sat down next to her and started reading. Van watched as a brief smile slowly crossed his face. She wondered whether it was the passage where Peggy talked about how Van looked at Ryan. It brought a smile to her, too.

"Son of a bitch," he muttered. "How many other places has Hector poked his nose into? But," he said, looking down at the paper again, "this is good, right? As Richard's son, we can have my Y-DNA tested and not even involve Richard!" He looked at Van, and the smile slid off his face. "Why are you frowning?"

"You may be Richard's son in spirit, but in case you've forgotten, your Y-chromosome DNA is one hundred percent Ryan Thomas, not James Hardy. It isn't any good to us at all unless we dig the old you up, and I'm certainly not going to do that!" Van shuddered at the thought of disturbing her son's grave. Even the idea of exhuming Jeremiah Harwell was too revolting to think about.

Ryan rolled his eyes. "Come on, it's more cut-and-dried than that. It's not like you're really digging me up. It's just a body; I'm still here." He smiled again. "So you really do believe I'm your son? That's good," he said, nodding. "I never really expected *this* level of validation from you." He dropped the letter on the window seat and put his arm around her.

"As for Richard," she said, "I don't want him involved any more than he has to be. I don't want to uncover a vindictive side to him. I'm terrified that HYA may have already contacted him." She paused. "And that brings up something else I've been meaning to discuss with you. If you feel so strongly that you are Richard's and my son, how should we break the news to Richard that you're . . . well, whatever you want to call what you are: reincarnated, reborn, redeposited, remade." She laughed at the absurdity of it. "We need to decide the best way to tell him."

"Oh, no, you can't tell him any of this," said Ryan, rising to his feet. "He can't ever know. I have absolutely no memory of him, although that picture of him in your living room was trying to pull some memory out of me."

"Are you out of your *mind*?" she said. "How fair is that?"

"No, you can't tell him," he insisted. "Someday, by chance, maybe our paths will cross. And when they do, if I remember him, then I may decide to acknowledge our relationship."

"But how could you let him go on hurting and thinking you're gone? Maybe *he* needs the validation to move on."

"This is what it is, and I don't think it's mine to question."

"But that seems so cruel. And if you never connect?"

"If not, then we'll pass like ships in the night."

"And that doesn't bother you?" Van asked.

"I can't help the way I feel or the way I react. But, Van," he said carefully, as if trying to choose the right words, "you have to figure out what you want from me. You seem to be jealous of my working relationship with Peggy, yet you want me to reach out to Richard to create a father-son relationship. You need to make up your mind. You're starting to make me a little crazy! Are your feelings for a son or a lover?"

"Maybe . . . I just don't know anymore," Van admitted.

"You don't believe me, or you don't know how to treat me?"

"Don't know how to treat you. I'm having a hard time relating to you as my son. I'm not saying you're not. Heaven knows, you have information that only my son would know. It's easiest just to think of you as the man I have met and fallen in love with. Deep down inside, don't you have any misgivings about this whole crazy scenario being true?"

Ryan sat back down on the cushion next to her. "Every day, bit by bit, I remember more, and there is no doubt in my mind," he said, looking her squarely in the eyes. "But, I don't think I need to discuss it with Richard or anyone else right now. In that way, I'm gone from your lives. I don't know why, but I've been brought back here for a purpose. I think I may have something in my life to finish. And it doesn't necessarily involve Richard. It's difficult for me, but I'm going to live with all my heart and all my strength, as free from Ryan's past successes, mistakes, loves, and losses as I can. I'm not saying I have this all figured out—God knows I don't. One minute I'm James, totally in control, and the memories just flow. But it's an illusion. My life has been out of control since I woke up in that hospital room. Still, every day I try to shake free, and every day I feel him fading away a little more. One day it's going to be just me in here."

"I don't understand," she said, "and I can't imagine the turmoil you must be going through. Just don't lose faith in me, even when I make it difficult for you. Okay? I'm still struggling here, too."

"Oh, I know. Van, I want to protect you here in Nevis. But we could leave this all behind. I could show you the world. We could go anywhere you want to go. We can see it all. I have the means to give that to you."

Van shook her head. "No. I love it here, and this is where I want to stay. And if it takes everything I have to protect it from HYA, then that's what I am willing to do."

"HYA has already started to buy up your neighbors' houses: the Jeffries, the Spencers, the Morgans, and others. They'll either continue buying up all the houses around you or they'll be able to document—legitimately or otherwise—an owner other than your family, from whom they can buy all this land. This is not over by a long shot."

Van nodded and reached over and took Ryan's hand in hers. "Jean and I have mobilized some of the movers and shakers in town," Van said, "but it's not nearly enough. I can't believe Nevis is going to make the same mistake twice. It's the over-fishing story all over again. They didn't learn a thing. Selling their houses for much more than they're worth—it's good in the short term, but in the long run, Nevis won't be able to pay the price. The town, our heritage—all lost, ruined, gone forever. Some of them just don't get it."

"We'll handle this," said Ryan, kissing the tip of her nose. "HYA is not going to steamroll us. We're not going to lose Nevis to those bastards—not if it's the last thing I do. I promise you. And I'm not mad at you for running Peggy off. I know what you thought. I saw it in your face. I just hated to see this opportunity slip away. But there are people outside of HYA that may be able to help us. I'm going to use my contacts and everything I know to beat these people." He checked his watch. "I need to go, but I'll call you tomorrow."

Van followed him to the door as they parted once more. "Won't you stay?"

"That would depend."

"On . . . ?"

"Whether I'd be sleeping on the couch again."

Van laughed and glanced up the stairs behind her. "Actually, I think you've made it to the second floor."

"Is that anything like second base?" Ryan asked.

"Perhaps. The only way you can find that out is to stay."

He laughed. "Okay, I'll stay, but I have to warn you, I was very good at stealing home."

Van laughed. "We shall see." She drew him inside and closed the door.

TWENTY-EIGHT

MORNING LIGHT

Van opened her eyes to the beautiful sight of Ryan, with his arm draped across her and his face resting against her bare shoulder. She resisted the urge to lean over and kiss him. There was no barrier between them. After last night, she just felt contentment. As she looked at his face she desperately wanted to run her hands along the planes of it, stroke the beard stubble along his jaw, and kiss his beautiful, perfect lips. Her eyes followed his form, now hidden in a swath of sheet, down to where his hand rested in sleep. She loved his hands, their warmth and strength when they held hers. They were hands that fit together perfectly. She returned her gaze to his face.

"Oh, you're awake," she said, startled to find him looking at her with serious, thoughtful green eyes.

"A bird," he said.

"Excuse me?"

"It would definitely be a bird."

"What are you talking about, crazy man? Are you really awake?"

"Your mosaic plaque in the kitchen—it would definitely be a bird."

"Really," she said, sitting up against the headboard. "Why do you say that?"

"Because you have a beautiful soul. Did you know that?"

"A very dark soul," she said, laughing ruefully. Snuggling back up to him, she placed her hand on his chest, over his heart. "You know, your heart is beating fast like a little bird's."

He ignored her. "Not at all dark. Maybe to begin with, when I first met you. But now you're like one of those sun catchers, with light shining through in different colors. It's like morning light: soft and soothing. And someday the full light of day is going to shine through you again. And I'm sure I will love you just as much then as I do now."

"Did you say you had nothing planned for today?" she said. "Because I just checked your calendar, and I think it's full." With a lighthearted giggle, Van took the edge of the sheet and flung it over both their heads, closing out the rest of the world.

Unlike the last time they had been together, they weren't concerned about who might see Ryan leaving.

"You know, Van, with the pickle boat house and the Tomato Tavern, I figure these must be our salad days."

"You are incredibly corny."

"I know, but I made you laugh, didn't I?"

"Yes, you did. You're very good at that. It's one of the many things I love about you."

"Are you sure you want to love me?" he said.

"I don't think I have a choice at this point. You really should come with a warning label."

"I'll make sure that happens next time," Ryan said, nuzzling her ear with light little kisses.

"There isn't going to be a next time," said Van, and she wiggled around in his arms and kissed him long and deeply.

They spent the rest of the day just enjoying each other's company, and at the end of it they shared a late meal before Ryan had to leave. He sat rereading Peggy's letter, with Ernest Pickett's little dog in his lap. Since Pickett had no immediate family, the authorities had decided that Susie could stay with Van. She seemed to take a particular shine to Ryan, who sat absentmindedly stroking her fur from head to tail. Susie didn't object, and lay motionless, very close to sleep.

"What's the deal with the dog?" Van asked.

"I always wanted a dog."

"I didn't deprive you, *James*. You were allergic to dogs!"

"What a coincidence. Poodles are hypoallergenic."

"Ryan, do you want that dog?"

"Yes," he said, and a big smile spread across his face. He tucked the dog under his arm and headed out the front door. "The first thing we have to do, Susie, is change your name. No self-respecting man would be caught dead with a dog named Susie. And the pink flowered collar goes, too."

"But it's a girl dog."

"That's irrelevant." He paused for a minute, looking the little white dog in the face. "Come on, Spot, let's go."

Van laughed and just shook her head. She kissed him quickly and stayed on the porch as he walked to his car. In the broad, bright scheme of things, the name didn't really matter. Only the loving relationship did.

A florist's van pulled up in front of the house as Ryan unlocked his car door. He watched as the delivery man got out and bounced up Van's steps with a vase of long-stemmed yellow roses.

"Should I be concerned or jealous?" Ryan asked, pausing before he got in his car.

"Don't be silly," said Van. "They're probably from Richard—one last attempt to get me to change my mind," she said, pulling a card from the flowers. "Ryan, wait . . . these are for you." Puzzled, she began to read: 'Congratulations on the Tomato Tavern. Will be contacting you soon.' Well, at least they have good taste in cards," she said as she flipped the card over to check the brand. "You'll have to introduce me," she said, waving a black origami crane for Ryan to see. "Ryan? You obviously didn't hear a word I said," she mumbled as she watched his car already disappearing down the road. "Catch you later, busy boy."

TWENTY-NINE

RISE OF THE PHOENIX

Whatever HYA's new game, the name and rules were unknown to Ryan and Van. It was now a waiting game—the calm before the brewing tempest. Ryan was determined to move his life forward in a new direction and wasted no time in developing the Tomato Tavern from a dream to a destination. It was amazing what money and dedication could build. With no-nonsense Jean handling deliveries and the books, Ryan worked like a whirlwind to transform the shabby old warehouse in the center of town into a snappy English-style pub. He seemed to be catching his stride again after his life-altering insights and revelations to Van. Walking away from HYA had freed his soul, and he had no intention of letting HYA take Nevis.

Graphics of tomatoes still adorned sections of the exterior walls, but the interior was a study in contrasts: bright walls and sleek, rich, dark wood tones—classic lines of a British pub. Once Van saw how much thought and care Ryan put into every detail, she suggested that he find a more fitting name. Together they decided on "the Phoenix"—rebirth from the ashes of death and despair.

"Sign here, please," said the delivery man, dropping the shipping invoice onto the makeshift desk in front of the red-haired woman. He held out a cheap disposable pen as he looked around the room.

Jean sighed, lifting her eyes from her pile of papers to another face in the endless procession of delivery men shoving pens at her. "Okay, which delivery are you?"

"Williams Transport, ma'am—balusters and turnings."

Jean pulled her glasses from the top of her head and scanned the master delivery sheet. She had it memorized. Deliveries had been nonstop since her arrival this morning. She crossed off the company name and finished signing the Williams Transport copy, wearily noting that as the day wore on, her signature had grown larger and more illegible.

"Are we good?" she asked, shoving the paper back across the desk. If you can get in close, stack up what you have over by that yellow cone. Thanks." She remembered to hand the young man's pen back and stuffed the receipt into the back of her ledger. If every day was going to be like this, she might have to reconsider her new job. She thought too much of Ryan to leave him in the lurch right now, though. Nevis wasn't exactly brimming over with jobs, either. She laughed to herself. The only things in Nevis without dust were the backs of the young people networking hard to leave.

Jean picked up her ledger and worked her way through the construction to find Ryan. He was in an interior room, deep in discussion with his architect and the framing contractor. She had to admire his taskmaster attitude. A lesser man would never have gotten the project off the ground, let alone moved it this far along in so short a time. She could hear their apparent disagreement as she drew closer.

"Rip it all out from here to the end," Ryan was saying, gesturing with his hand as he walked along the newly erected half wall. "This is all wrong. It's too short. Measure twice, cut once," he said to the carpenter. "Follow the plans, or I'll find somebody else who can. Are we straight now on what has to be done?" The carpenter nodded but offered no comment. Ryan nodded in turn, rolled up the blueprints, and began walking away with the architect to inspect the next room.

"Ryan, can I talk to you for a minute?" Jean said. "I'm about to call it a day."

Ryan whirled around at the sound of his name, his demeanor changing immediately. "Sure, Jean. Sorry. How long were you waiting there?"

"Just long enough to watch you kick some major butt. Very impressive, I might add. Got the invoices for today. We're short just a couple deliveries."

"Great, thanks," he said, taking the ledger and leafing through the book.

Jean clasped her hands behind her back and stared at the top of Ryan's head as she rocked on her toes.

"Something else, Jean?" he asked as she continued to linger.

"Um, I was wondering . . . You haven't, um, filled the one waitress slot?"

"No, still need one more, why?"

"I was, uh . . ."

Ryan raised his eyebrows.

". . . wondering if you might be interested in hiring Marla," she blurted out.

"Jean, I don't think Van would be too comfortable with that arrangement."

"I know, I know. She can be a flirt, but she knows you and Van are together now. And she does have a wonderful, outgoing personality. She'd get along great with the customers."

"I don't . . ."

"You don't have to give me an answer right away," Jean said quickly. "She really needs a job right now. Just consider it," she pleaded. If she doesn't work out, you can always let her go. I promise I won't hold it against you."

"Let me sleep on it, okay? No, wait, on second thought, have her come in and talk to me. I'll decide after I interview her."

"Thanks. I owe you one," she said. She reached up and grabbed Ryan by the neck and gave him a quick, awkward hug that took him by surprise. "See you tomorrow. My butt is dragging. I'm not sure if I can keep up with this pace every day."

"Don't get discouraged. I think it should get easier from here on out. Most of our materials are in. Barring something unforeseen, we should be ready to open in a few weeks. Which reminds me, Bennie will be in town late tomorrow. We'll probably run out for a late supper, if you'd care to join."

Jean gave Ryan a withering look. "I'll keep my own social calendar, thank you. Don't do me any favors. I'm sure you can find another lady friend to keep company with Bennie. See you tomorrow, Ryan." As she walked away, Jean had to laugh at Ryan for being so blatantly obvious. She didn't get why everyone wouldn't just accept that she was done with men and okay with it.

❧

"I feel like we're tag-teaming," Jean said to Van as they greeted each other at the front door. She gave her a high five as they passed.

"I know. You look beat. I'll talk to the boss and see what I can do to make your work pace a little more tolerable. Ryan is like a demon trying to finish this place. Everyone just needs to slow down. It'll all get done." Van could see Ryan move through the rooms, shuffling the paperwork for the day. He had been working around the clock the past few weeks—even sleeping in the half-finished space. Anytime an empty town building was concerned, arson was never far from anyone's mind.

"Hey, how's it going?" Van asked, walking up close to give him a hug.

"Not bad, and definitely getting better," he replied with a smile, tossing his papers back down on the table and pulling her a little closer to nuzzle her neck and ear.

"Quite a storm last night. They're calling it a *derecho*, whatever that is. I had to pull some big limbs off the deck. The patio table bought the farm, but everything else looks good. Any damage here?"

"Never heard of a *derecho*, but that was one hell of a storm. If you need me to send a carpenter over, just let me know. Got plenty of 'em. This is a tough old place. The power was off for a while, but other than that, we survived intact. So it's still full steam ahead. If I can get everybody to listen to what I'm telling them and not to what they *think* they should be doing, then we might be ready to open on time. Even the dog won't listen to me."

"Poor baby, where is she? I'll bet she misses old Mr. Pickett."

Ryan began to whistle, and the jingle of a dog's tags directed their attention to the little puff of white perking up from under one of the sawhorses on the far side of the room. "Come here, Hoffa, come on!" The little dog raised its head just long enough to see who was calling, and then flopped on its side and went back to sleep.

"See? Damn, dumb dog."

"Are you deaf? The dog's name is 'Susie,' not 'Hoffa'!"

"I don't like 'Susie'—too girlie."

"Girl dogs *are* girlie!"

"Doesn't matter. Besides, she reminds me of someone I used to know in Detroit."

"I don't think I want to know. What happened to 'Spot'? No wonder she doesn't come. You have her totally confused."

"Damn, dumb dog," Ryan repeated, shaking his head.

"What if I started calling you by a different name?"

"Like 'James,' for example?" Ryan asked, raising his eyebrows.

Van laughed. "Okay, one point for you, but you know what I mean. Cut the poor dog some slack or I'll have to take her back. I don't care how much identity conflict you two share."

"Nope, nothing doing. That's too much trauma, Indian giver."

Van laughed again. "Okay, she has been through a lot, but don't push me."

"I meant trauma for *me*. I'm stressing about it already. I think I need a hug at the very least," he said, waiting for Van to take the bait, which she did with little prompting. As usual, their chaste kiss deepened as the heat between them rose.

Ryan was the first to pull back as the sound of a clearing throat burst the bubble surrounding them. Reluctantly they separated and turned to the contractor, standing in the framed-in doorway.

Ryan heaved a quiet sigh. "Duty—see you later, doll." He kissed her quickly one more time and took off after the foreman.

"It's really looking good in here," Van said as she scurried behind him. "Are you going to hang anything on these walls?

They look a little bare. Hey," she said, a sudden wave of inspiration hitting her. "What about using some things from the museum? We could frame some of the posters and put them up. Not to put any thoughts into your head. I know you have a clear idea of what you want to do."

"Great idea," Ryan called over his shoulder as he disappeared from view. "I trust you. Surprise me—bring them over? Hands are kinda full . . ."

Van stopped. There was no use trying to keep up with him. He was a man on a mission. "No problem," she called back. "I can think of a few things that would look great in here. Do I have free reign—understanding, of course, that you have veto power? If so, I'll head over there tomorrow and grab some stuff."

Ryan poked his head back in the door at the far end of the room. "I'm sure I'll like anything you do. Sorry . . . these last few weeks. I'll do better once we open. It's just the final crunch, you know?"

"No, you're still good in my book," Van replied. "I like seeing you happy and occupied. You go ahead. You don't seem at all stressed about doing this. Are you? You'll get town people to come, but I'm still worried about you making a living off it."

"I'm not overly worried about the income. With the right advertising and promotion, it'll come. This town needs a draw—maybe lots of little draws—to reenergize it. Revitalization doesn't have to come at the expense of charm and history. You don't have to sell out. If more people came and saw what a gem of a place this is, they'd want to buy a home, spend time and money in quaint little Nevis. The more competition HYA has, the better. Nevis just needs promotion, and I'm going to do everything I possibly can to make this an uncomfortable place for HYA to sneak around."

"And I love you for that," Van said. "It would be nice if the tavern had a long run like Betty's," she mused, gazing out the window at the little kids racing by on their bicycles. "Bicycles—that's it! Ryan, have you ever seen the bicycle pelotons that come through Nevis? Sponsor a bike race! That could give you lots of press in some very strange places. It could be an annual event with prizes and T-shirts. A big whoop, you know? Feature microbrews from around the area."

Ryan bought right into the idea, and it wasn't long before Van found herself researching Maryland breweries and contacting bicycle clubs.

❧

In one of his last managerial decisions right before opening, Ryan agreed to hire Marla, but only as a favor to Jean. He didn't need a lot of staff and would have preferred someone with bar experience. Still, he had total faith in Bennie and his ability to draw out the best in anyone. He wasted no time in making Marla a project of Bennie's and not one of his own.

"Marla, I'd like you to meet Benjamin Bertolini, better known as Bennie. Bennie was the best bartender in Manhattan until he took the job here." Marla extended her hand and smiled as she gave Bennie the once-over, eyes settling at last on his shiny dome. She hated the style. It was impossible to decide whether a guy shaved his head as a fashion statement or was truly bald. It *did* make a difference.

"Bennie, this is Marla. I've just hired her as our hostess. She'll also be assisting you as barmaid. If you don't mind, she'll need you to show her the ropes. She's new at this, but I think she'll be a natural."

"Marla, it will be a pleasure working with you," Bennie said, smiling. "I'll teach you all the shortcuts—piece of cake. We'll have a good time. Our trial run is on Wednesday. Maybe you'd like to come in the afternoon on Tuesday—that is, if it's okay with Ryan."

"Bennie, like I told you, the bar is yours. Do what you need to, to make it successful. Just let me know what you need, and I'll take care of it." He clapped Bennie on the shoulder. "I have great faith in you. Now, if you'll excuse me, I have fires to put out, so to speak."

"Come on, Marla," Bennie said. "I'll show you what needs to be done. We'll start with garnishes. You drink? Yeah? You'll love this part. Oh, first, let me see your hands."

Marla timidly extended her manicured hands. Bennie took them in his short, meaty fingers, flipping them over to look at her palms and firmly placing them together in his right hand. He patted the tops gently.

"Just what I thought. You might want to trim your nails a little, hon. They get soft being in and out of water all day. You don't want to tear them up any more than you have to."

Marla fought back tears. "I thought I was mainly going to be a hostess. I'm not sure I want to be washing dishes and nasty stuff like that. Maybe I need to go back and talk some more to Ryan."

"Nonsense. You're gonna love it back here with me. Come on," he said as he wrapped his arm around her shoulders and steered her back behind the bar.

THIRTY

FAVORS AND FATHERS

The morning of the opening was just spit and polish. Bennie had conducted a successful dry run yesterday, and arrived on opening day with a wicked attitude and a huge smile. With Ryan backing him, he knew it wouldn't be long before a "Best in Bar" award hung from the main bar mantel.

The locals came out of curiosity. New businesses were a rarity in Nevis—interested parties lacked the capital, and disinterested ones flocked to greener pastures. Still, there was a customer base waiting to be served. And serve them Ryan did. Once it became clear that the food was going to be good, the prices reasonable, and the beer cold, the Phoenix had no trouble attracting customers. No need to send someone in a wine bottle-shaped sandwich board out to the main street to drum up business. With Van's help, Ryan scouted out a local cook who could serve up meatloaf on Mondays, spaghetti on Wednesdays, and she-crab soup Fridays. Topped off with Betty's homemade pie, pretty soon everyone in town was fitting the Phoenix into at least one day in their weekly planner. The place had a mystique of its own, and the potential to be the heart of a little town.

Van stood off to the side and observed comings, goings, discussions about the *derecho,* and general activity in the main room. Attendance was good. Most patrons were enticed by the promise of half-price fare and enough information to gossip about for quite a while. Ryan was endearing. He couldn't stop grinning as he worked the room, slapping backs and sharing drinks. Van was immensely proud of him and happy that he had succeeded in creating his dream. He was good at this. She watched as he headed, drink in hand, for the customers sitting at the bar.

"Officer McCall, glad to see you could make it," Ryan said, patting the policeman on the back. "Having a good time? Drinks on the house."

"You trying to bribe me?"

Ryan smiled at the curmudgeonly old cop and didn't miss a beat. "Drinks are three bucks," he said. "Pay Bennie at the bar, and don't forget his tip. He's used to getting a hefty percent in New York."

"My tip would be to keep his nose clean and go back to New York. Don't think for a minute that I'm not watching you and yours, Mr. Thomas. I just came in to check your liquor license. I didn't think you could get one of those in Nevis for love or money." McCall eyed Ryan over the top of his beer glass before draining it and dropping a bill on the counter. He took his time leaving, seemingly taking in everything that was going on.

"Everything okay?" Van whispered, coming up behind Ryan. "He's not bringing trouble in here, is he?"

"No, everything's good—better than good," he said, giving her a hug. "I really didn't expect anyone to show up—figured it would take more time. I didn't think they'd be this trusting of an outsider coming in and starting a business. This is terrific!"

"I'm pretty sure that not everyone here is what you'd call *trusting*," Van said, "but they know you're with me, and that goes a long way. Clearly, I have excellent taste." She kissed his cheek and took a sip of his drink. It was ice cold, smooth, and enticingly fruity. "What is that?" she said. "I want one."

Ryan looked at her and laughed. He whistled to Bennie, and a few hand motions later, Van had a drink in hand. "That's called a Bennie plenty," he said. "A few of those and you won't care what hit you. You're allowed one. I don't want you stumbling off into the night with one of our patrons."

"Yeah, right. I'll keep that in mind. Just a little warning for *you*, my friend. I don't know your usual intake, but I think you're pretty well on your own way to getting sloshed. Maybe you should start pacing yourself, huh? No more of these?"

"Yeah." A tickled smirk lit up his face like a neon sign.

Van looked around at the happy, drinking crowd. "I know word of mouth is a good thing, but it can't be so good that it's bringing in all these people. Half of them I don't even recognize. Where are they coming from?"

"It's probably this big spread we had in the *Washington Post* 'Weekend Getaway' section," said Ryan, spreading a newspaper out across the bar top. "They gave us a pretty good write-up and a lot of space. How could you *not* want to come see all this? This is more promotion and exposure than Nevis has gotten in the last eighty years."

"Ryan," Van said, narrowing her eyes as warning bells started to ring in her head, "why on earth is the *Washington Post* giving us such a nice piece? Do you know someone at the *Post*?

A smile spread across his face. "Someone . . . a favor . . . that kind of thing. Effective, huh?"

Van wasn't smiling anymore. "How are you going to start a new life if you can't walk away from your old one?"

Ryan laughed. "You worry too much. It's not a problem, so don't worry about it. Like I said, the last thing in the world HYA wants is attention. The more people come to Nevis, the less attractive it becomes for dirty business. This is a win-win."

Van remembered going down the "win-win" road before, and she found no comfort in his choice of words. "Don't get cocky," she said. "I hope that's the liquor talking."

Ryan leaned in close. "I haven't gotten this far along without knowing the right people. Relax."

"Just don't be the kind of man I wouldn't respect," she said, leaning away from him. "Sometimes it's not all about winning."

"Don't be naive about all this," he said, growing serious. "If you want to save Nevis, you may have to get your hands a little dirty. If you can't handle that, don't ask and don't lecture. This is all or nothing—half measures aren't going to cut it."

"Wow, that doesn't sound like the Ryan I know."

Rather than say more, Ryan walked off, leaving Van speechless and feeling a little rebuffed.

❧

With no one to keep her at home, Jean quickly claimed a place at the end of the bar. A week into the opening, she sat on her barstool, nursing a cosmopolitan. She laughed uproariously as Bennie leaned in close and whispered something in her ear.

"What kind of fool do you think I am?" she asked, pushing Bennie's arm off the bar top. "You are such a bullshitter."

Bennie's eyes sparkled in amusement, and he leaned in a second time to whisper something else, but this time Jean did not swat him away, and he made no effort to back off. Jean moved her hand to his arm, where it stayed as they continued to talk and flirt.

Across the tavern, Van stood watching the easy banter between the two, and as they began to touch, her expression changed to one of disbelief. With raised eyebrows, she turned toward Ryan.

Ryan shrugged. "Beats the hell out of me. It's been going on all week. I expect Bennie to have good customer service, but that looks more like pitching woo to me." He laughed and shook his head. "If they get much closer, they're going to be sharing the same stool."

"Well, I never saw it coming!"

"A good bartender is a good listener, Van. Maybe that's all she needed. Leave 'em alone. She could do a lot worse than Bennie. He is a gentle man with a heart of gold."

"You're probably right. I didn't pick *you* for your good listening skills," said Van, with a teasing light in her eyes.

"No, but I'm not a bartender, either," he said laughing.

❧

Watching Jean reminded Van of the loose ends in her life that were tying her down, preventing her from moving forward in her own relationship. She finally mustered the nerve to call Richard and asked him to come into the tavern for dinner and a heart-to-heart conversation.

As she expected, he didn't take it well. He agreed to meet, but the tone of their phone conversation went quickly from cordial to icy. The night of their meeting, Richard arrived at the

Phoenix early and sat in a corner away from the bar. There he sat, nursing one bourbon after another until Bennie cut him off.

Van saw him as soon as she came through the door—spouse radar after all their years of marriage. She realized how ready she was to close this chapter of her life when she chose at once to walk straight to his table. Months earlier, she would have pretended she hadn't seen him, and headed directly for the room in the back. "Richard, you're here . . . early. Let me get a couple of menus. We can—"

"Sit," he said. "Let's just skip the song and dance."

Van took a seat across from him at the table. She had hoped they could ease into the discussion, but apparently, it was not to be. Richard had obviously had a few, and he wore an air of belligerence on his face.

"Are you filing for divorce?"

"This is so hard," Van said. "It's time, Richard. I'm going to file. I hope we can keep this amicable. For the sake of what we had, I hope we can remain friends."

Richard said nothing but looked into her eyes with an unsteady gaze.

"There's no point in us staying together," she continued. "We had a beautiful life together, but it's over. Don't ruin the memories of what we had. I've moved on. Finally, I'm happy again. If you feel anything for me, let me be happy."

Richard shifted his eyes to study the bottom of his glass. Still he said nothing.

Van had seen him drunk enough times to know that she was wasting her time. He wasn't going to cooperate. Her eyes brimmed with tears that threatened to spill over. "Hon, let me go," she said. "I'll always love you, but we both need to move on."

Richard looked up at her again, and this time the emptiness in his eyes cut her to the core. "I can't," he said.

"You *can*," she said, putting her hands on both sides of his face and drawing him closer to her. "We both deserve to be happy."

"I'll be damned if I'll beg you to stay," he replied, his voice cracking from the emotional strain and the booze. He slapped her hands away.

Van stood up from her chair. "Excuse me, Richard," she said. "I have to go help with a few things." And she fled to the bathroom.

Even though she had had the guts to meet with him, she couldn't maintain the bravado all night. Still, hiding in the bathroom forever was no solution. She dampened some paper towels and wiped her face and neck. If a long stay meant she could keep from facing Richard again, she was all for it. When she thought enough time had passed and she was sufficiently composed, she pushed open the bathroom door and walked out—straight into the chest of a waiting Richard.

"Oh," she gasped. "I thought you'd be gone by now."

"I didn't think we were through. I was concerned when you didn't come back."

"There isn't much left to say. I wanted to let you know tonight that I've decided to file for divorce at the end of our separation."

"It's that tall guy that built the bar, isn't it? He's gotten in between us and destroyed our relationship."

"No. No one else is influencing my decision. I really think this is the best thing for both of us. We both deserve better."

"So you think he's better than me."

"Damn it, Richard, I didn't say that. This is about you and me."

"Do you really think I'm that stupid?" He tossed a large yellow envelope down on the table in front of her.

"What is this?" Van grabbed the envelope and ripped it open to reveal a series of pictures of her and Ryan together at various places around town, including her house, the boardwalk, and the Phoenix. They were pictures that could have been taken only by someone who was well acquainted with his subjects. While the pictures were not damning, there was no doubt to even the most casual observer that the subjects had, at the very least, an emotional connection.

"You started fooling around with him before you ever filed for the separation."

"You had someone watching me . . . taking pictures?" Van shouted, sailing the envelope back at Richard. The edge slid along his face and left a paper cut on his left cheek. "How dare you!"

Richard winced and ran his fingers along the cut. As he lowered his hand it clenched into a fist. "That would only be a problem for someone who had something to hide. You're just mad because I caught you with that son of a bitch."

"You damned hypocrite. If I had a picture for every person you cheated with, there'd be a paper shortage. There's a big difference between spending time with someone and being romantically involved. He's been a perfect gentleman, which is more than I can say for you. Once we're divorced, I'll enjoy whoever's company I choose."

"Oh, yeah, that's right. Those nights he spent at your house were strictly platonic. He just looked guilty as hell sneaking out early in the morning."

"Get out."

Richard grabbed Van by the top of the arm and yanked her closer. "Until we're divorced, you'd just better remember who you're married to."

"Ouch!" Van said, twisting her arm as she tried to pull free. "Let go, damn it! You've had too much to drink."

Richard responded by tightening his grip around her arm.

"Stop it," she said. "I'm—"

"Hey, get your hands off her." In two long strides, Ryan was in Richard's face. He shoved him hard in the chest, forcing him to let go of Van as he went careening into the next table.

"Do you know who I am?" Richard growled, getting to his feet as Van went to Ryan.

"I don't give a damn who you are. Nobody treats a woman like that. This is my bar. Now, get out."

"You don't have to introduce yourself, you little fuck. Stay away from my wife."

Ryan froze in his tracks as his eyes darted to Van and then back to Richard again.

As the eyes of Ryan and Richard met and locked, Van's breath caught and time ceased. Neither man blinked.

It was Ryan who broke the silence. "Get the hell out of my bar," he said evenly.

Richard turned to Van and said, "You'll wish you hadn't run out on me." He turned on Ryan. "And you, you little nothing shit. Keep your miserable fucking dump of a cheap bar . . . and my cheap wife, too."

The words were hardly out of his mouth before Ryan caught him with an uppercut under the chin, sending him several feet backward, where he sprawled in a heap on the floor. A grimace shot across Ryan's face as he drew his hand up and held it in his other hand. When Richard didn't get up, Ryan wrapped his good arm around Van and pulled her with him into the next room.

Cradling his injured hand, he headed to the kitchen, looking for ice. "Bennie, please have Officer McCall pick up the unruly drunk in the back room. He fell pretty hard. I think he smacked his face on a table when he passed out. Please ask him to be quick—it's bad for business."

"Ryan, let me see your hand," Van said. It was already beginning to darken and swell as she took it gingerly in both hands. "You probably broke something. You sit. I'll find some ice." He started to protest but gave it up as she pushed him down into a chair.

Ryan's eyes never left Van as she filled a plastic bag with ice, and when she nestled it over his hand he grimaced a little but said nothing.

"Are you in a lot of pain?" Van asked, running her palm down the length of his back. He glanced up at her, and she was startled by the conflict she saw in his eyes.

"It's all relative, I guess," he replied. There was a quietness in his voice that alarmed Van. "We need to talk, but I'm not sure now is the best time."

"Okay . . . are we talking about your hand?"

"We'll talk later," Ryan said, picking up the ice bag and heading back toward his office.

"No! You can't keep running away every time we get into an argument." Van grabbed him by the arm and pivoted him back around to face her. "Let's talk about it now. Please."

Ryan rolled his eyes. "I didn't realize we were having an argument. Fine," he said, exhaling deeply. "Let's do it here. I'm not sure you've been completely honest about the way you feel about Richard."

Van's mouth dropped open. "What are you talking about? You saw what just happened."

"I saw the two of you earlier."

"Well, what exactly did you see?"

"You holding his face, kissing him."

"You most certainly did not. We discussed divorce. There definitely was no kiss."

"I saw the way you looked at him."

"Ryan, what do you want me to say? I was married to the man for a long time. I still care for him very much, but our relationship is over. And I've made that clear to you from the very beginning."

"I thought you had already made a clean break with him. Have I been naive? I told you, I don't want to help drive a wedge between you two. It can't be both of us. I'm not going to play second fiddle to him, waiting for you to decide what you want. I can't do that—not with the way I feel about you. You have to make a choice, Van."

Van reached up and cupped his cheek in her hand. "I've made my choice. It's you. You're the only one I want. I don't know how to make it any clearer to you. But if you expect me to have no feelings for Richard, then you're going to be waiting a long time. I did, once upon a time, have a wonderful life with him. He gave me a beautiful son who was an absolute blessing. You wouldn't be standing here talking to me otherwise."

"Yes, I would, but I would be someone else." Ryan shook his head. "You know what I mean."

"Yeah, like nobody else would."

"I only ask that you be sure. Trust has to work both ways."

"I know, and I am," Van said as she tried to pull a reluctant Ryan toward her. "And actually, I'm pretty relieved that you two didn't recognize each other. I was holding my breath when you came face to face. He never mentioned HYA or Nevis. I'm pretty certain HYA hasn't approached him. I don't know how I would have felt bringing Richard back into my life permanently. Certainly, your and my relationship would have ended."

She looked at Ryan, but he was playing with a button on her shirt. "Are you listening to me? Ryan, look at me!" He slowly looked up and held Van's gaze. His look stopped her cold. "Oh, no . . . You did recognize him, didn't you?" she gasped. Don't turn away. Look at me. How could you deny your own father?"

Ryan shook his head. "There was so much drunken hate in him. He would never have acknowledged that I was his son. I hate the way he treats you. I owe him nothing in this life."

"How can you say that? He doesn't deserve to suffer needlessly. I don't understand you. Are you jealous? That's it: you're jealous of your own father."

"My father was Edward Thomas," Ryan said, and he turned on his heels and walked back out into the bar area. "Bennie, that drunk in the back goes on the top of our 'special customer' list. He's welcome like any other paying customer, but *limit* him. If he doesn't buy anything, throw him out. Got it?"

"Sure thing, Ryan. Don't give it another thought. I never forget a name or face."

❧

Ryan could walk away from the discussion, but walking away from these feelings wasn't so easy. He felt torn. He was in love with his mother and despised his father. God, Oedipus had nothing on him. He was the golden ring for shrinks everywhere.

THIRTY-ONE

MIND YOUR PS AND QS

Although business in the tavern was off to a good start, life in the personal sphere seemed to continue in an uncontrollable downward spiral.

"Bad news," said Ryan, sliding onto the stool next to Van and Jean. "Peggy just called. She'd been holding out, but she's had to release her research to HYA. Ellen found a duplicate copy of the deed in the courthouse, and Peggy couldn't stonewall anymore."

Van put her head in her hands. "Oh, God, they're going to hunt down Richard. I can't face him again. It's over. He'll sell us out. He hates me. To think that someone I loved could be responsible for destroying all this."

"All these years," said Jean. "I don't understand how all this land could have been owned by one person and nobody even knew it. It's a small town. Everybody knows everyone else's business. For goodness' sake, if they could remember that George Washington slept in this town, surely they could remember who *owned* the bloody place. "Nothing in all that stuff you've collected? There must be *something*. Have we looked through *everything*?"

"Everything but the boxes Mrs. Morgan gave me."

Jean looked incredulous. "What the hell? You haven't gone through them?"

"Listen, I've known Mrs. Morgan for years. She's a wonderful old lady, but—how do I say this politely?—she's a hoarder. Every so often, she gives me 'special' boxes, and all they ever contain is nonsense: receipts, collections of advice columns from the newspaper. She's never given me anything but junk. I don't want to hurt her feelings, so I take the boxes, keep them for a while, and then toss 'em. This time it's probably all her tax returns back to 1950."

"Damn it!" said Jean, pulling Van off the barstool. "I can't believe you didn't look. Come on. I hate it when bastards win."

"All right, we'll look," said Van. She couldn't argue with Jean's sentiment, although, truth be told, she had very little hope of finding anything. With a heavy heart, she followed Jean out. She hated I-told-you-so's.

❧

Their biggest fear glided into the Phoenix right after Van and Jean left, with a quiet smile that charmed the patrons at the neighboring table and prompted Bennie to press the silent alarm button connected to Ryan's office. Hector's and Ryan's eyes locked briefly, but this particular evening, Ryan was of little interest to Hector. He was keen on the activities of one Richard Hardy, who had arrived ahead of him and sat in the corner, sullenly nursing his bourbon. Information traveled swiftly at HYA, and the sharks had begun to circle.

Hector sat across the room from Richard for quite a while, studying every movement and mumble he made. As if attuned to an inner clock or some other subtle sign, Hector suddenly picked up his glass and approached Richard's table.

"May I join you?" he asked in a voice that was equal parts polish and authority. He didn't wait for a reply—just pulled out a chair and sat before Richard could respond.

Richard looked up but didn't seem to care that he'd gained a friend, or at the very least, a drinking buddy. His eyes were beginning to show the effects of one too many drinks, and he narrowed them to stare across the table at Hector. "Something I can do for you?" he asked as he drained the last of his drink.

"Not really. But perhaps there is something I can do for you. You *are* Richard Hardy, aren't you?"

"Depends on who's asking. You a damn lawyer my bitch of a wife hired to divorce me?"

"No," Hector said, chuckling. He loved to see someone get drunk and make an ass of himself, especially when it made business easier. "How would you like to make a boatload of money and stick it to your wife, all at the same time?"

Richard's mouth slowly morphed into a sly, goofy smile, and he leaned his head a little closer toward Hector. "I'm your man, sir. Let's stick it to her," he said, emphasizing each word with a jab of his finger.

Hector smiled and pulled out a carefully folded sheet of paper. "I would like to give you a fair price for the land you own in Nevis."

"I don't own any land in Nevis."

Hector raised his eyebrows and feigned surprise. "You mean your wife didn't tell you? Well, I guess I'm not really all that surprised. If she finds a way to prove you own it, she could take half of it in a divorce. You, on the other hand, could quietly sell it to me now. She would get nothing." Hector leaned in close.

"I can prove you own it." He tossed the paper across the table. Richard studied the page, squinting as if to squeeze the drunken double images into one. His face sank into a deep frown.

"What is this?"

"It's a land rent agreement your ancestor signed about three hundred years ago. It documents your family's ownership of most of the land here in Nevis. You are the only direct descendant of the man who signed this. The land in Nevis belongs to you. The people that think they own it are just renting it from you."

"Sure, it's yours. How much?"

"Six million dollars."

Richard's mouth dropped open as the words penetrated his drunken stupor. "No shit? Ha, ha, ha! Where do I sign?"

"I thought you'd be interested. This sells your land holdings in Nevis to my company. All you have to do is sign at the bottom. I know someone who can notarize the document for us." Hector leaned back in his chair and motioned for a friend on the other side of the tavern to join them. A little bald man with big ears scurried over and, in a few short minutes, notarized the legal documents. "It's a pleasure doing business with a man who understands the bottom line," Hector said as he pulled the paper back across the table.

Richard slapped his hand down on the paper, stopping its progress across the table. "The money," he said.

"Oh, yes, thanks for reminding me. I almost forgot," Hector said with a snicker, pulling an envelope from his coat pocket and handing it to Richard.

Richard took the envelope and frowned at the size. "What the hell is this?"

"You don't really think I'd be carrying around six million dollars in cash, do you? Do you have any idea how much that amount of money *weighs*? No, probably not." Hector tapped the envelope with his index finger. "Inside you'll find the name of a bank in the Cayman Islands, and an account number. The account is in your name. A call from me, when I leave here, will initiate a deposit into the account. You can draw from the account, but don't try to transfer the money in large amounts to a U.S. bank. Keep the deposits under ten thousand dollars to avoid triggering an alert to the Treasury Department. We'd like to keep this below the radar. Any questions?"

"Nope."

Hector extended his hand. "A pleasure doing business with you, Mr. Hardy." Hector slid the notarized document into his jacket pocket and, together with the little bald fellow, disappeared just as quickly as he had arrived.

THIRTY-TWO

SURVEYING THE SITUATION

Across town at the pickle boat house, Van and Jean started working their way through Mrs. Morgan's boxes.

Van yanked several notebooks out of the box and handed one to Jean. "Dig in," she said. "Now, you know what you're looking for, right? Just don't get disappointed if it's really goofy odds and ends."

About an hour later, they had emptied the boxes—boxes full of charming notes about local sightings of bluebirds and hummingbirds, what the Morgans did on their vacations over the course of their extraordinarily long marriage, and other random observations—all meticulously documented in Mrs. Morgan's lovely old-fashioned handwriting.

"Well," Jean said a little peevishly, "I was hoping for a little more excitement: antique jewelry, stocks, bonds, maybe a treasure map or two . . ."

"We're talking about Mrs. Morgan here, remember?" Van replied, refilling the last box of junk. "I didn't expect to find anything, but thanks for the motivation. At least now we can say we looked everywhere. Come on, let's get out of here. It's much too depressing right now." They pushed the boxes back against the wall and were halfway down the hallway when they heard a dull thud upstairs.

"What the hell was that!" Van gasped, pressing herself back against the wall and backing away from the staircase.

"Who's up there?" Jean hissed, tripping over her own feet in her haste to get out of Van's way.

"Shh." Van pulled her grandfather's walking stick out of its place in the umbrella stand, and before Jean could grab hold of her, she tiptoed quietly up the stairs. She hesitated at her bedroom door. "What the . . . Why is there plaster and horsehair all over my bedroom floor?" Her heart beat wildly as she crept slowly forward. "And a huge hole in my ceiling?"

Jean peered around Van's shoulder but looked ready to hit the stairs at a gallop if necessary. "No one's here? All this water—it looks like a water balloon exploded."

Van crept farther into the room until she could look up through the hole. "Oh, my God. I see blue sky and a tree branch. There's a *tree branch* sticking out of my roof!"

"The *derecho*? The branch that hit the deck—it bounced off your roof first? Oh, sweet relief! I thought someone was robbing you." Jean wrapped her arm around Van. "It's okay, hon. That's what insurance is for. I'll get a mop."

"Ew, look, there's even shingles in this mess," said Van, getting down on the floor. "And a box. Where did *this* come from?" she asked, peering back up into the ceiling.

"The attic?"

"Pickle boat house doesn't have an attic. You don't suppose that . . ."

"That you have an attic you don't know about?"

"Nah, not possible, but maybe a space just big enough to

store a few things. I'll get the ladder. There's a lock on here. See if you can figure out how to open this box."

Van's ladder gave a bird's-eye view of the poplar branch impaling her roof. "It's wet up here. Rainwater must have puddled between the rafters until the plaster couldn't hold the weight." Van waved her flashlight around in the space and let out a low whistle. "There's other boxes up here. Jean, I'm not sure I can get to them. You're gonna have to help me. Climb up and hold on to me."

"Not happening."

"Huh?"

"I'm afraid of heights. There's no chance I'm coming up that ladder."

"Oh, for God's sake, Jean, get up this ladder before I come down there and make you wish you had. I am so serious. Don't make me come down there after you; it won't be pretty. Now, sister!"

Jean looked up the ladder and shook her head. "Really, Van, I don't think I can. The last time I went up I came down a whole lot faster."

"Close your eyes and don't look down. Come on, Jean. I really need you right now. Please? Just two steps."

Jean grimaced and put her foot on the bottom rung. "Only for you, Van." Slowly, with her eyes closed, face taut with fear, she inched her way up until she could steady Van. Between the two of them, they wiggled and jiggled the two boxes until they were down and sitting safely on the living room floor.

"Why would anyone put boxes up there where no one could find them?" Jean asked, opening the bigger cardboard box.

I don't think they wanted them found. Maybe whatever's in here is too important to share with just anyone."

"Let's try this again. Anything that talks about land in Nevis, pull it. Set it aside. We can decide later if it's going to do us any good."

Jean rolled her eyes and pulled open the first notebook. And the second and the third, right on down through the box, without so much as a second glance at most of the documents: shipping invoices, indentures, births, death reports. In the end, she dumped the last one back into the box. "Sorry, Van, nothing here except lots of dead people."

"I know," she sighed. "I had such high hopes—make that one last hope." She pulled the last few loose papers out of the bottom of the box, preparing to shove them into the last ledger, when the name "Hardy" caught her eye.

"Stop. Hardy document." She scanned down the page. "Court proceeding, delinquent tax payment. This is a judgment against Coleman Hardy (alias Harwell). 'Given failure to pay taxes assessed against the property called Nevis Landing, cited in previous tax assessment . . . property seized to be sold for payment of taxes in arrears . . . title to the old property transfers to the purchaser at the time of sale . . . right of ownership to revert at any time within sixty days to former owner provided former owner pays purchase price . . .'" Van sat back on her haunches. "Coleman Hardy lost ownership of Nevis for failure to pay taxes? This is a miracle."

She pulled a small hard-bound book from the bottom of the box. A title was written in neat capitals across the top: "HARDY AND AFFILIATED FAMILIES, 1679 TO PRESENT. PRESENTED TO ALFRED HARDY ON THE OCCASION OF HIS EIGHTIETH BIRTHDAY, BY HIS LOVING DAUGHTER, BETSEY SEAGLE." Van flipped through the book and found an index in the back. Running her finger down the page, she stopped at an entry for Coleman Harwell (alias Hardy). "Jean, there's a whole section on Coleman Hardy in here. Wow, look at the family trees." Van stopped and glanced at Jean. "This is awesome!"

"Aw," said Jean, sticking her finger between the last page and the cover. They used cute little kid drawings of Nevis for the end papers. It's a map. Look."

"Jean, that's not a kid's pictures. It's a survey map . . . signed by *G. Washington*? Dated 1785? Get out! These are signed by *George Washington*! "Not only did he *sleep* here, he *surveyed* the place!" She flipped to the endpaper at the front of the book. This one's not a map; it's like a pictograph . . . a drawing of houses . . . some notes on the bottom."

"This couldn't be Nevis, could it?"

"It's hard to tell. I thought the pickle boat house was one of the older houses in town. The houses on Main Street don't look old, but then again, colonial Williamsburg hid in plain sight for over a century. We need something to compare."

"Don't you have any old pictures in the museum?"

"No. Nothing that would show an area this broad. Just references to the town that I used to make the model in the museum. The model . . . Jean, you're brilliant!" Van squealed, lunging at Jean and giving her a big bear hug. "HYA can't tear down or hide in a historic town, especially one surveyed by the father of our country! Come on. Let's check the model. I can't wait to see the look on Ryan's face."

When they got back to the Phoenix, Ryan was in his office, brooding about Richard and Hector.

"Ryan, we need to talk. Now," said Van, bouncing with excitement. "We found something that's going to save Nevis." She handed him the court document. "It looks like Coleman Hardy may not have been able to hold on to his Nevis property. He had tax problems. This says the property was seized and sold for nonpayment of taxes. I skimmed parts of the book. It discusses him losing his fortune shortly after he inherited it. If we can find documents verifying that various parcels were subsequently sold and not reclaimed by Coleman, we can make it very difficult for HYA to make an offer to a single descendant."

Ryan ran his finger down the page, backtracking occasionally, all the while muttering under his breath." Suddenly he looked up and grinned at Van. "Life is so good," said Ryan, nodding as an exuberant smile spread across his face. "Peggy appears to be firmly in our corner. I'll get her to comb the land records to see if the land was sold—whether Hardy was able to reclaim any of it. It's not exactly her area of expertise, but she has the patience and skill to look through a lot of records quickly."

"Ryan, it gets better. As I suspected, Mrs. Morgan's boxes were full of worthless musings. But when we were at the house, part of my bedroom ceiling collapsed. There's a hole in my roof, probably from the *derecho*. Half my upstairs ceiling has collapsed and there were boxes hidden up in the rafters. *Good* boxes! Besides the tax document, there was also this family genealogy book with Coleman Hardy in it. Open it up and check out the end papers."

Ryan studied the book for a few moments, then looked up at her. "No way! *George Washington?* This is real?"

"Right time frame. Hidden away in someone's attic? Could be authentic. Flip to the end paper in the front. It's a pictograph. These colonial houses pictured here may still be on Main Street. The model at the museum shows turn-of-the-century buildings in the same location—a similar block of structures. It'll take more digging by somebody that knows what they're doing. False fronts, additions—all kinds of architectural changes can mask older structures. I'll contact someone I know down at the Smithsonian. If we can designate this area as historic, HYA is screwed.

"Okay," said Jean, but I still don't understand why they hid and left them."

"Guess we'll never know. Perhaps they weren't even supposed to be hidden—just tucked away for safekeeping. My granddad died suddenly out on the bay. Maybe he never got a chance to tell anyone else. I doubt my grandmother got involved in his business dealings. Granddad was very respected in the community. Maybe he was a keeper of the flame."

"Maybe he knew he'd have a granddaughter who cared," said Ryan, giving Van a hug. "You're probably more like your grandfather than you know."

"That would be nice," said Van, beaming. With a whoop, she threw her arms around Ryan's neck and pulled an embarrassed Jean into their embrace. "We've won, Ryan! Now they'll have to leave us alone!"

THIRTY-THREE

A WHISPER BY NIGHT

"More flowers. When is this all going to end?" Jean asked as she hurried across the room with yet another vase. Ever since opening night, flower arrangements had been trickling in from well-wishers. This one was uncommonly elaborate, made entirely of white: bell flowers, delphiniums, lilies of the valley, white roses and orchids. A small flock of black origami cranes fluttered in among the petals in stark contrast to the white. And at the top of the entire arrangement perched a crane-shaped card, gleaming black as hematite.

"Your choice. Go to it, Jean," said Ryan, waving his arm around the room. But as she passed him by, his demeanor changed immediately. "Wait, come back," he said, his hand darting out to grab the arrangement.

"Oops . . . hang on. Damn, Ryan, I'm gonna drop it!" Only Ryan's quick reflexes kept it from crashing to the floor.

"When did this come in?" he said, lifting the arrangement out of Jean's hands. "Who brought it?"

"Harpers delivered it just a minute ago. No sender, unless it's in the card. Problem, Ryan?"

"*Jeesh*, I'm sorry Jean. I didn't mean to rip your arm off. This is spectacular. Let me have it. I think I'm going to put it in my office until I find out who sent it. Be right back."

Jean frowned and shot a sidelong glance at Van, who merely raised her eyebrows and shrugged.

Ryan wasted no time in getting back into his office and locking the door behind him. He set the arrangement in the center of his desk and then backed up until he hit the filing cabinet behind him. Origami cranes. HYA was calling. He ran the back of his hand across his brow and exhaled deeply. Slowly he walked forward and drew the card from the center of the arrangement. It read "Would like the pleasure of a meeting with you at the Phoenix tonight at nine o'clock. Looking forward to discussing present and future success." He looked at his watch. It was almost eight.

He put the card back in the flowers. It had been a pipe dream to think that he could shake free of HYA. He had been reckless and scattered in his negotiations, accepting Hector Senior's agreement at face value. What a mistake. A whisper by night and a shadow by day—HYA operated without a face. He didn't even know the price for walking away. He could only hope that it would be quick and relatively painless. Could he, in good conscience, answer? Circling around the desk, he unlocked the bottom drawer and pulled out the little five-shot revolver, checked that it was loaded, and put it in his pants pocket. One thing he was sure about: he would not be used and discarded as Earl had been. He relocked the drawer and returned to the public area of the tavern.

"Everything all right, Ryan?"

"Everything's just ducky, Van." He came up beside her and hugged her tightly. "I was just in my counting house, counting all my money. I've decided to close early tonight. We've done that well. Lock the door, Marla," he shouted across the room. "Everyone can start cleaning up. I expect this place to be deserted by eight thirty. No arguments. Go, get with it!"

Ryan didn't have to tell the staff twice. Even Marla was moving at double time. By eight forty-five, the last of the customers had been politely ushered out the door, and the place was empty except for Ryan, Van, and Jean.

Ryan put his arms around Van and Jean and started walking them toward the door. "Ladies, I have a little bit of paperwork to attend to," he said. "Would you like me to drive you home?"

Van ducked under his arm and pulled him away from Jean. "No, I think we're going to walk home. It's a beautiful evening." She hugged him lightly and pecked his lips. "You go ahead and finish. Stop by when you're done?"

"Sure, as long as you go right home so I don't have to worry about you."

"We promise, but we can't leave until we find Jean's purse. We've searched everywhere but the storeroom and the ladies' room." Van shot Jean a warning look. "Would you check in the back while we check the restroom? Then we'll be out of your hair. Come on," she said, grabbing Jean by the sleeve and pulling her toward the restroom.

Ryan's heart began to beat a little faster, but he kept a calm exterior. He hurried to the stockroom to find the purse and get Van and Jean out of the tavern.

❧

As soon as Ryan was out of view Van changed course and headed for his office.

"What's going on?" Jean said. "You know I never carry a purse. Stop right here and clue me in."

"Shh! Whisper! Call it women's intuition. I want to stay behind, but I need Ryan to think I've left . . . Leave without me. When you get to the door yell back that we have the purse and we're leaving. Then vamoose so that if he looks out the door he won't see you without me."

"Van, what are you up to? Whatever it is, I don't like it. There's 'trouble' written all over your face."

Van couldn't disagree, and at any rate, she didn't have time to. She gave Jean a friendly shove in the right direction and disappeared into Ryan's office. Dead center in the middle of the desk sat the flower arrangement. She snatched the card from the center and began reading. It didn't seem threatening. Her stomach knotted as she realized there was more here than met the eye. As she stood facing the cabinets lining the wall, she hatched a plan. She couldn't let Ryan face this alone. There was only one way to find out what was going on. Van put the card back where she had found it, and hurried to the office door to listen for Ryan. Nothing. Quietly closing the door, she turned her attention back to the tallest of the cabinets. It was empty except for an unopened package of tablecloths on the top shelf. She ripped open the package, pulled one out, and threw the rest back on the shelf. Billowing the cloth out, she covered herself with it from head to foot and slowly began to pull herself and the tablecloth back, one shoulder at a time, into the cabinet. The cabinet door swung back toward her to close but bounced back off her hip. "Oh, God," she prayed, "make me fit. I'll diet on Monday, I promise!" She pictured herself thin, wriggled back once more, and kept still as the door swung back toward the magnetic latch. *Click*. Van exhaled slowly, then inhaled. The latch held. She silently began reciting every car name she knew, beginning with "A."

After a seeming eternity, she could hear voices, which grew loud enough for her to identify as Ryan's and Hector Junior's, followed by other footsteps. They entered the room, and the door closed quickly behind them.

"Why are you here?" Ryan said. "Our understanding was clear. I'm done with HYA."

"As soon as you've done this little favor, as you promised," said Hector.

"What is it you want me to do?"

"HYA is anticipating a steady income to be generated from some current and future business activities in Nevis. We need to be able to move and deposit money that—"

"You want me to launder your dirty drug money through the Phoenix?"

Hector laughed. "You're a bright boy. I knew I wouldn't have to explain it. Consider it a tribute to Earl. The sums won't be too large for you to handle."

It was Ryan's turn to laugh. "Are you out of your fucking *mind?* Even if I wanted to do that, there is no way this place will even come close to turning a small profit, let alone bring in the kind of money you'll want me to handle. The feds will be on my doorstep bright and early the morning after I make the first deposit."

"See, the thing is, it doesn't have to be all at once. Small-sum deposits will do."

"No way," said Ryan, shaking his head as he began to pace along the row of cabinets. "I'd be depositing for you until I was old and gray. There must be another way, another business with bigger profit margins. This doesn't even make good business sense."

"What doesn't make sense is you thinking you could screw over the company and just walk away." Hector stopped and smiled at Ryan. "I thought you might want to know that Richard Hardy and I had a very fruitful conversation. He is now a very rich man."

"How much richer?"

"He's a happy millionaire now."

Ryan couldn't help but laugh in disbelief. "*You* gave *Richard Hardy* a million dollars? For what? What could the man possibly do for you that would be worth that kind of money?"

Hector stood silent, gloating.

Ryan exploded with laughter. "Hell, you tried to buy Nevis, didn't you, for one million dollars? Damn, you're funny! That much money for land he doesn't even own."

"Actually, it was six," Hector admitted with a laugh. Then he grew serious again. "But I'm not stupid enough to give that old boozer all his money at once. There was an initial million-dollar deposit." Hector's expression suddenly froze, as if he had finally processed Ryan's words. "*Doesn't own?*" he repeated.

"Hell, no. Hardy's ancestors lost control of the land in Nevis long ago for nonpayment of taxes. Come, now, you didn't know that? Your research skills are slipping, my man. You know better than to take all these things at face value."

"You're lying."

"Nope, got documentation to prove it." Ryan walked over to his desk and flipped open a yellow folder. "Copy of the court proceedings," he said handing Hector the top sheet of paper. "The originals are locked up in a safe place. HYA needs to take its dog-and-pony show somewhere else—there's no profit here."

"That son of a bitch," said Hector, and he picked up a nearby chair and hurled it into the opposite wall, where one leg broke through the drywall and stuck. Inhaling deeply, he glared at Ryan as he tried to regain some self-control. "So obviously, that brings us to a second piece of business. Richard Hardy owes me money. I'll need you to get it back from him."

"Me? Why can't you do that yourself? Oh, that's right, you've already been closely associated with one murder in Nevis. Anything less than choirboy behavior on your part would invite additional, unwelcome scrutiny. Not to mention that you have already been seen at the Phoenix, with the victim. Sorry, Mr. Hardy and I are not on the best of terms."

Hector laughed. "Can you blame the man? You've been banging his wife. You don't respect *anyone's* relationship." Hector sat down on the edge the desk. "Here's the deal: I want that money back—all of it. Either you get it back for me or I'll take the old man for a ride and shake him down where nobody's gonna find him. What's your girlfriend gonna think when she finds out you could have saved him and didn't?"

"Sorry, Hector, you're on your own. If you're smart enough to give a man a million dollars for land he doesn't even own, then you're smart enough to talk him into giving it back."

Hector slid off the desk and walked over to the liquor cabinet and poured a glass of whiskey. Taking a couple of swigs, he addressed the two men standing silently behind him, who had accompanied him and Ryan into the room. "Nothing on the face, boys. We don't need a walking billboard."

The larger of the two men grabbed Ryan by the shirtfront and slammed him up against the tallest cabinet, bending the handle down on the door. Van let out a gasp as she felt the cabinet shudder. Terrified, she squeezed her eyes shut and held her breath, praying that the runaway thumping of her heart wouldn't give her away. The door shuddered several more times, interspersed with Ryan's grunts and groans as he tried in vain to fend off the violent attack. Even more alarming was the sudden stillness and silence that followed. She strained her ears to hear whether Ryan was even still breathing.

In a heap, up against the bottom of the cabinet door, the two men grabbed Ryan by the arms and hauled him back to his feet. Hector walked over to Ryan and delivered one last punch to the gut, sending Ryan crumpling to the floor once more.

"Maggie still won't return my calls," he said. Then he picked up his glass of whiskey off the table and poured the remains over Ryan, tossing the glass on top of him. Hector's face was emotionless. "Money will arrive by courier on Monday with specifics. Use the usual communication channels. And either you ask Hardy nicely to return the money, or I'll go get it from him."

Van listened to the door slam. Then there was only Ryan's heavy breathing in an otherwise eerily silent tavern. Any other night, the silence would have been welcome. Tonight it was terrifying. She guessed she and Ryan were alone again. One look at the broken latch on the door told her she couldn't escape from the cabinet on her own. "Ryan!" she shouted, pounding on the cabinet door. "Open the cabinet! I'm stuck in here." She continued to pound and shout until she heard the sound of the latch on the door.

"Van? What the hell . . . can't get the cabinet open. The latch is . . . afraid I'll break it off. Oh, God . . ."

"Ryan, Ryan, are you still there? I'm so sorry. Please, don't hurt yourself. You can leave me here. I'm okay. Don't—"

With a shudder, the lock snapped. The cabinet door swung open, and there stood Ryan, with a cast-iron bookend of Abraham Lincoln, the great emancipator, in his hand. Van wasted no time pulling herself out of the tiny space and wrapping her arms around a battered and broken Ryan as he crumpled back down onto the floor.

Oh, please don't touch me," Ryan moaned, curling in on himself. "What the hell . . . ," he began again, but never finished the sentence.

❧

When Ryan awoke he was looking into Van's sad, tear-filled eyes. She was sitting on the floor of the office, cradling his head in her lap. Every part of him screamed in pain.

"Ryan. Oh, hon, are you all right? What should I do? I'm sorry. I couldn't lift you, and I wasn't sure you would want to involve the police."

"I'm okay, he said, trying to sit up. "Oh, almighty God, help me." He collapsed back into Van's lap, quickly abandoning any further attempts to get up by himself. "Thankfully, they were just sending a message, which I got loud and clear. Help me sit up, will you? Oh, slowly. No cops. I need to call Bennie."

"Does Bennie work for HYA?"

"No, but he put two and two together a long time ago. Good bartenders listen but never repeat. Like I said, Bennie is the best."

Ryan reached in his pocket to pull out his cell phone and managed to pull out the gun without thinking. Van's shocked eyes met his, but she said nothing. Ryan found his cell phone and called Bennie. The call went right to voice mail.

"He doesn't answer. I'll give him a few more minutes."

"Is your car outside?" she said. "Let me get you to your car. Then we can go to Bennie, or anywhere else you want me to take you."

"Car's right out front, but I'm not sure I can go that far."

Van grabbed him under the arms and helped pull him to his feet. With his arm around her shoulders, they moved slowly across the room, Ryan wincing in pain and Van panting from the exertion. A few paces from the door, it was clear they could go no farther. Van lowered Ryan back to the floor and collapsed beside him.

As they caught their breath, she asked him the question he was expecting. "Ryan, why are you carrying a gun? You were expecting this. What haven't you told me?"

He looked up into Van's eyes and wished that he could think of something to tell her that wouldn't hurt her. That was something he never wanted, though he continually managed to do it. She waited, hoping to hear the right response, but he could see in her eyes the wariness and the belief that it would not be what she wanted to hear.

"They wouldn't just let me walk away. There was a price. I'm sorry. I couldn't tell you. I needed more time before you found out. I couldn't just . . . couldn't just let you go. You wouldn't have stayed."

A single tear rolled down Van's face and splashed onto Ryan's cheek. "No," she whispered, shaking her head.

Van looked down into Ryan's face. "I wouldn't have stayed, but now I would never leave you." She reached down and brushed her tear from his face with her fingertips. "Now, let me have your phone so we can try Bennie again."

In spite of the pain he was in, the corners of his mouth turned up in the faintest of smiles. He reached up and handed her the phone, then grasped her other hand and closed his eyes.

THIRTY-FOUR

EVERY MAN FOR HIMSELF

Bennie arrived about twenty minutes after Van called. Calm and quiet, without question or comment, he helped her get Ryan outside to his car. Even if Van had been able to do so alone, the four flat tires on Ryan's car would have gotten them nowhere.

"What are you going to do about Hector's demands?" Van asked, stroking the hair off of Ryan's forehead as she sat in the back of Bennie's car, Ryan's head in her lap. "You can't safely pretend he doesn't exist anymore."

"No. Next time it'll be more than a beat-down and four slashed tires. I do have money stashed away. I'll pay off Richard's debt."

"Ryan, we're talking a million dollars here."

"Does that mean I should just let them kill my father?"

"Of course not! I thought you hated him."

"Anger and hate aren't the same thing. I got him into this mess, and I'll try to get him out. But that's it. I want nothing else to do with the man."

Van tried to hide her smile. "Okay, but you can afford this?"

Ryan rolled his eyes before closing them for the final few minutes of the trip. Minutes later, Bennie pulled up beside the residence and office of Van's physician, Dr. Alan Champ, who had agreed to see Ryan after hours.

"You, my friend, were very lucky," the doc said as he turned from the chest X-ray hanging against the fluorescent screen. "The seventh rib is cracked just in front—very common type of rib injury. Fortunately, the lungs look good. There isn't much I can do. I would prefer not to wrap the ribs.

"The best advice I can give you is to take it easy—no sudden moves, no heavy exertion. The ribs will heal by themselves, and I can write you something for pain. Was this a grudge match?"

"Excuse me?"

"There isn't much I haven't seen in my years of practice, Mr. Thomas. Bruises and cuts on your forearms indicating you were in a defensive posture, nothing on the face, ribs cracked, just short of major lung and rib damage. I would say someone wanted to send a message in a brutal but controlled way."

"Yeah, something like that," Ryan said, slowly shaking his head, not wanting to give away any more than the doctor had already surmised.

"Don't worry, everything here is confidential," the doctor added, gently placing his hand on Ryan's shoulder.

"Thanks for seeing me at this hour, Doc. Come by the Phoenix sometime. Drinks are on me."

"I might just take you up on that," Dr. Champ said as he led them back out to the office exit. "But only if you promise not to do any more brawling. Good night, my friends."

❧

Bennie dropped Van and Ryan off at Van's house and promised to pick Ryan up in the morning. Cracked ribs were not going to keep the man down.

While Ryan could struggle through the pain and personal injury inflicted by Hector, he was having a harder time dealing with Hector's demands. Bailing Richard out was not a problem. Laundering money, on the other hand, was a huge one. As much as he hated to admit it, HYA had him backed into a corner. But he wasn't having any dirty dealings going down at the Phoenix. He arranged to meet the courier the following Monday, just outside town.

Wary of being followed, Ryan slowly drove a couple of loops around town and then cautiously swung out onto the highway and sped off for the drop site. It wasn't clear whether Hector's laundering scheme was set up to punish Ryan for perceived personal injuries or to serve a higher HYA purpose. Either way, Ryan had to be there.

He arrived early and coasted to a stop under an old oak at a dead end. He didn't have long to wait. A sleek black car quietly pulled up behind him. Ryan stayed in his car and waited. HYA be damned—he wasn't just going to walk out and meet trouble.

A door swung open, and the driver got out. With his hat pulled down over his face, he wasn't easy to identify, but he had a distinctive walk. As the figure drew closer, Ryan let out a yip and scrambled out of his car. Three strides, and he had the man by the hand and shook it fiercely.

"Marcus, why I never . . . not in a million years," he said. "It's been ages. *You're* the courier? So you're having a midlife crisis?"

Marcus returned the hug, slapping him on the back and then pushing a wincing Ryan back to get a good look. "You're looking good, Ryan, but now isn't the time. Change of plans. Forget about Hector. That asshole is never gonna change. He's totally off the reservation.

"I'm in a hurry, so I'll make it brief. Hector Senior had a stroke day before yesterday, and he isn't long for this world. It's hush-hush, but it won't be long before a whole new world order is established. Hector Junior is out—too volatile for the senior partners. My guess would be Bishop—no friend of yours, obviously. I'm here to warn you. He's gonna clean house. Bishop isn't going to cut any deals with you like Hector did. He's already forced Hector Senior into backtracking on what he promised you. HYA is going to use you until they get what they want. When they find out you won't play anymore you're history."

"And you?"

"I'm on a one-way ticket out—Caymans."

"And the real courier?"

"You wouldn't have wanted to meet the courier they would have sent. Hector Senior sent me instead, to warn you and to ask a personal favor. He still thinks a lot of you. Listen up."

The two men walked in the shade of the trees as Marcus leaned in close, a hand on Ryan's shoulder, reciting instructions from HYA's most influential member. Ryan didn't speak but nodded occasionally as he looked up to study Marcus's face. It was deceptively quiet and peaceful except for the occasional crackle of a twig underfoot.

"I don't know," said Ryan, running his hand through his hair. "That's a lot of documents. It's going to put me in a very bad position."

"Realizing it's a delicate matter, he's giving you free rein to take care of it your way. Handle it, Ryan. If you don't do it for honor, at least consider whether it's worth landing on the wrong side of the fence. Even after death, Mr. Young can be extremely grateful . . . or very vindictive."

Ryan nodded. He had seen it all too often and had been smart enough—or, more accurately, greedy enough—to have experienced only HYA's gratitude. "All right, I'm in," he said, extending his hand to Marcus.

"Good. I guess there is some honor among thieves." Marcus laughed and shook Ryan's hand. "Wish I could stay and talk, Ryan. Watch your back. See ya again sometime."

Ryan couldn't say much about honor among thieves. There was something to be said, however, about finding one's true self and gaining a conscience in the process.

Marcus walked quickly to his car and was gone. Marcus and Hector—it was hard to understand how two brothers could be so different.

THIRTY-FIVE

KARMA'S A BITCH

Bennie wiped along the bar top, eyes pausing momentarily on a slight imperfection along the bar's inner bar edge. He sighed. It looked like greasy fingerprints. He rubbed a little harder, and slowly it disappeared from view.

"You gonna make out with that bar top all night, or go home to a nice warm bed?"

Bennie laughed. "No sir, Ryan. I'm heading out. How about you? Why are you still hanging about?"

"Van brought in these things for decorating. Pretty neat stuff—there's even a crossbow in here." Ryan pulled the bow out of the cardboard box, loaded a hunting bolt into it, and sighted down the shaft. "I think that would go right through someone. Interesting . . . in a macabre sort of way." He gently set it back down on the desk, pointing away from the two of them. "Van's busy, and I'd like to get these up on the wall, and this box out of here. Don't tell her I said that. It's just . . . this place is my castle," he said, laughing. "I don't want any outside-world distractions. Know what I mean?"

"Yeah, you need a place to call home—can't just drift forever. If you don't mind some advice, put some deep roots down here.

You could do worse. It's obvious you and Van have a connection. Mine it for all it's worth." Bennie shrugged sheepishly. "Tomorrow's deposit is counted and in the safe. See you tomorrow. I'll lock the door behind me."

Ryan smiled. "I'm putting down right here, until the day I die. Night, Bennie. And thanks, I really do appreciate everything you do around here. I probably don't say it enough."

"Once is plenty. Night," Bennie said, and flipped the lights off behind the bar.

❧

Just outside town, Hector put a bundle in the trunk of his car and headed toward the Phoenix. His mind empty, he drove along on autopilot until he reached Main Street, where he snapped out of his stupor and flipped off his headlights.

He could make out two cars in front of the Phoenix as he coasted down the silent, empty street. He pulled around the side of the building and parked, then walked back toward Main Street with his bundle, stepping lightly over the sandy ground.

"*Jesus!*" he muttered at the sound of a car door slamming. He flattened himself against the wall, hearing for the first time the rapid pounding of his own pulse in his ears. He peered around the corner of the building just in time to catch sight of Bennie's car pulling away from the curb.

"Perfect." Emboldened by his sense of luck, he headed straight for the front door of the tavern. The handle was locked. Stifling the urge to shake the doors, he instead pulled from his pocket a small plastic pouch of thin metal picks, selected two, and went to work on the lock. With a skill acquired in childhood,

Hector worked the tools, feeling the tumblers align . . . until he could hear the click of the lock mechanism surrendering. Quickly and quietly he slipped inside, checking from left to right to left again and seeing no one. He paused and listened. Strains of classical music floated from the rear of the tavern.

Hector studied the image of the mythical bird over the bar. "Rise out of these ashes," he muttered as he uncapped the can and began pouring gasoline along the outer wall of the front room and down the back. For a moment, he stopped short of the office door, where he could hear Ryan moving about. Sliding the handgun from his waistband, he breathed deeply and stepped into the doorway.

"Good evening Mr. Thomas."

To Hector's surprise, he was staring down the bolt in a crossbow held by Ryan, who sat calmly on the edge of his desk.

❧

"Good evening, Mr. Young. I've been expecting you."

Hector didn't blink, but a wave of stunned rage washed over his face.

"Don't look so confused," Ryan said. "Your brother warned me. I *am* surprised you're here so soon, though. Were you going to shoot me in cold blood, or should we talk for a while? Have a seat."

"I'll stand," said Hector, quickly regaining his composure. You think that contraption is faster than a bullet?"

"Probably not, but it's just as deadly and, unlike your pistol, already aimed at center mass. I'm a patient man—not something I can say about you. Unfortunately for you, you have very expressive eyes, and I can read them quite clearly from here. You, on the other hand, have *never* been good at reading people. Why aren't you heading out of the country, like your brother?"

"I am—just had some unfinished business. Millions waiting for me in an offshore account."

"Millions? I'm going to have to ask for a raise."

"Where did you see Marcus?"

"Outside of town, as he was leaving. I always had a lot of respect for him—he adopted?"

"Of course not," Hector sneered. "He just could do no wrong."

"Maggie going with you?"

Hector scowled. "No, thanks to you."

"This isn't going to turn out well. We're both going down. You know that, right? Why not walk away—millions of dollars and a chance that Maggie could come around? I'm not worth it."

Hector began to nod. "That's where you're wrong. You're worth it to me. You have to go . . . You just have to go."

"Why?"

"Because," Hector retorted, growing agitated.

"I've already tripped the silent alarm. McCall will be here shortly. I'm going to give you a five count to leave before this arrow mounts you on that wall behind you. Your choice. One . . ."

"Pull your head out of your ass," Hector growled. "You can't walk away. The shake-up at HYA is from top to bottom. They're going to come after you, get it? It's only a matter of time. You can't hide in this little two-bit fantasy life of yours."

"We *both* can walk away. I'm small potatoes. I'll deal with whoever HYA sends, just as I intend to do with you. I'm not giving up what I have here. Two . . ."

"That Hardy woman—she loves you."

"And Maggie loves *you*. Three."

"You're no small potatoes—you're HYA's best. They dream of cloning people like you. But you never deserved their trust. You were no different from me—just with more finesse. Always out for yourself. Why did you give it up? I'll never understand. You had everything—everything I ever wanted."

"People change, Hector. I changed. I've finally found something more important than me. I'm no longer any competition for you. Go to the Islands. Four . . ."

The crossbow's old cording pinged as it began to fray. Hector brought up his gun and fired. In the same instant the arrow caught him in the chest, pinning him to the wall behind him. Ryan dropped the crossbow and slumped to the floor as the bullet ripped through him. A moment of eerie quiet filled the room. As Ryan lay in the growing pool of his own blood he waited for the cascade of memories to carry him away to a more peaceful place—not memories of the despicable life he had led, but the smiling faces of Van, Bennie, and Jean as they floated through the happiest days of his life. But no memories came. He looked over to see Hector, skewered against the wall like some sacrificial Christ, atoning for no one's sins but his own. He didn't move, but Ryan couldn't tell if he was alive or dead.

"Hector?" No reply.

"Hector!" Ryan called a little louder, but there was still no answer. With agonizing difficulty, he began to crawl across the floor, propelling himself with his legs and his left arm. When he reached Hector, he grabbed hold of his pant leg and began to pull himself into an upright position. Hector screamed out in pain.

"You son of a bitch. You're not dead." Ryan pulled himself up until he was face-to-face with the man who had just robbed him of everything.

"Pull it out," Hector gasped.

"If I do, you'll bleed out."

"Better than this."

"Karma's a bitch," Ryan replied, and with a last effort, he reached up with both hands and broke the fletched end of the arrow off a few inches from Hector's body. Everything went black to the sound of a bloodcurdling scream.

"Fucking hell!" said Officer McCall, bursting into the room with weapon drawn. He recoiled at the sight of Hector still pinned to the wall, and Ryan slumped at his feet. "Clear, but it's bloody," he called over his shoulder. "For crying out loud, these assholes . . ." He reached out to check for any sign of life. "Little, get an ambulance here stat. This one has a weak pulse. I think the other one's gone. Trouble from the moment I laid eyes on 'im . . ."

THIRTY-SIX

FAITH

Van shifted her gaze from the window back to Bennie. "What am I going to do with all this?" she asked, with a sweep of her hand. "I don't know anything about running a pub. How could he have so much faith in me?"

"He has faith in you because he loves you," Bennie replied. "This was his dream, and he knew that if anything happened to him, you and I together could carry on and make this place work. We're not going to fail him. I'll be right here, and you can just be strong for me, okay? It's what he wanted. He was prepared. He was taking it all in stride. Hector warned him to make a will, and he did—and a power of attorney, too. Everything he has is under our control. HYA got nothing in the end—not Nevis, not Ryan, zippo. Ryan had the last laugh."

"I'm not laughing," said Van, teary eyed as she looked around Ryan's office. "Life has been nothing but day after day of putting one foot in front of the other and, at the end of each day, giving into mind-numbing fatigue. Then I get to get up the next day and repeat it all over again. Empty, mindless pattern and repetition. If he doesn't make it, I can't do this, Bennie." Van sat down in the nearest chair and put her head in her hands. She was too empty to cry.

Bennie walked over, pulled up a chair, and draped a protective arm around her. "He's going to make it, and I know that you can, too, hon. Stare this in the face, Van, even though you feel you can't. Dig deeper—you're stronger than you know. In fact, I've never met anyone stronger. You haven't come this far to give it all up now."

But how had they gotten to this point? And where, exactly, were they? Against heavy odds, Ryan continued to survive the shooting. It was still a waiting game—God's rules and God's call. Hector's bullet had come within an inch of Ryan's heart and right lung, and it was all the paramedics could do to keep him from slipping away as they rushed him to the hospital. Van worried that his purpose in life was complete and that he would once more disappear from her life. Even if he survived, who would come back to her: the Ryan she knew and loved, or the Ryan whose mercenary ruthlessness had made him the pride of HYA? Van didn't know. She spent every day sitting at his bedside, praying that she hadn't already lost him.

❧

"He's still heavily medicated," said the nurse as Van arrived for her daily visit, "but he's been alert a couple of times today. His eyes might follow you, but don't be upset if he doesn't talk—or doesn't make a whole lot of sense if he does. He's so full of medicine, he'll be loopy."

Every time Van entered his room, it broke her heart all over again. The tubes, the steady beep and whir of machines, the medicinal smell—it made her want to scream. She took the seat closest to the bed and wrapped her hand around his. Jean, with her for the first time, took the opposite chair. Her wide-eyed stare betrayed the anxiousness she had been trying so hard to hide. Van watched her eyes, so full of fear, darting all over the room, and wondered if she had ever been in a hospital.

"Ryan," Van said in a loud, steady voice, "it's Van. Do you know who I am? Blink once if you do. If you're confused, blink twice."

Ryan opened his eyes, but there was no other response.

Van winced. "This is Van. Don't you remember me?" The steadiness was gone from her voice now. She tried to keep down the panic rising in her like bile as she tried to decide whether this was *her* Ryan or *their* Ryan."

"Who? I'd like to buy a drink . . . for old time's sake."

"Old times . . . ?"

"Yeah. We've met before?"

"Is that the best line you've got?" Van asked, tears running down her cheeks. Who did he think she was?

"No line. We've met before. I'm sure. Just one? If it doesn't work out, I'll walk away . . . win-win."

"Win-win?" Van repeated. The phrase that she had learned to hate now sounded like music to her ears. She smiled, glancing at Jean for affirmation that this was *her* Ryan, the man she wasn't going to be able to live without. "Why is that?"

"Just because. I think we're good this time."

Ryan turned his gaze on Jean and frowned.

"Do you know who this is?" Van asked.

The frown continued. "Marla," he said with a sigh, and closed his eyes.

"No, not Marla. That's Jean, my next-door neighbor."

"The nosey one."

Van burst out laughing in relief, in spite of herself, as she watched Jean's shocked response. "Yeah, that's the one. We've been here waiting for you to wake up. Welcome back, Ryan."

"Where's Bennie?"

Bennie's fine. Everyone's fine. Nevis is safe."

Ryan chuckled as he groggily continued to meander through the conversation. "My wingman. He really likes you, but not as much as I do. I love you."

Van continued to laugh through tears of joy. "That's good, because I like Bennie, but not as much as I love you."

"Bennie loves Jean . . . *shhh* . . . but don't tell her, Marla," Ryan said, looking at Jean. "She'd bolt like a rabbit."

"Bennie really said that?" asked Jean, the anxiousness in her eyes giving way to an entirely different emotion.

"Hector?" Ryan said, ignoring Jean's burning question. Jean shot Van a desperate request for help.

"Are you going to take inventory of *everyone*?" Van asked, ignoring Jean's stare and the hand pulling on her sleeve.

"Hector," he repeated.

"He's down the hall in critical condition . . . bastard didn't die. They've charged him with attempted murder and enough other charges to put him away for life. Officer McCall still can't believe you both survived. He thought you were dead when he found you at the Phoenix. A few more minutes, and you would have been. Thank God for the silent alarm. Why . . . ?"

"Because," he whispered, and turned his head into his pillow. "I'm so tired."

"I know," Van said, wiping tears from her cheeks. "We'll let you sleep for a little while, but I'll be back. I've got to talk to the doctor about when we can get you home."

"To the pickle boat house," he whispered, squeezing her hand.

"Yes, to the pickle boat house. You'll get better there."

"Van?"

"Yes."

"Vanessa Hardy?"

"Yes, Ryan Thomas."

"Win-win."

"Uh-huh," Van whispered as she leaned forward and kissed him on the cheek. "It's a definite win-win."

"You believe in second chances?"

"Yes, Ryan." She squeezed his hand and felt him relax as he gave in to the soothing effects of love and sedation. And a sense of peace and joy washed over her in turn. "Now, get some sleep. Next time you wake up it'll be in the pickle boat house. God works in mysterious ways. We've been blessed with a second chance."

CHAPTER THIRTY-SEVEN

CODA

Van tossed the coffee grounds into the trash can and was about to close the lid when she saw the remains of a letter, torn into pieces and shoved down along the side of the trash can. She fished the pieces back out and carefully laid them out on the table. The legal-size envelope had a New York postmark. The contents, typed on plain white bond, read simply, "Always the best. 432.94.341227 647535314 8."

HYA? During his recovery, Ryan had been silent on the subject. But was he finished with them? Now she had her doubts. She walked to the front door, where she could see Ryan sitting outside on the porch steps, waiting for the sun to rise. She had memories of James sitting in that very spot. Their body language was identical. Van had never wanted to think of James as a memory, but at some point after meeting Ryan, she had stopped daydreaming about him. Despite her best efforts, he had disappeared into the golden mist of her memories.

Van let the screen door slam behind her as she walked outside and sat down next to Ryan. "Okay?"

"Yeah, good place. You?"

"Good place," she repeated. "Are you ready to go back to work tomorrow?"

"More than ready. You and Bennie have done great, but I need to take that weight back off your shoulders. And surfing the Net gets old, even if I did find you a mate for your carousel horse down in the museum. Dentzel. It'll be here in a couple of weeks."

"Dentzel? Ryan, that must have cost a fortune. What am I going to do with another carousel animal? I don't even know what to do with the one I already have."

"I have a plan."

"Oh, God. Isn't recuperating from a near-fatal gunshot wound and running a tavern enough for one man? What are you getting me into now?"

"That's what happens when you have nothing to do but recuperate and think. It would be nice if we rebuilt the Nevis carousel, somewhere near the green, as a sort of tribute to the town's heritage. It'll take a while to buy and restore everything, but it will be worth it when we're done. I can pay for it all," he said quickly, seeing the look on her face. "I'm sorry . . . I thought you'd like the idea."

"I do, but it's the money thing," she said, and she handed him a piece of his shredded letter. "I'm sorry. I wasn't trying to be nosy, but I'm shocked. Are you still working for HYA?"

Ryan's face fell as his eyes flicked from Van to the letter. "It's not what you think. When I went to New York to cut ties with Hector Senior I agreed to honor one last future request from him. I didn't know what it would be, but I stupidly agreed anyway. I'm sorry, but it was the only chance I had to walk away, and I took it. Well, Hector Senior is dead. He passed away a few weeks ago—complications from a stroke. HYA has been cleaning house ever since. Before he passed, he asked me to honor my agreement, and I did. That letter has the bank information for eight million dollars deposited in an account for me in the Caymans. Even in death, he was a generous man."

"What did you do for him that was worth so much money?"

"Don't look at me like that. I've done much more egregious things than what he requested. God knows, he could have demanded so much more. I handled certain papers and transactions for him that I won't discuss with you or anyone else. I fulfilled my end of the bargain, and he died with certain assurances. That's the end of it. I have no intention of taking the money. That's why you found the letter in the trash."

Do we have to worry about HYA anymore?"

Ryan looked at her, and she could see the wheels turning. "Don't lie to me," Van said, exasperated. "Why do you do that?"

"Sorry. There are still some inclinations I have to fight."

She nodded. "And?"

"They'll be back, and it'll be business in a personal sense—purely vindictive and punitive. But it'll be a while. They need to regroup first. We have time."

"Time. There's no guarantee of time. It's all borrowed."

"I know," Ryan said, "and good for us that we know it. I don't intend to squander a single precious minute."

"Me, either," said Van. How is it that our love has defied all this?"

He shrugged. "Does it matter?"

She shook her head. It didn't, really. The "why" and the "how" in her life still added up to "just because." She could live with that. She could really, finally, move forward.

"Do you remember all the times you sat here as a child?"

He shook his head. "No. I remember very little about James's life, but I'm sure I liked it. You do realize that the quiet days in Nevis are probably over? Now that people know there's something interesting here, you won't be able to keep them out."

"Yes, but they're the right people—people who care. They'll figure out a way to protect Nevis. That's more than you or I can do alone. Now we have help. The history buffs and the genealogists will turn over every will, newspaper, insurance policy, and history reference until they put Nevis in its rightful place. We give up a little, but we get a lot. There will always be a greedy HYA out there somewhere.

"Who would ever have thought that Nevis's history went much deeper than a turn-of-the-century resort, huh?" Van blushed. "Why are you looking at me like that?"

"I like your passion. You look beautiful when you're animated. Your eyes dance."

"And I know you obviously have no personal stake in saying that."

"Van, when we first met, I would have manipulated you into bed in a heartbeat, and left even faster. That would have been the end of it. Things are different now. I'm different now, and I don't want that. I want a relationship with you. Trust, respect—something that will go the distance."

"You have brought me peace, Ryan—something I never thought I would have again. I no longer look at Nevis as a hiding place. For the first time in ever so long, I'm looking forward to the future instead of living in the past."

"Richard has agreed to a divorce. You know you're the only one standing in the way of us being together."

"I know. I need to get out of my own way, but I'm not sure I can yet. It's overwhelming. You have no idea how hard these last few years have been on me. I struggle with the simplest things that break my routine, and I stress all day over them. It's a box of my own making. I used to think I could do anything I set my mind to, and now I know I can't."

"Then let me help you. Damn, Van, I really love you. I hope that doesn't scare you away. It should be obvious to you by now. Let me help you. 'Come Be with Me and Be My Love' and the thousand other love poems I could recite to you. All you have to do is take my hand, and I will love and protect you, forever. Come," he said, "and get out of your own way." He reached his hand out to her.

"I'm not sure it's as easy as you think," she said. "Though I do believe that we are the only two people who can put each other back together."

As the sun peeked above the bay, a rush of swans rose from the northern marsh and lumbered southward with long, slow wingbeats. Van reached out and grasped Ryan's hand. He put his arm around her and tucked her into himself so he could feel her heart beat. This gorgeous morning was a promising start.

Made in the USA
Charleston, SC
10 March 2013